Purgatory Hotel

Anne-Marie Ormsby

CROOKED CAT

Copyright © 2017 by Anne-Marie Ormsby
Cover Photography: Adobe Stock © chainat
Design: soqoqo
All rights reserved.

No part of this book may be used or reproduced in any manner whatsoever without written permission of the author or Crooked Cat Books except for brief quotations used for promotion or in reviews. This is a work of fiction. Names, characters, places, and incidents are used fictitiously. Any resemblance to actual persons living or dead, business establishments, events, or locales, is entirely coincidental.

Nick Cave lyrics reproduced with kind permission
of Mute Records Ltd.

The Ghost by
Charles Baudelaire

She Weeps on Rahoon by
James Joyce

First Black Line Edition, Crooked Cat, 2017

Discover us online:
www.crookedcatbooks.com

Join us on facebook:
www.facebook.com/crookedcat

Tweet a photo of yourself holding
this book to **@crookedcatbooks**
and something nice will happen.

*To Ray Bradbury
for writing the books.
To my parents
for buying them*

Acknowledgements

Thanks to Nick Cave and Mute Records for permission to use the lyrics to Loverman, it wouldn't have been the same without those words. Thanks to Carlo Rossi at Code 72 for all the work on my wonderful website. To Jamie Scott Beal for the amazing promotional images.

To Crooked Cat Books for their hard work and for seeing something worthwhile in my story.

And to my husband Neil and daughter Juno for always making sure I am not too serious for too long.

About the Author

Anne-Marie grew up in the company of her movie loving, crime fiction obsessed family consequently developing a passion for books and cemeteries. She has been writing poetry and fiction for her own pleasure since she was nine and has recently been working on screenplays with a production company, one of which was made into a short horror movie.
Finally turning her attention to allowing other people access to her brain, she has published her first novel Purgatory Hotel, and frequently writes vintage style articles for In Retrospect Magazine. She lives in South London with her husband and their tiny human.

Purgatory Hotel

ONE: Awake

Her body had no register for the sort of pain she was in. Something struck her head and she slipped away, and pain had no part in it – only numbness and fear. She was about to die and she knew it, as though there was always an awareness that this was how the end felt. In that moment fear left her, and it was like when a gust of wind came and went, the stillness that followed.

Before everything stopped, her life passed before her in a random barrage of images that arrived like photographs slipping past her eyes:

Her mother kneading the scone mix, the crucifix she wore around her neck glinting in sunlight; her father polishing his motorcycle, and stopping to smile at her; her sister styling her hair and laughing in front of a mirror; the photo in the hallway of the barren landscape of the Dakota Badlands; the blue dress her mother was wearing the night she died; her father looking smart in his suit as he closed the car door forever; the second she laid eyes on him and knew for the first time what love was; the hug he gave her as she wept at the hospital – "a murder of crows," he had said – and the words of a Baudelaire poem he only ever said in French; steady autumn rain falling on the garden and the first fall of apples; rain on the churchyard; the face of a missing young girl on the front of a newspaper; the burning in her heart that made her feel she had been in love, the kind of love she had read about in books, the kind of love that tore you to pieces, the kind of love that did more harm than good; the warm smell of his skin as they made love; the feeling that the only place that ever felt like home was in his arms; tears on her sister's face; the words he wrote for her blurred by her own tears; the crisp cold blue of his eyes, his eyes.

And she was gone.

In the moment before she woke she remembered rain and trees, the dark green, dripping night of the forest. It was more a sense of the place than actual sight; she knew how it looked yet it was just darkness and the sound of the rain. But in her head it was clear, the branches overhead framing the stars, the wet leaves dripping rain onto her face as she looked up. There was movement nearby, perhaps a fox, its eyes glinting in the gloom. Nothing was there and yet, from the sounds, she could see every detail.

In the seconds when her eyes began to flicker open, and the dark woods were being replaced by dim lights, she knew something bad had happened, something really bad.

The calmness of the woods was being replaced by a sense of urgency, of the irrational fear that rises when you don't yet know what it is you are scared of.

Her head was thumping. She was face down on the floor, her cheek squashed against a sticky carpet, and as her eyes blinked, her vision cleared slowly. An unpleasant smell was permeating her nostrils; something long ground into the carpet didn't smell good, and as she peeled her cheek off the floor she felt some of whatever was in the fibres still clung to her face.

As she sat up she noticed the blood, huge clots of it covering her hands and arms, her grey sweater losing its colour to the dark, rapidly spreading stain. Panic rose up her throat like bile. Her hands shook as she reached up and touched the source, a pulp of bone and brain matter at the side of her head.

That was when she knew she was already dead.

TWO: Checking In

Dakota was on the floor of a gloomy, Victorian-looking hotel lobby. The blood that had been pouring from a wound in her head was now gone, as was the wound. The dark gloves of blood that had covered her hands had now disappeared and she was left confused by the illusion for a moment. Her confusion soon spread to her location. She had no idea how she came to be in a hotel lobby, or indeed where the hotel was.

The walls bore a deep red colour velveteen wallpaper and the ceiling was a dirty gold as were the doorframes and window ledges. Curtains fell long and velvet from the tops of the high windows where rain was crashing against the black glass. It was like a museum of rotting grandeur; once rich, vivid colours were now dull, worn and faded. Wherever she was it was night now; she could not see anything through the windows, only the occasional flash of lightning showed the rain streaking across the glass.

The lobby would have been completely dark had it not been for the dim oil lamps that sat on tables and hung from the red walls. They cast a soft but unusual glow through tiny threads of cobwebs and dust, down onto worn and faded leather sofas and armchairs that lay around the large gloomy room. As she listened to the rain thrash the windows, she felt drawn to the fire that crackled beneath the mantelpiece where more dust collected. Her clothes were dry, but she felt cold and damp right down to her bones, as if she had just crawled out of her own grave.

To her left was a huge door that shuddered slightly in its frame and appeared to lead outside into the storm. To her right there was another door, surrounded by a multitude of clocks, which appeared to give the times all over the world. In England it was twenty minutes past midnight.

"Can you come over here and check in please, miss?" said a voice that snapped her awake again. Just along from the clock door was Reception, and behind the desk stood a tall, willowy-looking woman in a white suit. She stood out sharply in the otherwise dull room. It was only then that Dakota noticed other people sitting in the lobby, standing against walls, all in clothes so drab they almost blended into the furniture.

"Hello?" called the woman, beckoning Dakota across the room to her. The other people in the room seemed to acknowledge her, then deliberately ignore her. As Dakota moved warily across the dim lobby, eyes glinted behind drab fabrics, and from behind furniture, low whispers came to her ears like dry leaves tittering across concrete.

She was focusing so intently on not looking at anyone, she walked straight into someone who shoved her back so hard she fell over. A low murmur of amusement edged around the room as she looked up at an angry-looking woman whose eyes were so red she looked as though she had not slept in years. Bones protruded from her shoulders, and her cheekbones were so prominent she had the appearance of a skeleton with the thinnest layer of skin pulled over its features.

"Look where you're going, bitch," the woman said in a cold and featureless voice. For a moment Dakota thought she was going to cry but bit back the tears knowing full well that her bursting into tears would only makes things worse. She picked herself up and moved carefully around the woman making sure not to look up even though she could feel the bitter red gaze on her.

By the time she reached the reception desk, she felt like she was about to burst into huge body-shaking sobs, but the lady who looked across at her from beyond the desk put her suddenly at ease.

"Hello, Dakota" she said, her long finger pointing at a huge book that lay on the counter between them.

"Uh... I – I don't know I... can't remember... I don't know where I am..." she offered weakly. As she looked down at the book, she noticed that names were appearing on the half-full page, names and room numbers written in flowing script by an unseen hand, as the white-suited woman ran her finger down the long list.

"You are Dakota Crow." The woman smiled as she looked up at Dakota's worried expression. "Forgotten it all, have you? It's all right, it will come back to you when it needs to. You will be in room twenty, if you take that elevator over there. When the door shuts, say your room number out loud and it will take you right there, OK?"

"Uh – yeah um I'm um... I need to... um..." She paused. "I'm dead, aren't I?"

"If you go through the door opposite the elevator, you will find the Bar. Perhaps it would help you to have a stiff drink?" The smiling woman completely ignored Dakota's question. She reached under the counter and pulled out a golden key with a large silver tag bearing the number twenty. "If you need to ask any questions, I will be right here. My name is Ariel. Don't be afraid; I am always here."

Dakota smiled weakly at the beautiful pale woman, and began to wonder whether it would be wrong to ask her if she was an angel. Just as she was about to open her mouth a huge gust of rain-filled wind blasted through the still room. Dakota jumped and turned to see a ragged old man coming through the main entrance. Lightning flashed at the windows as he slammed the door shut behind him.

The handful of men and women in the room, lit up briefly by the storm, all looked sullen, weary and tired. Their clothes were drab and dirty looking, nothing brighter than shades of grey against the worn leather sofas. They all had different styles of clothing, modern and old-fashioned, but all grey. It was as though the place itself had leeched all the colour out of everyone.

One man looked as though he might only be around thirty, but his eyes were those of a much older man. They were tired and red, full of pain. To his left, far across the lobby, sat a woman with a mass of unkempt hair. Her dress was ripped and tattered, and her eyes were rimmed with red as though she had been crying for days. Closer to the main entrance sat a young man of no more than eighteen. He looked more afraid than the others – about as afraid as Dakota felt. His eyes darted around the room as though they were attached to two flies, buzzing around the room. Then they landed on her. For a moment they just stared at each other and she smiled softly at him, but this only made him more jittery. His leg began to bounce up and down as he scratched at his forearms with dirty fingernails. Dakota felt suddenly aware that nobody here would be friendly, nobody here would make her feel any better or any safer. When she breathed in, she felt she was inviting pure despair into her body.

The man who had just walked in was soaked with rain, his long thin hair sticking to his deeply-lined face. As he moved across the lobby people shrank away from him, sliding off the sofas, pinning themselves back against the walls and vanishing into the long shadows. It seemed that even the lights were dimming, juddering on the edges of his presence, allowing darkness to take over his face. Then he saw her.

She felt a temperature change in the room as his eyes fixed on her like sharp points of silver glinting out of the gloom of his silhouette.

Dakota suddenly felt terrified and began backing up until she smacked into the reception desk again and turned to find Ariel gone. When she looked back, the lobby had emptied save for low murmurs around the edges, and he was moving towards her. She felt frozen by his gaze, unable to move any further as he drew closer and closer to her.

A whisper that accompanied his movement sounded like beetles scattering across a cold floor. Dakota felt her skin crawl as though cockroaches were scurrying up her trouser legs.

A huge flash of lightning illuminated the edges of his shoulders and head one last time before he was beside her, his nose touching the side of her face, and a cold icy hand gripped her wrist.

"Nice to see you again… Dakota," he whispered.

A sudden urgency overtook her and she broke from his grip running straight to the Bar, not looking back but still hearing a low cackle coming from where she had left him.

The Bar was littered with people muttering to each other in the dim light of table lamps. The rain could still be heard pounding the glass, but thick curtains kept out the flashes of lightning. The high corners and edges of the room faded into darkness, leaving her with the feeling that they concealed secrets. The darkness was so pervasive, she realised she had no idea how large the room was; it just faded away, taking with it the secret of how many other eyes were on her. It was as though the dark was alive with things she could not see, but she knew they were there from the low murmur that reached her ears. She looked straight through the rows and rows of tables at the brightly lit bar area, where a few customers were collapsed, or sitting with their heads in their hands, mumbling to themselves. The music that was playing sounded familiar to her, but it took a few moments for her to remember that it was Elvis. She laughed slightly to herself as she recalled that she had liked Elvis before. At last she knew something about herself. However, *The Wonder of You* had a creepy sound to it as it worked its way around the dark, foreboding room. For a moment she wondered whether he was actually there in the Bar – had he become a seedy pub singer in the after-life? – until she caught sight of a stereo.

Dakota thought for a moment and managed to recall what being drunk felt like. She realised that was exactly what she needed and headed towards the bar through the layer of smoke that was hanging at about chest height in the room. Again, nobody seemed that interested in her, though a few of the women glanced up at her, looks of sorrow in their eyes. One woman swigged from a bottle whilst cradling a bundle of rags in her arms. For a moment Dakota thought there was a baby there, but it was exactly what it looked like – a bundle of rags that looked like a baby. She shared a brief second of eye contact with the woman before looking away, realising she did not want to know her story.

"What can I get you?" asked the barman, a tired looking man of around sixty. Somehow he looked different from the other men here; his eyes seemed softer.

"I can't remember what I like, so give me something strong," she said quietly, sitting down on a barstool, far away from the nearest customer who seemed to be asleep with his head in an ashtray. "Uh… cigarettes?"

"We have plenty of those. Can't do you much damage now, can they?" He half laughed. "Here's yer drink and you'll need matches, too, for them fags." Dakota knew his accent but could not place it as she lit up a cigarette. The drink looked like extremely watery coke, but whatever it was tasted like paint stripper. She gasped and coughed slightly, taking a puff on her cigarette in an attempt to dull the fire in her throat.

"Hehe, guess that wasn't yer favourite back home. You look more like a vodka drinker. I'll fix you one of those, too." As he returned with another drink he said, "I'm Danny, by the way. Who are you?"

"Well, according to Ariel my name is Dakota Crow, and I'm pretty sure I'm dead." She laughed as a tear rolled down her face and necked the vodka he had brought her. The man seated along from her at the bar slid off his stool onto the floor with a thud. The noise distracted her from the pale look that had flitted across Danny's face.

"Head injuries, was it?" he asked, pouring her another drink.

"I think so, yeah. How'd you know?" she replied, the hallucination of blood still fresh in her mind.

"The ones who get here with no memory usually died of some kind of head injury – you're not the first. It takes some people ages to remember. Others who come here with no memory have actually completely blocked it all out of their heads because it's too much."

"Yeah, but it's not just my death I can't recall, it's my whole life. I can't remember anything. That's," when Dakota thought about how old she was, she seemed to know, "twenty-one years of memories, just gone. Oh, except the fact that I might have liked Elvis, and I remember a forest."

"A forest?"

"Yeah, just before I woke up, it was like a dream, I was in a forest and I had been there before. It was night time and it was raining heavily. It seems like a dream but I know it was real somehow... I knew those woods." Her thoughts distracted her for a moment.

"Danny, am I having a psychotic episode or something?"

"No love, yer just dead, as dead as everyone else here, as dead as me." He smiled at her, a sort of pity in his face. Dakota glanced around the dark Bar and saw other people acting like normal people, arguing, looking depressed and confused, and it felt like life to her. This place, though a little odd, could have been somewhere on earth, a hotel somewhere, in need of decorating, perhaps in a washed-out seaside town. She felt as though she was alive, just a bit down, like she had been walking for miles or hadn't slept well in days. The thoughts angered her. Why could she recall feelings and basic knowledge, yet she could not recall a single detail of her own life, of who she had been, of what she had done in her life. She felt so frustrated as she lit another cigarette. She didn't even know if she had ever smoked before, but she seemed to enjoy it so maybe she had. She swallowed down another drink and waited for Danny to fill it up again.

"I don't feel dead... I can breathe, I can move... nothing feels different, except... I don't remember what I was like..."

"I know, it all feels the same as life – just darker. The breathing thing is just a habit – you only do it when you think about it. Oh and the lack of a heartbeat." He laughed and put his hand on his chest. She did the same and realised he was right – her heart was still. Not a whisper of life came from its dark, dead chambers, and her eyes welled with tears.

"Oh god, is this hell? I know it's not Heaven, so this must be hell.'

"No, it's not quite hell, it's the place in-between. The

place where they put you when they aren't quite sure where you belong yet."

"Purgatory," she whispered to herself as tears began to roll over her dry lips. She recalled images from a book, distorted faces, horror.

"No point crying, love. You have to learn to accept it quick as you can, and get on with it," he said softly so only she could hear. She sniffed and wiped her eyes. "Crying won't do you any good in here. It just makes people think you're weak and you can be picked on. Don't let anyone see you cry, you hear?"

Dakota nodded obediently and glanced around to check no one had seen her moment of weakness.

"Why are you here? I mean, how'd you get here?" she asked, a mild slur in her voice.

"I was run over – got drunk and stepped out into the path of a lorry."

"Sorry… hang on... " She put up her hand as her dead mind threw forth a piece of information. "Purgatory. I thought you only came here if you had been bad or sinful or something?"

"Well done, love," Danny smiled in recognition of her memory twitch. "Yeah, that's right. You come to Purgatory to atone for your sins. There isn't a person here who didn't do something bad in their life. Guess it's a bit like prison, only everyone here is actually guilty." He laughed and lit a cigarette for himself.

"What, you mean sins like lying or stealing or coveting oxen?"

"Oh no, you only come here for the big ones. The rest is forgivable as far as the almighty is concerned. But I guess they feel that some things... well... need to be paid for." His voice changed tone and Dakota felt cold suddenly.

She was here to pay for something she had done wrong.

"Shit, what did I do?" she muttered feeling her head start to throb again.

"Well I'm sure it'll come back to you, and when it does... you'll wish it hadn't." He paused and took a drag on his cigarette as lightning lit the edges of the curtains and thunder followed hard upon its heels. "You see, that's part of your punishment. Remembering what you did, understanding how it affected everybody else, feeling their pain, too... feeling the guilt and how it eats away at you."

The rain began to sound like the sea, arriving at the window in waves, travelling on the gusts of wind. The Bar seemed quieter, most of its customers either gone or passed out. Dakota knew if she was sober she would be afraid, but right now, she was numb with drink and tiredness. Her wandering eyes fell on the motionless body of the man on the floor. Since sliding off his stool earlier he had not moved.

"Where are you from?" she asked as she took a cigarette from Danny's cigarette packet.

Danny smiled at her and lit the cigarette she put to her cold lips, and for a moment watched her rake strings of her brown hair from her face behind a veil of smoke.

"Ireland," he answered, stubbing out a butt in the ashtray.

Dakota froze. The room around her began to spin as a wind rushed through the corridors of her dead brain and one of the many locked doors of her memory burst open and poured its contents out into her still veins.

"Oh my god, I remember..." she managed as her head grew heavy with a torrent of lost images and faces.

Her first memory was sitting at a dining table. She was four years old and eating breakfast with her sister and her parents. She stared into a perfect pile of porridge oats that was waiting for the hot milk her dad was making and without any word she blew the oats from the bowl and watched as they settled on the table cloth.

Then she was lying down awake beside her sleeping mother as the summer sun poured into their lounge; the TV was playing cartoons.

"Come on, darling, brush your teeth. It's past your bedtime," said her mother in a strong Irish accent, as she walked her up a darkened staircase.

Dakota Grace Crow was the youngest child of Hannah

and Jack Crow, two Irish immigrants to a small village called Little Mort, in the south of England. Dakota had one sister, Lula, who was ten years older than her. There had been other babies after Lula but none had lived beyond a week – some miscarried late, some were stillborn, others died of cot-death. Lula had found the two that lived for a short while, cold and still in their beds, moonlight spilling in onto their closed innocent eyes. As a result of her experiences with dead babies, Lula ended up under the care of a psychiatrist; Dakota would lie awake at night and listen to her sister's sobs coming from the bed next to hers. Often times, Dakota would wake to find her sister standing over her bed shaking her awake, crying desperately then relaxing into a huge hug when her baby sister finally woke up and looked back into the stormy green eyes they shared.

It seemed that Lula never recovered from finding two of her siblings cold and dead in their innocent baby cotton wool sleep, and when Dakota was born she would creep in to check on her all hours of the night, terrified she was not doing her job as big sister properly. When Dakota got older, Lula would tell her all the time about how she used to come in to watch her sleeping.

Dakota could see her sister clear as day – when she was fifteen years old, with eyes the colour of a storm-tossed sea and a swathe of dark brown hair that fell down to her shoulder blades. She read poetry, Mills and Boon books, listened to opera and cried a lot.

Dakota remembered the perfume her sister wore: Dewberry, and whenever Lula hugged her, she would bury her face in Lula's thick dark curly hair and breathe in the sweet smell. She remembered that Lula was beautiful in a buxom 1950s way, all pale skin and eyeliner.

She remembered that she had often hoped she would be as beautiful as her sister one day. Then she realised she was unsure of how she looked now, having not seen a mirror since she woke up dead.

Hannah Mary Crow had brown hair in a bob and green eyes that sparkled whenever she looked upon her children.

Sometimes Dakota noticed a sad lost look in her eyes, and she knew that her mother was thinking about all the little babies she had given back to Heaven. All the big sisters and brothers Dakota should have had, lost to the earth under neat and tiny headstones.

Hannah nearly always wore an apron, and her hands were often covered in flour. She always seemed to be baking cakes and scones. Dakota remembered the smell of her mother's Tweed perfume mixed with the smell of flour and icing sugar when she cuddled her.

Jack Crow was a loving but distant father and Dakota's memories of him were scant but clear: he was building a swing in the back garden for her, his thick dark brown hair falling into his eyes; he was passing her a sausage roll as they picnicked on a stony beach somewhere in Ireland; he was closing the bedroom door and whispering goodnight to her and her sister.

Then she was playing on a sandy beach in the sunshine, her sister trying desperately to get a suntan, laid out like a pale corpse in the sea of sand.

Then it was raining as her mother ran out into the back garden to try and get the washing in before it was soaked through, Dakota scurrying after her, collecting the clothes pegs.

Her father was reading to her from a Hans Christian Anderson book that had been his as a child, streetlight seeping in through a crack in the beige curtains.

She was eight years old, and had won an award at school for best picture in a drawing competition.

She remembered walking out in the fields that surrounded their village, corn shifting gently in the breeze of a summer evening, the sunlight painting the landscape gold.

Her sister came home late at night wearing too much make up and a mini-skirt that left nothing to the imagination. As Dakota lay pretending to be asleep, her father put Lula into bed, a smell of alcohol and vomit filling the room; she listened to her sister's weak drunken moans. It was Dakota's ninth birthday.

Then something bad happened.

It was late on a Saturday night. Lula was eating popcorn and Dakota was half-asleep on the sofa beside her. Rain spattered the windows of the darkened room as the horror movie Lula was watching came to violent end. The clock struck midnight and Dakota awoke properly, turned smiling to her sister and cuddled her as the phone began to ring.

Then, moments later, a hysterical Lula dropped the answered telephone, and Dakota ran to her and begged her to tell what was going on.

"Oh god D, they're dead! Mum and Dad! We need to get to the hospital!" managed Lula between sobs. Dakota hung up the phone and called a number; it was Lula's boyfriend; he could drive them to the hospital. Somehow Dakota was taking care of her twenty-one-year-old hysterical sister, comforting her, wiping away her own tears and helping her into her boyfriend's car.

Then at the hospital, Dakota listened to her sister's screaming tears as she identified their dead parents. They had gone to a wedding reception. Hannah had worn a blue silk dress. There was a car accident; they were dead on impact. Dakota was an orphan. It was her eleventh birthday.

Dakota sobbed into her hands, uncontrollable tears streaking her face as she shook, her body suddenly wracked with pain and sorrow. The horror of losing her parents at such a young age washed over her, all the sadness and fear at once rushing through her as though it were the very blood that once coursed through her dead veins.

Danny was beside her trying to comfort her, but every time she heard the lilting tones of his Cork accent, the one he shared with her parents, she felt a fresh wave of grief drowning her senses.

No one else in the Bar even looked at her for more than a minute. They had seen it all before, the moment when something from the other side creeps back into the afterlife, some long gone memory that shatters the confused and lost souls trapped in the walls of the decrepit hotel. They also knew that before long, her tears would become more frequent for a while before drying up to revisit briefly from time to time – just occasionally, when the demons of the past reared up and brought up some horrific memory, dragging the poor souls into guilt or grief. People often just broke into tears without warning, because all they had now was memories and the secrets that came with them. Everybody here had something to feel guilty about, and every one of them deserved to stay awake for days on end, with bloodshot eyes and hollow hearts, wishing for deliverance, hoping for forgiveness and the presence of God.

She was no different, and no amount of comforting would help her.

But Danny could not help but try to calm her. When the hysterics subsided and all that was left was calm and red eyes, he passed her a bottle of vodka and replenished her cigarette stash.

"I can't believe I remember something! Well I can remember loads actually, up until I was eleven, all the happy childhood years..." Dakota trailed off and wondered if she could even be bothered to drink anymore, but in the same instant knew the numbness of alcohol would be good.

"Can you remember anything after the night your parents died?"

"Yeah, not much. I know that we kept the house and Lula's boyfriend came to live with us. I can't remember him, though – just that he was there. The funeral is sketchy... it rained and Lula had plaited my hair... she said it was just us now, that she'd be my mum from that day on... she seemed odd though, sedated. I think she was on a much higher dosage of medication by then. They put her on anti-depressants when she was about sixteen, I think, when she first went into therapy... had been on them ever since..." Dakota stared at her burning cigarette. Maybe it would have been better if she had never remembered anything of her life. She began to think she did not want to know how she died or why she was here in the first place.

"I remember Lula telling me that I'd see my parents again

one day when we met in Heaven." Dakota choked on tears that made her throat swell. "I'll never see them again, will I? They aren't here; I'd know by now, wouldn't I? Why would they be here anyway? They were good people... loving... wouldn't have done anything that would have sent them here."

"So, you obviously didn't die when you were eleven. How old were you when you died?" asked Danny, changing the subject and sitting down again.

"Twenty-one," she said as her mind offered more information, a tease of what else was hidden from her. "I'm twenty... -one. I remember it was 2004. I was born in 1983."

"Right, so that's a whole ten years after your parents died... So why can't you remember? I mean, why would you only remember up to that point?" She could tell Danny was trying to help her, but he also seemed to want to be somewhere else, as though the whole thing was stressing him out as much as her. He was shaking slightly as he lit another cigarette, and he ran his old fingers exasperatedly over his lined and tired face.

"I don't know... I think I need time to just deal with what I remember so far. You all right?"

"Yeah, I'm grand. Just feel a bit bad is all... that my accent brought all that back."

"Well at least I can remember something now. I guess I have plenty of time to remember the rest." She paused as her mind floated off. "I wonder what my funeral was like..."

"Won't have happened yet; time moves very differently here. It's something like a month passes here for every day on earth. Still it's hard to keep track of time here, being as we don't have any days."

"What did you do, Danny?" she slurred, gulping down another drink.

"It's getting late; you should go and settle into your room. I'll see you later."

"Yeah, in the morning," she muttered, standing up and stubbing out her cigarette.

"No love, we don't have those," he said, moving away.

"What?"

"Mornings... just night, always night here. That's part of the punishment, too. No sun, no blue skies." He gave her one last pitying smile and turned away to tidy up the Bar. As Dakota stumbled through the collapsed customers and tables, she began to understand why everyone had that pitying gaze when they looked at her. She felt as though there was so much she didn't know about this place, and she suspected none of it was good.

THREE: The Rapist and The Widow

Glancing down the corridor towards the lobby, Dakota could see that people were still milling around, but the laughing man had gone quiet. Facing her were the big shiny doors of the elevator. She only had to wait a moment before they opened and out wandered a man, looking sad and dejected. When he looked up at Dakota she could tell he registered her as a new face, but he did not offer any greeting. He just brushed past her in his dirty clothes and headed for the Bar.

She felt hazy. She had drunk too much for her to actually feel good, but she knew she had felt worse before drinking the bottle of vodka. As the doors shut she remembered what Ariel had told her to do, and looking down at the key in her hand, she called out her room number. A sharp jolt knocked her to the floor as the carriage rocketed up at an alarming speed, motion sickness washed over her and she feared she would vomit on the faded brown carpet. Then as soon as she began to acclimatize, another sharp jolt that nearly sent her into the fluorescent light above her signalled the end of her ride. The doors slid aside and she crawled out into the corridor.

She paused there on all fours for a moment, breathing deeply.

"Get inside."

Dakota looked up and found the corridor empty. It stretched into inky blackness to her left and her right, dull wall lamps lighting part of the way, but she could not see any further than a few feet either way. The voice she had heard whispering had no owner that she could see, but she had the feeling someone was watching her.

"Hurry! Get inside!" repeated the voice. This time,

Dakota tracked the sound to a door bearing the number twenty-one which lay a foot or so from her.

"Hello?"

"Please, just get into your room!" reiterated the frantic woman who was obviously behind door twenty-one. Dakota was about to approach the door, when from the corner of her eye she saw movement to her right. She sat back on her heels and looked down the hall. A few doors down from where she sat the wall lights had stopped working and the blackness was absolute, but she could feel something was there, waiting beyond the curtain of dark, watching. Lights flickered.

The moment she stood, the darkness cackled at her.

Fear lunged in her belly as a figure began advancing towards her.

Panic took over as she lunged towards door twenty and, shaking, thrust the key into the lock, seconds lasting too long as the lolloping figure lurched towards her, laughing and dragging its feet. It was the same chilling laugh she had heard in the lobby earlier. The same man was now slouching towards her, and her mind raced with all the things he might want to subject her to. As soon as she opened the door she slammed it shut after her, feeling blindly for locks and bolts which she was relieved to find.

Whoever was in the corridor had stopped outside.

She waited, ear against the door.

Nothing.

Then a huge thud shook the door in its frame. Dakota jumped back screaming as the creature in the corridor threw its body weight against her door.

"I know you're in there, little girl!" rasped a voice that made her hair stand on end.

The only light in the room was the dim glow coming from the corridor through the cracks in the door.

"Go away, go away, go away!" she whispered, more to herself than anything. One more cackle and she heard the sound of the intruder sloping away, dragging its feet.

Dakota leant her head against the door, breathing erratically as panic subsided in her. Turning to the room she saw a dim glow coming from an oil lamp beside her bed. Darting across the room she fiddled with the knob on the side until the flame grew and threw more light on the walls. Just as she stood straight again, a sudden knock on her door made her jump.

"It's OK, it's me, he's gone. Can I come in?" asked the soft woman's voice from beyond the panelled pine. Dakota was feeling wary of trickery and slid the chain across before opening the door. Out in the hallway stood a plump, short and nervous-looking lady of around fifty, with a bouffant of black hair, smoking and holding a packet of cigarettes and a lighter in her hands. Dakota slowly opened the door with the reasoning that she couldn't possibly harm her.

"What do you want?" quizzed Dakota standing firmly although she felt as though she might wobble.

"Thought you might want some company... please, before he comes back."

Dakota stood aside and let the woman in, closing the door swiftly behind her and re-locking the door.

As she turned she looked at the room she was in more closely. It was small with only enough space for a bed and a single armchair, which the woman was now seated in. Beside the bed was a small table with an ashtray, a full box of cigarettes and a box of matches.

"Christ, they do push you to smoke here, don't they? Free booze, free fags," mused Dakota. Beyond the armchair was a curtained window. The draping worn velvet moved slowly as a draft manipulated it. She realised she had not yet looked outside, and moved past the woman smoking in the chair to pull back the curtains.

"That view will make you wish we didn't have windows. The woman laughed knowingly.

Out beyond the glass was the blackest night Dakota had ever seen. What seemed like miles below them was a forest of dead, twisted trees shaking madly in the bracing wind. Beyond the mass of shuddering trees, she could see a lake, only made visible in the moonless dark by the great white ridges of panicked water surging insanely under the black fingers of the storm. Lightning broke over the lake and she saw, for an instant, a small black boat tossed and storm-crazed making its difficult path through waters that seemed intent on sinking it. There were two passengers, one a tall white figure that stood steadily at the bow of the boat, facing away from the other, a crouched dark being that held onto the side of the boat for safety. In the instant the light failed, she could no longer see them. There was no horizon, there was no distance, and she was only able to see as far as the edge of the lake by the dead forest. Despair filled her as she dropped the curtain back.

"Best you don't look out there too often. Sends people crazy," said the woman, leaning over to pull a bottle of whisky out from under Dakota's bed. "Here, get some of that down yer neck."

"I've already had a bottle of vodka. I can't drink any more," replied Dakota throwing herself onto the bed. It was stiff as a board and almost bruised her as she landed on it.

"You won't throw up, don't worry. You'll have a hangover but it's not like you have anything to get out of bed for, is it!"

"Why do they give you so much booze and cigarettes here?"

"I have no idea! It must help with the transition or something, being allowed to have the things you used to turn to when you were down. For most people here that's booze and fags. Though I hear that once you've been here for a while you get so sick of it you just stop." She laughed and swigged the tobacco-coloured liquid down with a grimace.

On the floor by the door, Dakota noticed, stood a small stereo and a collection of CDs. Although she could not recall what music she liked, she knew that she had always enjoyed listening to music.

"Be wary of anything that looks like a treat. They'd give you your favourite albums to listen to, but they don't allow loud music so the stereo has no volume control! Not everyone gets them, though, so I wouldn't go telling everyone. They will all be trying to steal yours." The woman laughed again, and lit another cigarette using the butt of her last one. Dakota wondered what music she had liked, but felt so drunk she was unsure if she could get off the bed again.

"What's your name?" asked Dakota, lighting another cigarette.

"Betty."

"Well I'm Dakota, and thanks for the warning earlier. I think I saw him in the lobby earlier. He'd just arrived, I think."

"Don't know who it was for sure. There's always someone roaming the corridors, trying to put the frighteners on you. But there's one, worse than the others." She drew sharply on her cigarette. "I hear them all the time. They wait for people to come back from the Bar or wherever and then chase them around till they get bored. Some of the rapists are the usual culprits. That's why I warned you to get in. Rapists might not have the right parts to do the deed when they get here, but they'll still have a good go at raping someone."

"What do you mean, they don't have the right parts?"

"From what I've heard, that's one of the punishments rapists have when they get here. They don't have a… you know…" Betty looked slightly embarrassed as she motioned with eyes and hands into her lap.

"Oh! I see… so they disarm them in a way? Removing their weapon of choice, as it were?"

"Yep, how frustrating eh? They still have the desire but not the equipment!" Betty allowed herself a chuckle. "But the annoying thing for the women here, is that even though the rapists can't do what they want, they will still attack whenever they feel like it. A lot of them hang out in the woods when they aren't patrolling the corridors."

"Well I think I'll call him in the corridor Woods, then. I don't fancy actually asking his name. What was odd was that, well, he seemed like he knew me."

"What makes you think that?"

"Well he… he said my name." Lightning lit the edges of the curtains briefly.

"Maybe he just overheard you checking in?" Betty

offered.

"I could have sworn he didn't come in till after that, but I could be wrong. It was just odd."

"Did you recognise him?"

"No... I don't think so. I don't remember a lot, you see."

"No? Head injuries, eh?" She shook her head sadly. "So you don't remember how you died? Or why you are here? Shit, that's tough."

"What about you? What did you do to get in here?"

"I'm a murderer," Betty replied with an innocent smile that seemed wrong considering what she had just said.

"Oh? Anyone in particular?" Dakota asked, hoping she wouldn't say young women.

"Two husbands." Betty broke into laughter before wiping away some tears.

"Why?"

"What can I say? I had bad taste. I was young when I married the first one, only seventeen. Then one night after four years of being beaten black and blue, I stabbed him."

"Did you go to prison?"

"Yeah, for a few years. I got off light cos it was self-defence, you see. Then when I got out I met Mick. He seemed lovely and perfect. Until about two days into our honeymoon and he punched me so hard I ended up in hospital. I realised straight away that I had made a big mistake and as soon as I got out of hospital, I laid out an elaborate plan where everyone thought he had gone away on business, only he never arrived at his hotel, because that morning as he was eating his breakfast I smacked him round the head with a hammer until he was dead."

Dakota found herself appalled and yet interested in Betty's tale of murder. She didn't know if this place was making her like this, but she wanted to hear more about it. So she listened to Betty for hours as she told her what he looked like after she had bust his head open, and how she buried him in the garden, and put decking and a pagoda over where his body was interred. And as fate had it, Betty would get run over by a police car as she left the police station after giving a stellar performance as the confused and worried wife checking on police progress to find her missing husband.

"That's karma for you." Betty chuckled. "Now I'm stuck with both of the fuckers for eternity maybe!"

"Are they here?"

"Oh yeah, they are on a different level so I can't see them, but sometimes I think they will just appear, like ghosts, that's why I don't leave my room. This is the first time I've left my room for weeks. Well I say weeks, could be years for all I know, no way to tell where you are time-wise. All I know is I am dead and this is my punishment for murdering two people."

"But it was self-defence! You wouldn't have killed them if they hadn't been beating you up constantly!" Dakota said angrily.

"You'll get it all together soon, love; you'll understand how it works. It's only self-defence if they are trying to kill you. All I had to do was leave; I didn't have to kill them. I guess I just wanted to."

Dakota was stunned. She realised she knew nothing about the rules of punishment. This wasn't a legal system she was dealing with.

"So if you're such a bad person why aren't you in hell? Why isn't the rapist in the corridor in hell?"

"Uh, I don't know. I don't understand any of it. As far as I'm concerned this is hell. Every time I go to sleep I dream about them. It's like it's happening all over again. Other times I dream that they are out in the corridor trying to get in. The dreams... they feel so real."

Lightning lit the curtains for a moment and Dakota realised she felt tired, after all the vodka and the whisky she had reluctantly shared with Betty.

"I need to sleep... do you mind?"

"No, you give it a go. You might need more whisky. You can finish that off; there is more where that came from." Betty got up and moved over to the door. She paused to listen for a moment then bolted out the door, slamming it. Dakota heard the sound of dragging footsteps and cackling again as

Betty hurried into her own room. Dakota got up and re-locked the door, listening to the sniffing noises the rapist in the hall was making. She felt alone and very afraid again.

She needed to know what had happened; she was dead and that was it but she still needed to know how and what she had done to deserve such an awful afterlife.

Lying down on her bed she closed her eyes and listened. Over the sound of the storms, she could hear crying, low moans and manic laughter. The sources of these noises seemed to be above and below her. It was all around her. People in other rooms, on other floors and on her own floor, were suffering terrible moments of pain and guilt.

She lay there for hours, just listening to them all until the sound became a lullaby that sent her to sleep.

FOUR: Loverman

The room was dark, but it was hot. The curtains fluttered slightly in a breeze from the open window, and in the distance she could hear cars passing, far off in their late night journeys. Beside her bed the time glowed red for 1.30am.

Low down and faint she could hear the words to a song playing:

"*Loverman, since the world began, forever Amen till the end of time...*"

The door to the room was haloed in a dim yellow light coming from the hallway.

Then a shadow broke up the halo as a figure moved outside the door. It was a man and he was humming along to the music that was playing somewhere in her room. When the door opened, all she could see was the silhouette of a man with long hair that just touched his shoulders, wearing a pair of trousers and nothing else. She could not see his face; he was just a black shape moving slowly and silently save for his low humming.

Although she seemed quite still and at ease there was a great knot growing inside her, twisting and turning her stomach over. As he closed the door and made his way towards her bed in the dark, she realised it was fear she felt.

"*There's a devil waiting outside your door... weak with evil and broken by the world... shouting your name and he's asking for more...*"

He had put the song back to the beginning and it was playing over again as she felt the weight of him lie down on the bed beside her, all the while singing along quietly. Fear was becoming confusion; she knew this man. Why was she so afraid of him? He said nothing to her; he just sang along, low and soft to the words of the song. He was faceless movement beside her in the dark, and he drew closer to her ear as he whispered the words:

"Take off that dress... I'm coming down... I'm your Loverman..."

The room seemed to be growing hotter and she could feel her body beginning to perspire, as she smelt moisture growing on his skin. Then he put his hand under her nightdress and buried it between her legs.

Dakota woke bolt upright, sweating and shaking. The light was still on, and she could see that she was still alone. She felt terrified and confused again. Though her head throbbed she reached across to the bottle of whisky to take a swig. Thunder rolled outside and she jumped, dropping the bottle on the floor. Glass shattered and the smell of whisky rose up from the dirty grey carpet. She pushed the images from her dream out of her head and concluded that it was the fear of the rapist in the corridor that had made her dream such a creepy dream.

She was still clothed in her grey sweater and jeans, but her boots lay on the floor by the bed, scuffed and old. Quickly she pulled them on and made ready to leave her room and go back downstairs. She didn't want to be alone anymore, and she didn't want to fall asleep again, so grabbing her room key and putting it in her pocket, she unbolted the door and raced out, locking it behind her.

The corridor was brighter. It appeared as though more lamps had been lit and she could see that the corridor stretched away for at least a mile. Though she wanted to investigate more, she was sure she could hear dragging footsteps approaching from the distance, so without a thought she got into the elevator and asked to be taken to the lobby.

FIVE: The Great Outdoors

The lobby seemed to be no different than before; people still lay about in various stages of drunkenness and despair. Dakota stood warily in the doorway looking around, wondering if she dared enter. She felt drawn to the door across the room that led outside. Without further thought she bolted across the room, bumping into furniture and narrowly missing another resident who had stood up as she crossed his vision.

As soon as she was through the first set of doors she breathed a little easier, looking back through the glass panels to make sure no one was following her. Rain howled against the doors ahead, but still she needed to go out there, and throwing her weight against the doors, she fell out into the rain-soaked night.

Dim light from the hotel flooded down in patches onto the mud that surrounded her. Taking steps forward was harder than she thought; the thick black mud clung to her feet as though it were trying to drag her down. As lightning flashed she saw a path ahead of her, so as fast as she could, she trudged forward to hard ground, where she stood to rest her legs. Rain whipped at her mercilessly, her hair and clothes were soaked within minutes and she was freezing under the icy gales that tried to knock her to her knees.

Dakota wanted to cry, but instead she screamed angrily at the storm. The great grim hotel sneered back at her, its windows like eyeless sockets beyond the great sheets of rain. A few yards away, the dead trees of the forest rose up out of the mud like the twisted clawed hands of old ladies. They seemed to be beckoning her into the endless night, calling her into the deep sickening dark of the forest. Anger was replaced by a weak sobbing noise that she realised was coming from her own throat. Dakota fought the urge to disappear into the dark throng of the trees and turned back to the hotel. Gargoyles leered at her and their clawed fingers reached down from above, where the walls seemed to have no end; they just stretched up into the abyss of the storm-filled sky, the dim lights at the windows blinking out into the clouds.

The wind rocked her back towards the hotel, whipping her face with her own hair and the cold sharp rain. Trying again not to be pulled into the mud forever, Dakota slouched back to the door. A gloomy lamp swung above the dark wood and she looked up at the windows beyond it.

Someone was watching her from a window high above the door. It was just a silhouette, but she knew it was a man. His gaze seemed to sink into her skin and gnaw at her bones. All was still in her. The storm raged and yanked at her tiny form, but she was frozen to the spot, eyes locked on the shape at the window. The curtain dropped back and he was gone.

Suddenly Dakota felt sick, as though her stomach was swimming around her midriff, eating into its own tail. She gagged uselessly, nothing in her body to empty out – she was dead all over. All she did was suck in air to fill dead lungs. The air was thick, it smelt bad, like something was rotting, and she gagged again.

Moments later she was back inside, on the other side of the main doors. The glass doors ahead swung in the burst of wind she had let in by re-entering the hotel. Weakly, she prodded them open and dragged mud into the lobby on her wet feet. Residents looked up momentarily and sniggered behind their cigarettes. Unamused, she moved past them all in the direction of the Bar. Rain dripped from every part of her and she shivered in the chill air of the drab, dull room.

At the doorway to the Bar she felt as though she was being observed again, the image of the faceless man at the window squirming like an eel in her mind, but a quick look around proved she had imagined it.

SIX: Remembering

The Bar looked the same; a few more people sat at the dirty tables as she made her way back in a trail of rain and sorrow in her wake.

Danny sat at the end, smoking and watching her approach through the dim and dirty room. He did not ask why she was soaked through; he just got up and poured her a drink, cigarette dangling from his lips, smoke curling across his face.

"You all right?" he asked. Dakota looked up and again recognised his accent as she had the night before. It almost hurt to hear it, making her think of things that did not belong here, in this damp mildewed room where whispers slithered out of the shadows and gave life to its flickering edges.

Moments before, she had reached into her pocket and pulled out the sodden clump of paper and tobacco that had been her own stash, and dropped them on the bar with a thick slap.

"So what are all those clocks for in the lobby?" she asked.

"Well, if you're going to visit the living it helps to know what time of day it is there. That door takes you back to wherever you need to go, if you want to try and contact them that are still alive," he explained.

"Ahh, so there is such a thing as ghosts then? So I can go back and spook people then?" she asked, almost laughing.

"If you want, but it takes a lot of energy to communicate. It's tiring – people who try to do too much end up right back here, exhausted, unable to move or do anything. This place seems empty a lot of the time – most of the residents go back to cause havoc, others just go back to watch. A lot of them hang around clairvoyants, hoping to God they might be able to get through to someone. They're all so fucked up, they just want to stay with the living."

"But if we are here to be punished, how come we can just do what we want? If it makes them happy to go back and wreak havoc, surely they aren't being punished anymore? They could just stay there forever!" She found herself asking the strangest questions.

"It's not nice going back, you know! It's terrible to see your loved ones and not be able to communicate or be acknowledged by them. I went back once and I'll never do it again; took me months to recover. It's a natural thing to try and make amends for what sent you here. You can't stay there anyway." He got up to serve another customer. "They bring you back when you get too weak. Being there is draining for us, and communicating can really take it out of you. There are those who do the whole 'poltergeist thing' and you have to be strong to do that. They can't do it all the time, but they just enjoy the interaction with the living – makes them feel less dead, I think. The less you do when you are there, and the less emotion it causes you, the longer you get to stay. But no matter what way you look at it, you are still being punished whether you are here or there."

"I guess that's the idea though, isn't it? Everything about this place will make you insane eventually." She looked down the bar to the other customer. He had obviously just arrived. He was confused and shaking as he gulped down the sickly whisky he was given. He jumped, smacking into the bar, as a drunk, dirty young man fell against him, dribbling and mumbling incoherently.

"Danny, how come there aren't more people here? I mean I'd expect to see millions of residents from different times and stuff." Danny wandered back down to where she was sitting as the new arrival grabbed the bottle of whisky and raced out of the Bar.

"It's got something to do with dimensions. There are millions of people here – you just can't see them all." He shrugged. "I heard someone say once that you can see them all if you concentrate hard enough. Must be like being psychic or something."

Silence sat between them for a while as Dakota tried to understand the whys and wherefores of the hotel. Then she realised it was as pointless as trying to understand the depths of space and whether there was an edge to the universe. As a child, she had imagined that there was a point where space and the stars ended, and beyond was just white nothingness. As though the universe was a fruit bowl on God's dining table. That his cupboard was full of other universes that lived in tea cups and coffee mugs.

"So you went outside, then?" Danny asked, changing the subject and pointing to her boots that oozed with mud. Dakota looked down at them and wrinkled her nose at them, suddenly aware of the thick wet contents and how it felt between her toes.

"Yeah, didn't get far, I wanted to see the lake, but the rain was so heavy it hurt."

"I don't think there's a person here who hasn't tried to get out there. Nobody gets very far. Of course some of the residents are mad enough to go out to the woods."

"Yeah that guy, the rapist, goes out there, I think. What's in the woods? Why would he keep going out there?"

"Which rapist?" He laughed. "We got loads of 'em!"

"Looks about sixty, long grey hair, laughs a lot? Why would he want to go to the woods? There's no girls to rape out there, is there?"

"Oh him. Some of the worst ones don't ever come in here; they just stay out there, lurking in the dark to frighten newcomers as they arrive on the shore. Besides, I imagine part of his punishment is never being able to rape a woman again."

"So some do arrive without just waking up on the floor?"

"Yeah, the ones who pass over naturally, their deaths are easy, so when they get here they have the punishment of having to walk up to the hotel through the woods. It's usually the old men who pass on nice and easy of a heart attack or of old age, but when they were still mobile they used to fiddle with children," Danny replied, shaking his head slightly.

"So do you know what crimes you have to commit to come here?"

"Well, so far as I can tell, you have to be a rapist, murderer or child abuser. Or you have to have committed suicide – that's a big one here, I think, but they don't usually stay here as long as the others, for some reason. It's amazing how far those three things stretch. I mean you get people here who allowed abuse to continue even when they knew about it. You get politicians and world leaders here – even though they didn't pull the trigger they allowed thousands of people to die in wars and conflicts. There are other things that get you sent here, I'm sure. I just haven't met many who didn't commit any of those particular ones. It's a bit like being in a hospital for the criminally insane."

"Maybe I killed myself?" Dakota wondered out loud. It seemed to fit with her memories so far. Perhaps she never recovered from her parents' deaths.

A drunken brawl kicked off behind her and two men began punching each other as tables and glasses scattered.

"Why do they let people drink for nothing here?" asked Dakota. "I mean the kinds of people who end up here are hardly going to be pacified by huge amounts of whisky!" She jumped out of the way as one man flew up against the bar, smacking his head and crumpling to the floor.

"It's a trick," replied Danny, pulling her away and whispering in her ear. "It was in the bible – '*wine and drunkenness take away the understanding*'."

"What do you mean?"

"They give us alcohol and booze to cloud our judgement and the chances of us ever leaving grow smaller as the years pass."

"I never see you drink,"

"Heh, that's part of my punishment. I can't leave this room, but I can't touch alcohol. I am forced to remain where I spent most of my life, but without the help of drunkenness." He smiled.

"I don't get it. Surely they want us to repent? Doesn't God want us to get to Heaven?" she asked, slightly dismayed.

"I'm not sure. I don't have all the answers, but it seems like they make it as difficult as possible for you to leave, without giving you an easy ride. It's like God tests you and tests you until you can truly prove that your soul is worth saving."

"What did you do to get in here?" she asked, but was unsurprised when he avoided her question yet again and began to clear up the broken glasses.

An image from the past surfaced: her mother reading the Bible to her at Easter. In her soft Irish tones, she told Dakota how Judas came to kiss Jesus and betrayed him in the dark and malevolent garden.

Dakota felt the sadness rise to her throat again as she thought how much she wanted to see her parents, have her mother play with her hair as she laid her head on her lap, be safe and warm in Daddy's arms again. But it could be a very long time before she'd feel safe again; she couldn't atone for what she couldn't remember. And there was no soft light, no sad-eyed Christ to answer her tears. She was amongst the fallen, put away from the presence of God and all his angels that she had seen in the pages of the Bible. She remembered Gustav Dore's drawing of the circle of angels, the gateway to Heaven shimmering with love and light, the flutter of wings, huge and white. It was all wrong; she had never seen this place in paintings, and she wasn't prepared for this. She had expected angels and flowers and Jesus and Mary Magdalene and his friends would all be there, and maybe even Judas was allowed into Heaven.

Dakota was weeping quietly in the dark corner of the Bar. All her childhood images of death and Heaven were useless now. All she had left was despair, rain and endless night filling her up with every passing moment. She had done something bad, something that had made God angry, and he had sent her here to make up for what she had done.

SEVEN: The Boy in the Hallway

Dakota wiped her face clean of tears and swept out of the Bar. She didn't want to go up to her room. She didn't know where to go to feel safe. The Lobby was full of people shouting and fighting, so she looked the other way down the hallway that ran outside the Bar. She realised she hadn't been down there, so she headed towards where it turned a corner and stretched on forever. It was unbelievable – the corridor had no end that she could see and she sensed that it went on for miles. Curiosity had her walking down it, though, wondering where it led.

In the available light from the oil lamps she could see the same velveteen wallpaper that grimaced in the lobby, but out here it was in a worse state, peeling weakly, its colours insipid and rotten. Spiders had lived amongst the wrought iron lampstands for some time, their webs now a haven for dust old as time. The air smelt old and musty, as though it was composed entirely of the same dust and cobwebs that she had to swipe from her eyes.

The dim wall lamps offered little help. Shadows crawled in towards them like cloaked figures and it felt like the dark was trying to suppress the light, pushing it back into the source. She felt uneasy; she had the perception that the deep shadows concealed things she did not want to know about; darkness pressed in on her like a mantle making her feel a little claustrophobic. Just as she decided she didn't want to go any further, something moved beside her.

She froze. The sensation was cold, as if someone had coated her in ice water, but it was caused by someone watching her at very close quarters. The darkness stared into her and she looked back, trying to see who was there in the shadow.

"Who is that?"

Silence answered her. A cold wind was whispering down the hallway, disturbing the flames of the wall lamps, and the shadows danced momentarily, freakishly. A lamp on the wall beside her came back to life after fading out the moment she stood still. The new glow of light brought her face to face with a boy who was an inch or so shorter than her.

Dakota leaped back in fright – if her heart had been beating it would have hammered itself out of her chest – but the boy stood very still, watching her reaction with an expressionless face.

Steadying herself, she recognised him as the boy from the lobby she had seen on her arrival.

"You scared the shit out of me! What are you doing?" she asked, half-angry.

"Nothing, just standing here," he replied, so still and calm in comparison to his demeanour when she had last seen him. His legs were still and his eyes no longer darted about. Dakota felt kind of sorry for him, strangely unafraid of the boy lurking in the shadowed hall.

"Sorry if I startled you. I'm Dakota. Who are you?"

"David. I saw you arrive the other day. You said to Ariel you didn't remember what happened to you?" he asked, his voice low and steady.

"Yeah, head injuries or something, can't remember anything... well, I just remembered stuff from my childhood, but the rest is gone." She shrugged. "Do you know why you're here?"

He said nothing but raised his arms up towards her, wrists uppermost. Dakota jumped back against the dark dirty wall as she saw great deep gashes appear on his forearms. Blood flowed away from the wounds in great fat rivers dripping, panicked, to the floor.

"I hate blood. Now they make me bleed all the time to punish me for stealing my life from God." He spoke steadily, his eyes wide and dull, boring into her. "That's why I'm in the dark. I can't see it if it's dark. I can just feel it, wet, all over my hands." He looked down at his arms and she followed his gaze to see the cuts in his wrists were gone.

"Why did you kill yourself?" she asked, relieved the blood was gone. "You don't look any older than eighteen."

"Couldn't take it anymore. My dad beat me almost every day of my life, and I was too much of a coward to fight back. You'd do it, too... years of abuse, bruised and battered so bad I couldn't leave the house half of the time. I wanted to kill him, stab him in the neck and watch blood pour down his fat useless body. But I didn't want to go to hell, so I killed myself instead."

"How long have you been here?" she asked, trying to forget the imagery he had just introduced into her brain.

"I don't know... time passes strangely. It could be years or weeks, but it's been a long time. They all blend in the end and it never gets any better, you never feel any safer. It's a nightmare you cannot wake from. You can't even close your eyes to it." He muttered on, staring intently at her, as though he was expecting a reaction from her. "There is no justice here. You might have lived a good life, but one mistake, or one choice, makes all the difference. I was always the victim. Maybe if I had stayed the victim all my life I could have gone to Heaven. But no! They send me here, among murderers and rapists, to pay my dues! What justice is that? Where is that 'just God'?"

A laugh escaped from his throat, and suddenly he was laughing manically, tears pouring down his face as he turned away from her and ran up the corridor, deeper into the bowels of the hotel.

As his laughter faded off into the distance, the wall lamps flickered further up the hall from her, the lights around her died off and a sudden burst of light from a lamp in the distance revealed another person standing about ten yards away. Dakota felt fear burning in her stomach as the spectator stood very still, watching her in the weak light. A second later the lights faded again and he was swallowed by the surging shadows as they fought to gain control of the hallway. Dakota bolted back towards the lobby, suddenly afraid of the dark again and all it contained. The light around her rose and fell as she raced back to the more substantial light near the door to the Bar. The darkness seemed to follow her, and she realised the whole lower floor of the hotel was even dingier than before.

As she raced into the Bar she came face to face with Danny, who seemed about to lock the doors.

"You best get back to your room – it's getting darker. All the crazies come up from the basement when it gets like this. It's not safe down here. Go to your room and lock the door."

"Why is it getting darker?" she asked, panting and panicked by Danny's warning.

"It just does. It means the Punishers are coming out. It usually lasts a while, so just stay in your room. Go on, get out of here!"

"Punishers?" she asked frantically as distant wails reached her ears.

"For some of the residents, just being here isn't enough punishment. If you behave badly here, you get punished. Get to your room and hope you haven't been bad!" he shouted, slamming the Bar door to lock it.

Dakota felt the dark surging up around her, and the air began to fill with an even mustier smell than usual. Low cackles and screeches began to fill the air and she darted into the elevator as a bald man with no teeth ran at her, laughing sadistically.

EIGHT: The Punishers

When Dakota arrived on her own floor, all was quiet. She listened out for Woods, but his laughter must have been ringing through the twisted forest instead. She paused outside her door and listened to the sounds coming from the other rooms. There was a low hum of music, too quiet for her to identify, and the occasional sound of weeping. Further away, a man was crying out loudly.

"I'm sorry! How many times do I have to say it?" Followed by his own wailing and moaning.

Then other voices began to become clear: a hundred people talking to themselves or to others.

"I'd do it again if I had to, believe me!"

"You deserved everything that happened to you!"

"It was an accident; it went off in my hand!"

"I couldn't help myself. They were so cute, I had to take them home and keep them."

"They asked for it! Every single one of them!"

The voices faded in and out, all in their own private hells, all trying to excuse their crimes.

Movement down the corridor made her focus again. The wall lamps flickered and sneezed in the gasping dark, the corridor grew and shrank in length as lamps in the distance breathed in and out again.

Then once more the silhouette came into view. He was watching her again, silent and foreboding. Just before the wall lamp behind him flickered out, she saw him begin to advance on her again.

Before he could complete his first step, Dakota was in her room with the door bolted. She wanted to scream at him to leave her alone, but she was afraid he would speak again.

Instead she whispered into her hands, "Go out to the woods, leave me alone!"

The oil lamp flooded insipid light over her tiny room as she crossed to look out of the window again. Beyond the faded velvet, the storm still raged, like a monster trying to smash its way into the hotel, its fist throwing bolts of lightning into the earth.

In the mud that led to the woods, she could see people rolling around, some fighting, others just rolling in the filth. Still more were running riot, chasing people, dragging them down, stamping them into the ground before running into the forest.

It rose up like many groping fists, its dead black branches scuttling in the whipping winds, lashing them with the stinging rain. Dakota could only imagine what it was like out there in the woods, a thousand places for crazed lunatics to hide and torment, the screeching wind trapped under the branches, sick laughter carried on the air. She shuddered.

As lightning crackled across her vision, she dropped the curtain and turned back to the room in its decaying splendour. The walls looked tea-stained and the pathetic wallpaper was peeling. The dingy high corners of the room kept their secrets but Dakota imagined that they were full of spiders and dust. Occasionally she noticed a string of cobweb trailing down the wall.

She sighed woefully at the decay around her and threw herself down on the bed. As she moved, a crackling noise came up from under the bed sheets. Dakota paused a moment, then pulled the moth-eaten sheets back to reveal a piece of paper lying slightly crinkled, bearing neat writing in capital letters.

She froze, her mind racing, then moving into a better position she began to read.

Like an angel of wild eye,
I shall return to where you lie
And towards you, noiseless, glide
With the shades of eventide.

I shall give you, dusky one,
Kisses icy as the moon,
Embraces that a snake would give
As it crawled around a grave.

When the sombre morning comes
You will find your lover gone,
My place cold till night draws near.

As others reign through tenderness,
Over your life and youthfulness,
I want, myself, to reign through fear.

Dakota was shaking slightly. Fear burnt a hole in her stomach as her mind raced. The poem had not been there earlier, as she had slept beneath the covers and would have noticed it – which meant that since she had left the room a few hours earlier, someone had broken into her room and put this in her bed. Nausea lurched in her. She had not considered the fact that someone could get into her room; she'd thought it was the only safe place in the hotel. But it seemed that breaking and entering went on here, too. Could anyone get in while she was in here? Surely not with all the bolts and chains on the door.

Dakota needed to speak to someone, and she was aware that going downstairs to Danny would be risky, so it would have to be Betty. Tears burned in her eyes as fear grew in her. Was the rapist still out there, waiting for her to come out?

Deciding that she would rather not wait in the hall while Betty decided whether to let her in, she knocked on the wall that joined Betty's room and waited.

A knock returned through the wall.

"Betty, can you hear me?" she half whispered, afraid that if he was outside her door he would hear.

"Yes darling, walls like paper here, what's wrong?"

"Can I come in? I need to see you. Get the door ready cos I think he's out in the hall and I don't want him to catch me."

"OK love, I'll wait by the door," came the disembodied

voice.

Within moments, Dakota was in Betty's room, still listening against the door for the sound of Woods moving in the corridor.

"Must have gone outside," she suggested as Betty opened her bottle of vodka. When Dakota saw it, she wanted to tell her what Danny had said about alcohol and how it would keep you here longer, but changed her mind as Betty showed a look of immense happiness at swallowing the clear liquid.

"God, I love this stuff. Bit harsher than the stuff I used to drink but the quality of the booze here ain't all that anyway." Betty laughed, and motioned to the chair by her bed on which she was sitting up against the wall. "Sit down and tell me what's up."

Dakota handed her the piece of paper and waited quietly while she read it through.

"Nice poem. Bit creepy though. Did you write it?"

"No. But it was in my room, in my bed. It wasn't there earlier, which means someone came up and put it in there," Dakota surmised.

"I never heard anyone go in after I heard you leave a couple of hours ago. Are you sure it wasn't there before?"

"Positive. I slept under the covers after you left; I would have felt it. Are you sure you didn't hear anything? They would have had to pick the lock to get in; you would have heard them, surely? I thought our rooms were safe. I don't feel safe anywhere now." Dakota's voice rose with panic, her hands beginning to shake as she fumbled with a cigarette.

"Don't panic. That won't help. Look, it's probably someone winding you up. There's not a lot else for people here to do."

Dakota fell quiet for a moment and listened to the rain whipping the window. "It just seems a bit sinister. Plus I don't like that someone can get into my room."

"They can't get in when yer in there if you have all the bolts on. Besides, not like there's anything in your room worth stealing, is it?" Betty chuckled and glanced around her own carbon copy room, with its stained walls and cobwebs.

Suddenly there was loud movement in the corridor outside, making Dakota jump.

"Shhh... stay still. I hope you haven't been up to anything naughty while you have been here." whispered Betty, visibly afraid and taking an extra-large swig of vodka.

"What? What is it?" But Betty put a finger over her lips and sat very still.

Beyond the peeling door something or someone was rummaging about in the corridor. Dakota had a feeling that there were others, further up the corridor. She could hear shuffling and sniffing noises.

Dakota froze as a shadow crept under the door along with a foul odour as the sniffing noise lingered on the other side of the wood. Something hideous was out there, something worse than Woods and his cackling. There was a change in the air, like electricity, as if pure hate and anger had been made palpable and was moving around looking for someone to blame, someone to take its rage out on.

The moments it paused there stretched unbearably, and tension made Betty's grip on Dakota's arm a little tighter.

The sniffing stopped.

And the rage moved on, away up the corridor.

Moments later, a few rooms away, a door was kicked in, and amongst the thrashing and screaming, she sensed that a huge creature made of infinite malice and vengeance, dragged a soul away down into the bowels of the hotel. The screams didn't stop, but faded into the distance.

Dakota found she was shaking, and spilt vodka down her chin and chest as she gulped the offered bottle down till she gagged.

"Have you ever seen them?" Dakota asked, trying to hold the shake in her voice.

"No, I think you only see them if they are coming for you. I've heard them loads of times, but never seen them."

"Christ, I hope I never have to see them!"

"It's OK, you know you have been behaving. They won't touch you," reassured Betty, passing a lit cigarette to her companion's lips.

"Why do they send them? What are they?" she asked.

"They live in the basement. Some say they were the most disturbed psychopaths when they were alive. Others say they were never people, that they are manifestations of all the hate and anger in the world. Whatever they are, they have been recruited by Them to mete out punishments for misdeeds even in the afterlife. I've heard it said that they take them off to... well... somewhere worse than this."

"I guess there must be some discipline here then. Silly to think God would stick all the bad guys in one place and say: 'well, do what you like!'"

"Exactly. We are all here to *do our time* which means we can't go around being as evil as we were on earth."

"What kind of things do you get punished for?" asked Dakota, feeling the vodka was helping slightly even though it had made her feel sick.

"Well, violence for one, you get a lot of bullies here, and they think they can beat up anyone anytime. But the main thing people get punished for is misbehaving on earth. Scaring people, poltergeist activity and stuff. Not that the Punishers actually make everyone start behaving. Some people just don't care what happens to them. That's when people have really got no hope of getting out of here. When they just do what they like and take the consequences. Makes me wonder if they enjoy whatever the Punishers do to them." She shrivelled up her nose and shook her shoulders.

Dakota decided she wanted to not think about anything like that.

"How can you stand just staying in here all the time? Don't you ever want to just go and look around?"

"No thanks, I don't want to run into my dear departed husbands, and anyway, they let me have books to read now, so I just sleep and read and drink." She motioned to the pile of books by her bed.

"Wow that's good, wish I could have some books, I'd be quite happy to sit in my room and read."

"Heh yeah, but the only draw back is... well, take a look at them," Betty said, and handed Dakota a book, open at the last page. Dakota looked closer and, flipping the page over, realised that the final page of the book was missing. When she examined another, she found the same.

"They let you read them but don't give you the last pages?" asked Dakota incredulously.

"Heh, yeah and I thought I'd done something good to be given such a treat as having books to pass the time. Nope, nothing here is a reward, nothing is as good as it seems; there is always a catch." She looked slightly less jovial now, as the thoughts in her head began to move around.

"Bastards! How horrible! I bet the CDs they've given me to listen to are all blank or of bands I hated!" Dakota spat with a grimace on her face. That particular gift seemed like a booby prize now, and she had been so looking forward to hearing music again. "I really fucking hate this place."

"Well you're supposed to, I guess." Betty shrugged and gulped some more vodka.

"I need to find out what I did wrong, otherwise I'll never get out of here. How can I find out? Can I have hypnosis or something? Are there people like that here? Surely there must be a way I can find out?" Dakota was up on her feet, pacing up and down the small space of the room, her arms flailing dramatically.

"The Library of Remembrance will help you," said a voice that was not Betty's. Dakota spun round to stare at Betty who was staring at the wall beside her. Without speaking she motioned to Dakota that the voice had come from the other side of her wall.

"Hello? Who is that?" asked Betty loudly.

"Just want to help. The library is where you need to go," answered the croaky voice. Dakota was unsure if it was a man or a woman.

"Where is it?"

"You need to take the corridor by the Bar – you'll find it down there. Not many people know about it. Don't let anyone see you go there," warned the disembodied voice.

"Thanks... what's your name?" Dakota asked brightly.

Silence. And though the question was repeated several

times, the person in the next room did not speak again. The wind howled outside and Dakota turned to Betty to ask whether she had ever heard of the library, but Betty had passed out with an empty bottle of vodka in her lap. Dakota sighed and made her way back to her own room, slightly nervous that someone might be waiting for her in the shadowed room.

To her relief she found it empty. The draught that was creeping in through the sash windows stirred the curtains slightly, and even though she knew it was just a breeze, she had to check that no one was hiding behind the faded velvet curtains.

Folding the poem in half, she stowed it in a drawer in her bedside cabinet. Before closing the drawer, she discovered an old alarm clock; she was surprised to find it there as there seemed to be no clocks anywhere else in the hotel. Except by the door that led back to the land of the living. Her brain clicked into gear as she saw the time: 12.21am. If this was the time in England, then only a minute or two had passed the whole time she had been in the hotel. This also meant that if she went back now, she would be at the scene of her death.

Dakota's mind raced. It was a long shot, but if she hurried maybe she would get back in time to understand more about what had happened to her. Without a thought for Woods or any of the other crazies roaming the hotel, she bolted out the door and headed for the lobby. Maybe seeing her own death might help her remember more of her life. Perhaps it would be all she needed to trigger her memory back into working order. As she entered the brightness of the elevator she saw, out of the corner of her eye, the figure of a man standing further down the corridor.

NINE: Death

The lobby was emptier than Dakota expected, but she could hear the sounds of people hiding in the shadowed corners of the huge room. She knew if she didn't do it quickly she wouldn't do it at all. So, with one brief glance up at the clock labelled England, she pulled the door open and left the lobby before the revellers returned to the warmth of the hotel.

She found herself in the rain again. She could hear it thundering down through the trees above her but could not feel a drop of it on her skin. It was night and she was in a forest so dense that she could see only an inch or two of starless sky beyond the whispering leaves overhead. It sounded like a million voices speaking at once, whispering dark secrets, cackling.

When she looked down, she jumped back screaming and landed in the mud. At her feet lay her own dead body, drops of rain dribbling down her lifeless cheeks. It was hard to see in the dark, and she did not want to get closer to her body, but she knew she had to see it for herself. Getting up on her feet again, she moved around the body to inspect it.

Her head had caved in completely on the left side. Black blood and brain matter were oozing gently from the gaping wound, dripping down into the mud. Dakota gagged and pulled back, remembering the odd illusion she had seen when she arrived at the hotel, the blood pouring out of her head and down her clothes. She knew now she had been remembering possibly her last moments. Hand over her mouth, she looked back at herself. Her hair stuck to her face like tiny black snakes creeping across her cheek, past her still open eyes, glassy and staring past her own ghost into the rain-heavy sky and the wild screaming trees. She wanted to cry, grab her own body and shake herself awake. It was all a dream, an awful frightening dream and she could wake up and walk home to bed, wherever that was. But Dakota's hands only melted through the body on the forest floor, reminding her that it was all horribly true. She was dead. For a flash of a moment, as she stared into her own, dead gleaming eyes, she felt she had done this before. She felt that at some time, somewhere, she had stared into a pair of dead eyes, glassy and free of expression, looking forever into endless night. She shook the memory away, beginning to believe that being dead was driving her insane.

Dakota gathered her thoughts and began to look around for whoever had smashed her brains out, but she was too late. Her murderer was gone, and she had no idea who it was. Her trip back to her death scene had been a complete waste of time – she had no other memories, it had not triggered her forgotten thoughts to return, and she was none the wiser. Except she now knew that she had been murdered – she could not have smashed her own skull in, and there was nothing around that suggested she had been in an accident.

As she looked around she noticed a rock, about the size of her fist on the floor, roughly a metre away from her head. Bending down to look closer, she saw it was covered in blood. Black chunks of matter sat on its surface, slowly dissolving as drops of rain fell on it. Dakota felt suddenly afraid – of what, she did not know. After all, she was already dead; nothing could hurt her here. She had been murdered just after midnight in a lonely part of the woods where she couldn't even see any wildlife. Her poor body lay lifeless in the mud, rain slapping her face, creating movement that gave the illusion she was still alive. But she was dead and alone in the woods. No one would find her, perhaps not for days. Her body was lying in a grove of trees that was off the beaten track and only luck would allow her body to be found at all.

She stepped out of the grove and into a small clearing that lay beyond a huge tree that hid the entrance to the grove. Looking back, she was shocked to see that the huge tree seemed to have a face. It was clearly dead but looked oddly like a woman screaming with her arms and hair raised to the sky. The sight of it sent a murmur through Dakota's mind, scaring her slightly, but she felt she had seen it before. Perhaps it was one of the last things she saw if she died out here. Her last image before death could well have been that screaming tree.

Dakota waited. She waited all night long in the rain and the dark, staring at her own lifeless body, waiting for someone to come along and close her empty eyes.

When the first bright fingers of morning began to creep through the trees, Dakota stood and watched the growing light with tears in her eyes. There would never be a sunrise in Purgatory, but here she could watch it and appreciate it in a way she never had in life. Each leaf that caught the early sun was worthy of a few moments' pause, and all she could do was cry as though she had never seen it before and it was the most beautiful thing in the world. The sky was bright and she felt she should just keep looking at it to store up the brightness within her, as though she could carry that light back into Purgatory with her and make up for those sunless skies and endless night.

It was not until that evening that anyone took that particular path through the woods, and when the man walking his dog came into earshot, Dakota found herself shouting and screaming as though he could have done something to save her. The man did not hear Dakota, but the dog started barking in her general direction as she rushed out onto the path. It was useless, though. The man kept walking and pulled his dog away with him. From where she now stood out on the path, she looked back and realised she could not see the grove, or the small clearing that lay in front of it and the screaming tree. Her body was in a place nobody was going to pass by or chance upon. It was like a terrible story in a newspaper: *Body of young woman found in remote part of a forest, decomposed and lying undiscovered for several months.* She knew she must have read it a hundred times before, in books and in the papers, but it couldn't ever happen to her. Dakota knew she could be waiting there for days or months for someone to find her, so she decided to go and leave her sad remains behind in the lonely woods, hoping that someone would chance upon her. Who would want to kill her and what had she done in her life that could not be paid for by her own brutal murder?

She contemplated the same questions as she found herself coming back through the door into the Purgatory Hotel lobby.

She felt suddenly weak and feeble. Her legs gave way under her and she hit the floor hard. Arms wrapped around her and carried her to a chair, where she sat to regain composure.

"You'll be OK in a moment. It must have been a shock for you," said a voice she recognised. Dakota looked up to see Ariel leaning over her, her unearthly blue eyes burning coolly in her face.

"I saw myself... it was awful," Dakota managed before tears came to her eyes again.

"Do you want me to take you to Danny?"

"Yes... yes please... thank you Ariel."

"He missed you. So did Betty," said Ariel as she helped Dakota to her feet and manoeuvred her towards the Bar.

"Betty?"

"Yes, she must like you. She actually left her room to try and find you when you didn't come back."

"Was I gone for a long time? I guess I would be – I must have been there for about eighteen hours," muttered Dakota, counting on her fingers.

"Yes, that's around three weeks here! Betty was quite worried. She thought the crazies had carried you off into the woods. She said someone had been in your room?"

"Yeah, someone broke in and... put a poem in my bed."

"I'm afraid you can't stop criminals from being criminals. You'd think their incarceration would make them change, but it doesn't." Ariel shrugged as she pushed the door to the Bar open.

Danny came rushing across the dark room to take over from Ariel.

"Geez girl, I was starting to worry you wouldn't come

back!" he said franticly, throwing Dakota's arm over his shoulder.

"Thank you, Ariel," Dakota said softly as her helper smiled and left the Bar.

Danny guided her to a table close to the bar and sat her down.

"Where did you go?"

"To my death," she said weakly and took a cigarette from his offered hand. Someone in the shadows began to choke on his cigarette, and table lamps shuddered in the draught that whistled through from some cracked window somewhere. Danny went away to the bar and brought back a glass and some vodka. Dakota took one sip and spat it back out.

"I can't drink that shit anymore!" A low cackle rose out of the distant corner of the Bar, but Dakota ignored it, instead looking past the oil lamp into Danny's lined face.

"OK, what did you see?" he said, pushing the bottle aside.

In a low voice, Dakota told him everything she had seen, and also about the poem in her room.

"Ahh, that's probably some fella's idea of fun – I wouldn't worry about that. You get plenty of people trying to shake others up." He paused and blew cigarette smoke from the corner of his wide mouth. "At least you know how you died, now. That's something."

"Yeah I know, but that doesn't explain why I'm here! I was the victim. What had I done to deserve that or this? I was upset at first, now I'm just fucking angry!"

"OK, OK, it will all come back. Don't worry," he said and patted her hand.

"Do you know about the Library of Remembrance?" she whispered to him. An odd look flashed across his face. She almost thought it was fear, but dismissed it.

"Yeah, I heard of it, like. Not heard of it from a lot of people though."

"Do you know what it is? Or where it is?"

"No, sorry love, I don't," he replied abruptly. "I think you should go and lie down for a while. You need to rest after that."

"Yeah, whatever," she sighed and got up. After staggering slightly, she moved out of the Bar, ready to thump anyone who even looked at her. She felt that Danny was being deliberately unhelpful, and didn't know why. Whatever the reason, she would just have to find the library alone.

TEN: The Library of Remembrance

Dakota turned down the hallway she had investigated before. It was still as dimly lit, the lamps flickered in and out of existence on the dying walls, the floor below her feet was still littered with bottles and cigarette butts.

A tiny thread of fear tightened around her stomach as the darkness closed in around her, but she felt determined that no one was going to stop her from finding the library. She had no idea why she needed to go there, but if nothing else perhaps she might find out who wrote the poem. The name of the author might mean something... anything. Anything was good enough for her now. She was so desperate to know what had happened in her life that she would take any help, even the help of a voice from another room whose owner she had no knowledge of, even though he could have sent her here to trick her, and the library might not even exist.

As the thoughts raced through her head, she kept telling herself that she had to just see if the information she had been given was of any use.

The hallway stretched on, occasional cobwebs brushing her face. She even suspected some other people were in the corridor too, but they were hiding in the shadows, watching her. As she went further and further into the bowels of the hotel, she began to see people – the back of a head, an arm, a leg, never the full picture – as the silent strangers drifted in and out of the dense shadows that lined the corridors like sentinels. She heard murmurs bringing the dark to life. The deep shadows had a voice, sounding like many lost bitter souls whispering bleak warnings and trickery in her ears. She could occasionally pick out a word or two: "little girl," "mistake," "wrong way," "trouble," "go back." They drawled out of the dark, the words like flies buzzing around her aching head, making her skin crawl. She had the perception that hands were reaching out, brushing against her body, trying to feel her with invisible fingers.

Blocking out the faint words and hands, Dakota realised she could not even see if there were any doors, so turned to one of the wall lamps to see if it would come off the wall. Her hands found the wrought iron base growing from the bottom of the glass shade that protected the flame inside. Sweeping cobwebs aside, shuddering slightly as spiders ran across her fingers, she tugged gently at the lamp where it met the wall. A tiny sprinkling of plaster powdered her knuckles and she tugged again. This time the whole lamp came cleanly out of the wall, chunks of plaster thumping to the floor at her feet, and she stumbled back across the hallway, the oil in the lamp sloshing about and causing the flame to flicker nervously.

"That's better," Dakota muttered to herself, pleased that she had a source of light she could carry herself, instead of relying on the sparse and unfaithful hall lighting. It seemed that as long as she was holding the lamp, it did not suffer from the same sickness as all the other lamps that shifted in and out of life. Movement and whispers scuttled beyond her vision as she continued on, fear still tightening in her belly. She began to inspect the walls looking for doors, but there were none – just peeling wallpaper and insects. She could not see any more residents; they seemed to have decided not to come as far in as she was. Still she felt as though someone was behind her, leading her to suspect the occupants of this corridor were more comfortable sticking to the shadows. Speeding up slightly, she did her best to ignore the feeling and took in everything the light cast by her lamp allowed her to see. Bottles no longer littered the floor, just dust and insects. It felt to her that no one had come this far up in the corridor for some time, but other footprints in the thick dust on the floor told her otherwise.

After walking for some fifteen minutes she came across a door on the left-hand side of the corridor. At the side of the door was a plaque, covered in cobwebs and dust that Dakota had to wipe away before she could read it.

"The Library of Remembrance," she whispered as her eyes scanned the engraved plaque. As she put her hand on the gilt doorknob, someone kicked a bottle up the corridor behind her. They were about twenty feet away, she guessed, although she couldn't see a shape or silhouette in the dim light down the hall. As the fear tightened, she turned the handle and pushed the door in far enough for her to get around it before closing it behind her.

The room she was in was also poorly lit, but there were more lights dotted around. They revealed high blocks of shelves containing hundreds of leather-bound books with gold writing on the spines. She could not tell how far up they went, nor could she see how long the room was as it all just seemed to fade into the distance as far as her eyes could see, but the little lamps continued to glow far off in the distant shadows, taking on the appearance of stars in the gloom. It was not a wide room. A high bookshelf stood a few feet away, and beyond that stood another up against the wall. A tall window beside it flashed as the storm threw itself at the hotel, and momentarily the room was awash with light, highlighting the thickening cyst of dust that lay over every surface, from the tops of the books to the long table that sat below the window. The rain continued at the mercy of the howling winds that threw its course from the window pane back into the endless night.

She could not tell if there was anyone else in the room, but a continuous noise permeated the dark. It sounded like tiny scratching, as though a million mice were alive in the room, scuttling beyond her lamplight. As she moved into the room, it seemed to get louder, so she followed her ears to the nearest bookshelf and lifted her lamp up to read the spines of the books. They all bore names of people: Mary Jane Barrows, Mary Kerry Barrows and on and in alphabetical order. Intrigued, she pulled down a heavy volume entitled Matthew Arnold Barron. It seemed to be the heaviest book she had ever held and she almost dropped her lamp as its weight surprised her into an unsteady wobble and a few swear words. Dropping to her knees, she rested the book on the floor, leaning the lamp precariously against the wall.

The scratching noise grew as she pulled open the heavy binding and looked at the first page. She read in flowing script:

The Life of Matthew Arnold Barron, formerly known as Henri Luc Pepin.

Dakota shrugged and pushed the pages on until she found the words: *Matthew was born in 1963 to Frank and Maria Barron.*

It went on to describe his birth and early childhood, and Dakota took it to be a biography of some kind. Grabbing a thick wad of pages, she flicked towards the back of the book. About three quarters of the way through, she stopped to discover the source of the scratching. The life of Matthew Barron was being written right before her eyes. Words appeared on the pages as though some spider was running across the large paper, leaving a trail of ink behind it, all the time scratching like the sound of a quill nib on thick paper. Dakota recalled seeing the same thing happening on the hotel register, but she still couldn't believe her eyes. Suddenly the writing stopped. As she leaned closer to the book, she read that Matthew Barron had just died.

Dakota put the book back on the shelf and decided she should start looking for the book bearing her name. She wondered if it would still be recording what she was doing. Or would its pages be silent, bereft of the scratching ink that recorded her life, silent since the moment she had died?

As she moved along the shelves, she marvelled at the thousands of names – all these people who had been alive or were still alive now, totally unaware that somewhere their biography was being penned by invisible hands. She had to walk a long way to get to the area where her name would be, only to discover that her book was probably about ten shelves up towards the ceiling. To her right she could see a ladder that ran all the way up to the shady top shelf. A light tug revealed that it rolled along the length of the bookcase on castors, so holding her lamp in one hand, she began to climb up in search of her book.

The air was full of dust, and it smelt ancient. From the depths of her mind she recalled how second-hand bookshops smelt of old paper and damp. Words from someone else's mind mouldering on pages unread for decades, useless and lonely. Looking around briefly, she could see lamps set at intervals along the bookcases, but the shadows in the room appeared to be winning the battle for control of the huge endless library. The continuous scratching began to become a background noise to Dakota. The millions of words being penned in the millions of books had no definition. It was just a low hum of perpetual sound, the events that brightened or shattered lives reduced to a dull scratching.

Dakota searched amongst the hundreds of books belonging to the Crow surname, until at last she found it. A huge leather-bound spine, embossed in gold lettering: *Dakota Grace Crow*. Her volume was thinner than others around it, which made sense, she realised, for her life had been so very short in comparison to some. She hadn't even outlived her grandparents on her father's side; if she looked she would find most probably that grandmother Crow was swearing at the television, still unaware that her youngest grandchild was dead. Granddad Crow was most likely making yet another model of an aeroplane that he would go and hang up with all the others in his dead son's old bedroom. The books that bore their life stories would be about three times as thick as Dakota's.

However, she was not in the dusty old library to read about her grandparents; she was there to read her own life story. So, nervously, she reached for her book and yanked it off the shelf, her lifetime of dust suddenly disturbed. Surprisingly, it was not as dusty as Matthew Barron's had been. Had someone read about her while she was still alive? Perhaps some dead relative. Pausing for a moment, she listened to see if her book was still alive with the scratching of words. But it was not. Silence drifted out of the pages to her, her life was over, nothing left to say about the girl she used to be. On the earth, her body was already decaying, her heart as quiet as the book she now held in her hands.

No matter, she thought. She had some reading to do, and began to descend the wooden ladder, the book clamped under the arm that also held the lamp.

When she reached the floor, she wandered off in search of a place to sit – there had to be some chairs somewhere. After walking a shadowy length of book case, she found a group of tables and chairs. They bore an undisturbed veil of dust, and the oil lamps that sat on them sent out a dim light from under a thick layer of grey cobwebs.

Turning off her own lamp and leaning it against the leg of the nearest table, she laid her book down on the dusty table, and watched as a cloud rose up around it and danced sluggishly in the light.

As she pulled out the chair and went to sit down, she noticed another person sat at the same table. The man had a mass of wild white hair and a look in his eyes that made her think of a frightened animal. He had a book laid out before him, and from a cursory look, she could see he was about half-way through reading it.

"Hi," she said unsurely as she sat down. "Didn't expect to see anyone else here."

"You are only the third other person I have ever seen in here. I hear people here but never see them," he replied, his voice low and wispy. "I come here all the time. I just go away to sleep for a while then I come back. Feels like I have been reading this book for ten years. Maybe I have?"

"Is it… about you?" she asked, looking across at his book, which was somewhat thicker than her own.

"Yes, it's mine," he said almost sadly, his eyes falling down onto the pages before him. "I don't want to remember it all, but I can't seem to stop reading… like I am addicted to it. Sometimes I just have to stop and put it away, go and have a drink at the bar. I didn't come back here for weeks after I first read it. I got as far as my eighth birthday and couldn't handle it anymore." He stopped talking and ran a withered hand through his mane of hair.

"Did you have a... um... bad life?"

"No! That's why it's so hard to read. It was wonderful. I was loved and looked after. But when I grew up, I fucked it all up. I... made such a mess and now I am here in this awful place and reading how... how good I had it. What a joke." He shook his head and a tear rolled down his drawn grey cheek. "Perhaps you are best off not reading that book if it's about you."

Dakota looked down at her own book, its pages a mystery to her beneath the red leather and her golden name.

"I have to read it. I just need to remember... I can't remember what I did to be sent here. I don't remember anything about my life, except the first ten years," she explained.

"Hmm, perhaps you forgot the rest of your life for a good reason?" he said, almost whispering.

"Yeah maybe, but I can't atone if I don't know what I did wrong, can I?" He nodded and looked back down to his own book.

"If I could forget, I would. I'd never read this book. I'd be happy to be ignorant," he muttered dimly, probably more to himself than to Dakota.

Deciding that she would never get anywhere if she didn't look, she opened the book at the first page.

The life of Dakota Grace Crow, formerly known as Miriam Diana Page.

"Sorry to bother you, but what does this 'formerly known as' stuff mean?" she asked the white-haired man.

"That's what your name was last time," he replied without looking up.

"Last time?"

"Your last incarnation, before the one you remember. You know what reincarnation is, don't you?"

"Uh... yeah, actually I do. So it does exist? People really are reincarnated?" She suddenly was amazed at her recollection of her previous belief in it.

"Oh yes, it usually happens around five or six times, until you reach the final judgement. And here we are. We have had our turn. Time to atone for what we have done with our lives. You only remember when you read the books. Some people remember past lives through dreams and such, but it's only patchy. You only get the full picture from reading the books."

"So there is a book here that will tell me about my past lives?" she asked glancing around her at the shelves.

"One book for every life. Each book will give you your previous name," he answered, becoming agitated, as though she was bothering him.

"So then—"

"Look, missy! I am trying to read here... just let me read! Work it out for yourself – *I* had to!" he began screaming at her. Dakota shrank back into her chair and resolved not to say another word to him. She began to read her life as it began, and it was oddly like reading a well-written biography. It left out the obvious things and told stories that would be of interest and have sentimental meaning. As she read the words it was as though they immediately transformed themselves in her head to the memory itself, as though she were not even reading at all, but merely thinking about her past. They became her memories as she flitted across the words, and not a moment sooner. Soon she realised she was reading things she had already remembered when she sat with Danny.

Urgency and curiosity took over and she turned directly to the last page in the book.

It was blank, as were the preceding pages. In fact the only pages with writing on were the ones she had already read.

"Hey, what is this?" she muttered angrily to herself, half-tempted to disturb the man down the table again. But as she returned to the blank final page, she stopped, stunned as a sentence formed before her.

To understand, you must return to the start; there is no end without the beginning.

Dakota felt suddenly like a naughty child, caught cheating at an exam. Humbly, she returned to the page she had been reading and read on and on until at last she found something she did not recall. It seemed there were things previous to her parents' death that she had forgotten.

ELEVEN: Back to Life

Lula Crow met Jackson Shade for the first time when she was eighteen and Dakota was eight. The story of their first encounter was one that Lula would relate to Dakota at regular intervals. Her desire to recall and share that particular event came more frequently as the years went by, and that desire usually came when Lula's medication made her emotional. Dakota remembered everything her sister told her.

Lula was visiting the graves of her dead siblings on a winter afternoon. The cemetery was sleeping under a blanket of dried leaves. Soft winds disturbed them occasionally and it reminded her of someone muttering fervently in their sleep.

The cemetery lay beside the church they had attended every Sunday of their lives, St Brigid's, and beyond the church and graves fields lay for miles. It was at the edge of the village and the next village lay miles beyond the woods, known as Pan's Wood, which sat to the right of the cemetery. Little Mort was a beautiful country village buried amidst the farmland of south-west England, but in the fouler weather it seemed lost and abandoned.

Lula visited the graves often, usually when she felt particularly plagued by the depression that haunted her life, bringing with it feelings that her medication wasn't working and that it was all a waste of time.

She had not had a full night of natural sleep since Dakota was born. For the first two years she would get up in the middle of the night, to shuffle across her bedroom and peer into her sister's cot, sometimes encountering her mother doing the same thing. Her mother had no idea that Lula's watch over her baby sister was so obsessive that it was keeping her awake most of the night. It was only after

Dakota's sixth birthday that Lula decided to get help. Her sleepless nights were soon put to an end when she was prescribed sleeping pills and anti-depressants. Hannah and Jack Crow felt terrible for not having noticed their daughter's insomnia or depression, but Lula never felt anger towards her parents. She just made her mother promise to keep an eye on Dakota for her while she slept.

So for the past year and a half, Lula had dutifully taken her tablets every night and slept through till dawn. But over the previous few weeks she had found her sleep growing lighter, even waking once or twice to check on her sister again, as though wakefulness in dark hours set an automatic mechanism off in her body.

With the wakeful moments came tears and thoughts of loneliness, anger at her state of mind and wishes that she could forget the memories of the dead babies she had found, still as churches at night.

Depression was moving sluggishly through her that day as she entered the graveyard. Clouds overhead promised rain and she hoped that it would come soon. She wanted it to pour down so she could walk on, soaked to the bone, and perhaps it would make her feel cleansed and refreshed.

When she reached the four tiny graves she sat at their feet and let her eyes skim over the names engraved on them:

Montana Ezekiel, born asleep.
Beatty Amos, aged 3 months,
Nevada Elijah, aged 2 weeks.
Alabama Delilah, born asleep.

Before Lula and Dakota's parents had settled in the South of England, they had toured the United States of America, working their way from state to state using the money they had inherited from Jack's parents. Photos of their travels adorned the hallways of their home, permanent reminders of the life they once lived, and as a homage to the land they had traversed, they named their children after places they had visited. However, their Catholic upbringing was also in their hearts and they gave all the children middle names from the Bible. All except Dakota. They gave her the middle name of

Grace because, as her mother said, it was by the grace of God that they had been allowed to keep her.

Beatty was the first boy and had been the first one that Lula had found dead. She was only five years old then. Montana had died two years earlier and she still remembered the sound of her mother's grief in the dead of night when the midwife had delivered the silent child. The sound of her mother's screams was what kept Lula awake whenever there was a new baby in the house. She would lie awake waiting to hear it again, that dreadful sound of pain and horror. However, the only sound she heard after her own terrible discovery was the sound of her own grief, her own terrified cries as she stared into face after tiny face searching for some sign of life.

Lula was beginning to wonder what she would do if she ever found Dakota dead. Wiping away the tears, she looked up at the cheerless sky and blinked the blur from her eyes. Dropping her gaze back down, she focused beyond the four white, angelic headstones. Some of the much older graves were in that section of the cemetery, and about two rows away began the deluge of elaborate and oversized grey headstones and tombs. In her direct line of vision was a sarcophagus bearing the name Finchley on its side. On top of the tomb lay a man on his back, reading a book held up above his face.

Lula blinked her eyes a few more times, thinking she was seeing a ghost, but as he shifted slightly she realised he was real. Unsure whether to reprimand him for disrespecting someone's grave – both Lula and Dakota had been brought up to think it was rude to step all over someone even though they were dead – or whether to feel sorry for him, she stood up and walked towards him.

Sensing movement, he turned his face to her and she stopped moving, a single gravestone between them.

As she was to tell Dakota many times, she had never seen a man more beautiful. He made no move to get up from where he lay on the cold concrete tomb. Instead his crystal blue eyes flashed at her from beneath his heavy brow, his face sharp and gaunt yet somehow soft, fractured by strands of his long black hair that had fallen across his face. Lula thought he might be a fallen angel. His black trench coat could have concealed wings that rose out from a strong but lithe torso that revealed itself from beneath a thin t-shirt.

"Do you like Baudelaire?" he asked, motioning to the book in his hand.

"Yeah," she lied successfully. She liked poetry and had heard of the French poet but had never actually read any of his work. The man continued to look at her as silence hovered between them, leaves blowing across the floor.

"You know this person, then?" she asked, pointing at the tomb he was lying on.

"No." He laid the book across his chest and stared up at the scudding clouds. "I don't know anyone here; I just like how quiet they are."

Lula found she was hanging on his every syllable, as though she had never heard a person speak before. His voice was deep and flowing. It blew away across the quiet graves as though he were preaching to the cold stones and grass.

"Who are you visiting?" he asked her. She looked down and away from him, suddenly not wanting to share the deaths of her family with this stranger. Just as the words began to rise in her throat, and the urge to share everything with him began to surge, he spoke again. "Don't worry, forget I asked. You can tell me next time." And with that he picked up his book and began to read again.

"Next time?"

"Next time I see you here. I come here all the time; I'll see you again," he explained, not looking at her.

She found she had no words left in her apart from rash declarations of love and sudden profound words of passion. So she turned away and walked home, looking back three or four times at the man on the grave.

She was in love and she didn't even know his name.

When she got home she wrote five pages in her diary about the two-minute encounter in the graveyard. That night she went to bed early just so she could lie in the dark and think about the raven-haired man with eyes the colour of Caribbean waters. Once she had finished writing it all down, she repeated it out loud to Dakota, who wasn't entirely sure of what her sister was telling her, but she was just excited to be the centre of her sister's attention for the time it took for the story to unfold.

The next day Lula went to work at the local bookshop and scoured the shelves for a book of Baudelaire's poems. The one she bought that day was the one that Dakota would read when she was eleven, its spine cracked and corners of pages turned down to mark Lula's favourite poems.

Lula read them over and over again, lost in the beauty of the words, imagining the mysterious man reading them to her. After holding out for two days, Lula returned to the graveyard after work. October had set in and the day was almost gone by five-thirty. Leaves scuttled across the slumbering residents as she walked up the path beyond the cemetery gates. Spits of rain were in the air, threatening the earth with a downpour.

He was sitting on a bench to the left of Finchley's tomb, book in hand. Lula's eyes dropped momentarily as she passed by the graves of her brother and sisters.

He did not look up until she sat down beside him, and at the moment, that very second when he turned his blue eyes to her, the Heavens opened and heavy cold rain trickled down her face. He did not speak; he did not smile. He closed his book and took her hand in his own. his long fingers slipping between hers, and he stood to lead her deeper into the cemetery.

Lula did as she was silently instructed and walked quietly beside him down the long avenue of trees, rain spattering their faces like tears, fresh and reviving. Then he led her off the path to a large tomb with an unlocked door that sat buried at the back of the rows of graves. Inside, large sarcophagi lay still and cold and the air smelt of stagnant flower water and dust. The final resting place of the Boncoeur family was quiet as Lula and her companion sat down on the huge tombs. Rain clawed at the tiny stained glass window that peered down from the back of the tomb, its leaden angel staring at them. Lula wanted to speak, but was afraid of sounding stupid, so she just sat and listened to the rain. A gust of wind blew the tomb door open allowing a slither of autumn light to crawl in before a gale slammed the door shut, plunging the dead room into darkness.

"My name is Jackson Shade," he whispered to her.

"I'm Lula Crow," she replied, and he leant over and kissed her passionately.

Lula never went into the details of what happened next, but Dakota had a feeling that Jackson and Lula had consummated their relationship right there in the tomb on a rainy October evening.

Lula would meet up with her enigmatic boyfriend three times a week at the same tomb. Each time she'd put a finger over her lips and say 'Shhhhhh' to Dakota with an excited giggle. She kept Jackson a secret from her parents because of the age gap. She knew they would disapprove of their eighteen-year-old daughter dating a twenty-three-year-old man. Even though Lula talked to Dakota about him, she continued to keep his existence from their parents. Lula said she liked the secrecy and so did he. Every time her parents asked about a possible boyfriend, she kept her cards close to her chest and never told them anything. Even though she was old enough to do as she liked, she still lived with her parents and this alone meant pretending to abide by their rules. Her clandestine meetings with Jackson were the most exciting thing in her life, and she felt her parents might ruin it if they knew about him.

"And anyway," Lula said one day, brushing her hair in the mirror, "we don't want to be boring and be like everyone else. It's more fun that no one knows about us."

"But I know about you!" Dakota laughed.

"Yeah, but you're good at keeping secrets, aren't you, D? You will keep my secret for me, won't you?" Lula laughed, and Dakota promised again to keep her sister's big secret.

Dakota did not meet Jackson until she was ten. Lula never brought him home before that, and the only reason he came by that night was because Mum and Dad were having a rare night out and Lula was babysitting.

Jackson strode into the lounge where Dakota was watching TV. When she looked up at him, he seemed to freeze to the spot. They stared at each other for what felt like the longest time, both unsure of what to do or say. She felt peculiar as she looked at his long black hair and his black clothes. She had a feeling that they had met before, but she had no idea where.

The moment was broken as Lula entered the room. Grabbing the TV remote, she turned up the volume and said, "Stay down here, OK sweetie?" Then Lula turned and took Jackson upstairs to the room that she and Dakota shared.

Dakota sat still and listened. After a few moments, she heard her sister moaning as the bed creaked rhythmically. Dakota knew all about sex already. She had learnt all about it from reading her sister's copies of Marie-Claire and Cosmopolitan. She would read all the juicy details while Lula was out. There was also a book that had come free with one of the magazines and it had fictional stories about sexual encounters. Dakota found them fascinating and had even learnt to masturbate from reading through the seedy stories, and the various articles about improving 'self-love' techniques. She practised secretly under her duvet while Lula was out getting drunk or having sex in graveyards.

After a half hour of moaning and creaking, Lula and Jackson reappeared looking flushed and dishevelled.

Jackson was putting his black trench coat back on as he stared at Dakota. She looked back at him silently. He looked like he was about to say something but Lula began to usher him out of the house and the moment was gone.

Dakota often quizzed Lula about her relationship with Jackson. The sisters sometimes went out for walks after dinner into the local woods where they could talk away from the ever-listening ears of their parents. Usually they waited until they went to bed and Mum and Dad were downstairs. Dakota would ask questions: was she in love? How did she know? How did it feel? Was she going to get married?

"I don't know if we'll get married, but we want to live together," Lula whispered to her little sister in the dark bedroom.

"Don't move out! You can't leave me!" Dakota replied, tears welling in her eyes. Lula was her only friend. She had no friends at school, and she didn't fit in with anyone she had ever met. Her play-times were spent alone reading book after book, looking within the stories for some kind of life she could live when she grew up. Without Lula to gossip to at night, Dakota felt she had nothing. Her mum and dad were great, but they were adults and she wanted to hear about her sister's life – the parties, the sex, the drugs.

"I'm not leaving yet! I can't afford it. I have to get a better job and save up, and Jackson still lives with his mother and has to pay rent to her, so he finds it hard to save money. Maybe when I am twenty or twenty-one I will be able to move out. You have me for another couple of years."

"I wonder if I will still live with Mum and Dad when I am nineteen," pondered Dakota aloud.

"No! You'll be a model in Paris or New York." The two girls giggled in the dark room as the lights of passing cars briefly haunted the ceiling.

"I'll have five kids with Jackson and you'll marry someone rich!" Lula laughed.

"You want to have kids?"

"Yeah, it feels like you're my child though," replied Lula thoughtfully." I always tell Jackson that you are my baby. He says he'd be happy for you to live with us one day."

"Really? He said that? That would be so cool!"

"Do you like Jackson then?"

"I only met him once and we didn't even talk!"

"But he is soooooooo gorgeous, don't you think?" Lula giggled dreamily.

Dakota closed her eyes and she saw him, the way he was in the lounge that evening, tall and dark with a swarm of unnamed thoughts brooding behind his crystalline eyes.

"He's OK," she said before saying goodnight. Something about Jackson made her stomach burn, something about his sharp eyes drew her in, and she felt the tiniest twinge of fear. He never came to the house again.

Some time later, on a late summer night, her parents died. As her sister dissolved into hysterical sobs of grief, Dakota's first thought was to call Jackson, which she did by retrieving his number from Lula's phonebook that sat beside the dropped telephone receiver. The first words she ever said to Jackson Shade were: "My parents are dead. We need you... to take us to the hospital."

And he replied a simple "OK" before doing exactly what Dakota had asked of him.

The night her parents died in a horrific car accident was the second time Dakota had met Jackson, but after the phone call they did not say a word to each other, even though they sat in an empty waiting room together for hours. Their eyes met once or twice, but she looked away swiftly each time; she did not want him looking at her. Her eyes were red and swollen and her cheeks were stained with tears and all she wanted was to be held. She wanted to be back in her daddy's arms again, on the rare occasions that he hugged her, safe and warm in the smell of his clean clothes, dozing as he watched the television, his arm around her a comfort to drive away the bad dream she had had, the terrible dream of his death, the cold white hospital corridors that led to the room where he and Mum lay, gone from the earth.

But she was not going to wake up from this, and Daddy would not be downstairs in the lounge while Mum made cocoa for them both. This was it. They were gone. Lula was talking to the counsellor that Dakota had refused to talk to, and there was no one around to comfort her, except Jackson, the dark stranger.

After she could take it no longer, she burst into huge body-shaking sobs. Jackson did not move; he just watched her from across the room. Suddenly she was on her feet and running towards him. He simply opened up his coat and wrapped it around her as she fell crying into his arms, curling up on his lap and burying herself in his chest. After a few moments she began to calm, and the tears dissipated. They stayed that way; she lay enfolded in the wings of his coat for another hour before Lula returned, sedated and bleary eyed. Dakota was asleep in his arms by now, and he stood to carry her out to the car. Lula told her later that she thought it looked like one of their mothers' religious paintings: the angel carrying the sleeping child to safety. She always said she was relieved that Dakota had been comforted by Jackson during the time she had to be calmed by a therapist. She never said a word to Dakota about what their parents had looked like at the end. The sight of their mangled bodies would be her memory alone; she never wanted her little sister to think of them that way, and Dakota had the sense to only ever ask Lula about the identifying process once.

By the time they got home it was around 3am. Dakota had awoken in the car and heard Lula say that she needed Jackson to stay with them that night. But when they got into the quiet empty house, the two girls went up the stairs hand in hand, to their parents' bedroom, and lay down on the bed in the darkness. Jackson stayed downstairs in the lounge to practise his own insomnia in front of the TV.

Lula and Dakota lay side by side recounting memories as they came to them. Mum's scones, the songs she used to sing at bed-time when they were little.

"'Where have all the flowers gone' was my favourite," offered Dakota, as a passing car threw a slanting light across the black ceiling. Everything became so precious suddenly, every memory needed to be spoken, given life again, from the time Mum lost her wedding ring in the scone mix to the smell of her father's Argyll sweater.

They went on for hours, remembering and crying until, when dawn came, there was nothing left to remember, only to understand.

As pale morning rode up to the windows of the still house, the two dark-haired sisters looked into each other's eyes and promised to be strong. Dakota's eleven years of life had suddenly developed meaning and substance. She was alive because two wonderful people had fallen in love, and even though their hopes of a big family were dashed by death's dark hands, they had not lost faith that God would give them another child. That morning, through grief and pain, Dakota and Lula vowed that, no matter how low they got, they would never take their own lives. For no matter how difficult it got or how pointless it seemed to go on, their lives were evidence that Hannah and Jack Crow had lived and had been in love.

TWELVE: Death's Dark Veil

In the days that followed, Lula was distraught and depressed, and Dakota stayed home from school to tend to her sister.

In the evenings, Jackson came over, to cook and take over the watch on Lula. Dakota became peripheral as Lula grew worse, unable to sleep at all anymore; the doctor eventually prescribed new medication, strong sedatives for night-time and anti-depressants for the day time. She worked like clockwork from then on as long as Dakota and Jackson ensured that the correct medication was administered at the right times of day.

Dakota was informed eventually that her parents had died in a car accident out in the country; her father had lost control of the car and ended up in a ditch. But sometimes she heard Lula talking when she thought she wasn't listening and it seemed her father had had too much to drink at the party and that's why they crashed. Lula seemed angry with their father, but Dakota couldn't feel anything but sadness.

Jackson began to help with the funeral arrangements as the mere mention of them threw Lula into deep dark hours of sobbing. Dakota did her best to help but she was only young and there was only so much she could do.

The funeral was the same as all funerals, dull and painful. As her grief was pulled out of her, put on display and stretched out endlessly, Dakota tried desperately to cope with it. At the graveside, she looked across at Lula hidden behind the net veil on her black hat, make up streaking down her cheeks as Jackson put an arm around her shoulders to comfort her. Dakota felt a pang of jealousy; she wanted to be comforted and cuddled, but Lula had been too distraught all day to do any more than hold her hand briefly in the church;

she was too lost in her own grief to comfort her baby sister.

Various people, friends and family, gathered at the house for the wake and spent the afternoon looking mournful and pitying every time Dakota entered their field of vision. She was upset but had no tears left. She did her best to avoid conversation and wandered in an out of rooms full of loud Irish people.

In the downstairs hallway there was a wall of framed photographs of Hannah and Jack Crow's journey around America. The largest and most central was a beautiful image of a dry rugged landscape, full of jagged rocks and unforgiving ravines. It was a photo her father had taken of the Dakota Badlands, and her mind pushed forth the memory of talking to her mother about that picture.

Sunlight slanted across the hall and Dakota asked her mother what that place was called.

"That's called the Badlands, and it's in the state we named you after, Dakota. In fact we named you that because we liked this place so much," explained Hannah, stroking her tapered fingers across her daughter's face.

"It looks so... lonely there," managed the seven-year-old girl with dark brown plaits in her hair.

"It *is* a very empty place. Nobody lives there and all you can hear is the wind."

Tears began to roll down Dakota's cheeks, as her heart filled with loneliness and despair thinking of being alone there, in the dark rippling rocks and canyons, not another soul for miles of dark road and night. Alone with the wild animals and crying winds, calling out over and over that she was lost and alone.

"What's wrong, darling? Why are you crying?" asked Hannah desperately, kneeling down beside her quietly weeping daughter.

"I'd be scared to be there, Mummy, on my own," replied Dakota sadly, unsure of why the image in the photograph had filled her with such loneliness and fear. Deep in her heart somewhere she feared that one day she would feel that way again, the way that photo had made her feel. She felt that her parents had cursed her somehow by naming her after such a desolate and mournful place.

And there in the same hallway, Dakota stood and stared at that same photograph and realised she had been right all those years before. Those feelings of loneliness and despair had returned to her again, and she felt her heart may have resembled that sharp rocky terrain, dry and haunted.

The wake carried on around her. Occasionally she caught sight of Lula, beautiful in her fitted black suit, her hair perfect and her make-up re-applied every half hour when her tears got the better of it. Jackson tried to avoid everyone, responding politely monosyllabic to anyone who tried to engage him in conversation.

The extended Crow family looked vaguely worried by Jackson's appearance. They muttered to each other, rolling their eyes and pursing their lips. Dakota heard Auntie Kathleen say he looked like a drug addict, while cousin Deirdre pushed red curls from her eyes whispering sentences that contained the words: 'cult,' 'witchcraft' and 'devil-worship,' all the time crossing herself at intermittent bursts of Catholicism.

Dakota looked at Jackson. He was staring from his glass of whisky to the wall behind Uncle Patrick's head and back again, as Patrick tried desperately to get Jackson to say more than one word answers. Jackson was very handsome. He looked like a cross between an illustration from an Edgar Allan Poe book and Jack Kerouac. His long hair swept away from his sharp face and down the back of his neck to where it rested behind his shoulders. They still hadn't really spoken to each other – they just shared the occasional look – but she didn't feel uncomfortable about him. If anything, she enjoyed the fact that she didn't feel obliged to speak whenever he was around.

As the day wore on and the Crow family got more and more drunk, slipping in and out of arguments and renditions of old Irish songs, Dakota wished they would all go away and let her get on with her life.

As Jackson made his way out of the room to get away

from the noise, he leant down and whispered to Dakota: "Now I understand why they call a group of crows, a murder," and moved off as she giggled quietly.

When it was all done, life slipped into a routine again. Dakota returned to school to find she had been put back a year, Lula returned to work and Jackson moved into her parents' bedroom with Lula, leaving Dakota alone in the room she had shared with her sister her whole life.

Jackson continued to manage the local library; Dakota cooked her own microwave meals every evening while Lula and Jackson ate in front of the TV when they both got home from work.

It was another year before Jackson began to communicate with Dakota.

She loved music and spent most of her time shut away in her bedroom listening to CDs and writing in her diary. All the music she owned was taken from her parents' room after they died. Her mother was a big fan of Bob Dylan and the Doors; she used to sing along to the songs at the top of her voice, a voice so sweet she should have been a singer herself. So every night when Dakota played the music, her mother came alive again, her voice almost audible behind the melodies. Occasionally Lula would come in on her way to bed and sing along with Dakota to their mother's old favourites, and for a moment they were both young again and innocent; Mum and Dad were still alive, singing along too, the years rolled away and Dakota was free in her heart, unburdened by the terrible weight her parents' death had placed on her.

And when Lula got the sadness in her eyes, the singing stopped and Dakota's joy dissipated. She knew that Lula would then leave, go and take her medication in her bedroom and slip away into an impenetrable slumber to dream of her Jackson reading Baudelaire and preaching to the dead.

Now that Lula had to be sedated at night, Jackson was left alone to stay up till 3am, when hours of music, writing in his notebooks and drinking whisky would eventually send him off to sleep. He played his music loud enough for it to seep upstairs and under Dakota's bedroom door. No noise would wake Lula, and it made Dakota sad; she felt sorry for her poor sister with her mind a mess of death and corpses, years of therapists telling her it would be OK, that the dreams of dead babies would go away if she took her drugs: one to sleep, one to wake up. And in her heart, all she wanted was her dream Prince Jackson to marry her and give her her own baby, another life to make up for those she could not save.

But at night when Jackson was lonely himself and he needed her most, she was wrapped in a tight cocoon of forced sleep that locked her out of the world she had with Jackson.

Dakota heard the sounds of sex less often these days as Lula and Jackson slipped into a new routine. She found that if she turned her music up loud around eight o'clock, she could drown out the noise of them in the room down the hall. At least they were still doing it after all this time, she thought, although it wasn't as often as it once was.

It was late at night, a week or so after Dakota's non-existent twelfth birthday, the clock on her wall read 12.10am, and she had just smoked a cigarette she had stolen from Lula's handbag. The August night was hot and she sat on cushions beside the window that was opened wide onto the night. The distant hum of occasional traffic rose up to meet her as she flicked the butt out onto the back garden. Since her parents had died on her birthday, she had the feeling that she might never celebrate that day again. It seemed wrong somehow.

Lately she hadn't been sleeping so well, staying up later and later each night, waiting for sleep to arrive and fall on her eyelids, but it always came so late now. She pondered how odd it felt, sitting alone, knowing that somewhere else in the house, Jackson was alone, too, listening to his music as always.

A book lay open on the bed. The rest of her books sat worn and over-read on her shelves: one classic after another and a copy of her father's favourite book, *On the Road* by Jack Kerouac. She read it over and over, trying to discover her father there in the pages. He was a man she hardly knew and in her mind he was only explained to her by the words in that book. He became one of the characters, telling the story of his life before she or Lula were born.

Bob Dylan sang out of the speakers softly about wanting someone, and Dakota felt that maybe she wanted someone, too, but she was only twelve and she knew it was stupid to even think about such things. She had been reading too much poetry lately. Her heart seemed to be large and empty, populated only by the saddest words that rose out of the pages of her books. She had no friends at school, she did not fit in with anyone and she was lonely. She no longer had her late-night chats with Lula, and she felt as though she had lost her only friend.

The hours between dusk and dawn stretched out lonely and dark, full of someone else's words, low music from downstairs and the fear that life would always be this sad.

Her storm green eyes filled with sadness as they flicked over the images of her parents, and the other images on her wall. A picture of Our Lady of Lourdes with her Heavenward eyes and golden roses on her feet hung opposite Dakota. She always thought that her mother looked like the Virgin Mary; she had that air of unrecognised beauty, a simple woman with flour on her apron and the biggest heart in the world, eyes cast Heavenward for answers.

Beside the Virgin Mary was a picture of the Sacred Heart of Jesus. Like the picture of Mary, it was recovered from her parents' bedroom and seemed a must have in every Irish Catholic home. Lula had abandoned their birth religion – she hated God for taking away so many loved ones – whereas Dakota clung to the iconography of her mother's religion. A sad-eyed, soft-cheeked man with long hair and a bleeding heart wound round with thorns looked down at Dakota. He was an icon of suffering and sacrifice. She thought of his loneliness in the Garden of Gethsemane and wondered how it felt to know you were going to die.

Her mother's spirit was in the room. She could feel her, and she was saying the rosary and staring in Jesus's soft eyes looking for eternity and endless stars.

Besides all the poetry, Dakota had her mother's Bible and prayer book on the shelf. She thought that whenever she took it down to read it her mother was happy with her somewhere.

Crickets sang in the lawn below her window, and in the distance she could hear sirens. The music from Jackson's midnight world crawled up the stairs, sickly haunting as the vocals kicked in with a sonorous melancholy voice.

"I found her on a night of fire and noise..."

She recognised the song. The album it was on was obviously a favourite of Jackson's as he played it regularly. She reached across and turned her own stereo off so she could hear the song from downstairs properly. She didn't know who it was but she liked it; something in it reached out to her as it crept under her door, penetrating her private space like an uninvited guest she could not turn away.

Then there was a light tap on the door.

"Lula?" she said to the closed door. But when it opened she was surprised to see Jackson there. The hall light was brighter than her dim candle-lit room and he seemed more silhouette than anything else. Without words he walked in, a glass of whisky in his hand, closing the door behind him. The voice from the stereo downstairs asked feverishly, unsurely: *"Do you love me?"* over and over.

Jackson moved across the room towards where she sat by the window, the closer he got the taller he seemed until he was standing over her like a giant. As he sat down on the floor, his back turned to the window, she realised he hadn't been this close to her in a very long time. There was a mild smell of whisky on his breath and his hair slipped from behind his ears as he leant forward. From his shirt pocket, he took a box of cigarettes and offered Dakota one before taking one for himself. She looked surprised but took it anyway, wondering if he was about to tell her off.

"You like Baudelaire?" he asked, lighting her cigarette before his own.

"Yes, but that's Lula's book," she replied, glancing at the book resting open on her bed.

He nodded and looked at her for a moment, seemingly

contemplating her hair. Looking away from her, he peered into the starlit sky and Dakota felt confused but comforted by his silent presence in the room. She smoked her cigarette still wondering if he was working up to lecture her on the dangers of smoking, but instead he just sat, head rested back on the window ledge, picking the details of the room out of the shadows.

He reached out his glass of whisky to her with the words: "It helps."

The music tinkled on downstairs, slow melodic ballads filtering up the stairs past her sleeping sister's room and under Dakota's door.

"It helps with what?" she asked, sipping the dark liquid before grimacing at its sharp, hot taste.

"Loneliness. I know. It doesn't taste great, but it takes the edge off," he muttered, taking the glass back from her.

"Why are you lonely? You have Lula. At least you have someone," she asked, suddenly completely at ease talking to him.

"It's worse, you know. Being with someone. If it's not right… you feel even lonelier." He looked sadder than she had ever seen him before. She remembered that night at the hospital when he wrapped her in his coat, the smell of his skin. A sadness overtook her and she wanted so much to reach out to him.

It was a hot night and the breeze that blew in was just hot air moving over her. Perspiration prickled on her brow and the silence was only disturbed by the new song beginning on the stereo.

"There's a devil waiting outside your door…"

The song went on and she listened intently to the words, singing slowly up the stairs. Jackson turned to Dakota and when their eyes met, the singer began to scream against a sudden crescendo of music.

"Loverman! Since the world began…"

Dakota moved suddenly as if inspired by the surge of sound. Reaching across to him, she put her small hand on his chest. He looked up surprised and removed her hand slowly.

"Dakota," he said shaking his head.

But she felt overtaken. His presence in the room, at that moment, was all that mattered. It was like it all made sense to her suddenly; she didn't need to be alone, neither did he. She moved over to him and kissed him on the mouth, quickly and uncertainly, unsure how he would react. Would he slap her, shove her away? Wake up Lula?

He grabbed her by her shoulders and held her back from him, his eyes suddenly alert and sober.

"What are you doing?" he said, the grip on her shoulders tightening.

She didn't reply. She pushed herself forward, kissing him again. The feel of his lips was like a memory on her own. Addicted, she needed to feel it again; she wanted to feel nothing, apart from how his lips made her feel. She persisted until she was kissing him hungrily, angrily, almost biting him as hot tears streaked down her face, her hands reaching for the zip on his trousers, desperate to feel more of him.

What followed would forever remain broken up in Dakotas mind. Hands and lips, her nightdress discarded to reveal her small figure, a pain that burnt up through her as he entered her quivering body. She had never felt anything like it before. The rest of the world melted away. All the sadness and loss, the loneliness was gone. She felt for the first time since her parents had died that she belonged. That she existed and mattered.

In the background, she could still hear the singer's voice and all the words he sang became suddenly important and memorable.

"*L is for LOVE baby*
O is for ONLY you that I do
V is for loving VIRTUALLY everything that you are
E is for loving almost EVERYTHING that you do
R is RAPE me
M is for MURDER me
A is for ANSWERING all my prayers
N is for KNOWING your loverman's going to be the answer to all of yours..."

THIRTEEN: Revelations

Back in the Library of Remembrance, Dakota slammed the book shut and staggered back, knocking her chair to the floor as she hit the wall. The clattering sound echoed around the edgeless room, the deep shadows returning the echoes of her fresh sobs.

The memory of that night had returned to her quiet and almost empty brain with screams and horror. She shook with uncontrollable tears as the clearness of the experience repeated over and over in her head, the smell of his skin, the pain and the elation it brought to her.

Her memory did not extend any further than that night, but she felt, deep down somewhere, that it would not be the last time Jackson Shade had touched her.

As disturbing as the memory was of her sister's boyfriend being the one she had lost her virginity to, what made her feel sick now was a knowledge of how wrong it was, and yet her twelve-year-old self had wanted that, had instigated that. To feel loved. At any price.

Looking back at it now, she could see, with the mind of an adult, how back then her childish mind had no way of knowing how bad the situation was. The first flushes of wanting to be an adult were upon her and the loneliness she felt, that gap that existed between her and the rest of the world was bridged by Jackson, and she could not help but grab a hold of what his presence offered her.

Intimacy.

How sad she felt now to realise how dangerous those feelings were, and while she still did not know what was to happen next, she was certain that her need for intimacy being met by a man fifteen years older than her could only damage her in the long run.

If only we could have the wisdom of adulthood in childhood when it is needed, she thought. But she could remember so clearly how right it had felt at the time.

Looking up with tear-blurred eyes, Dakota could see that she was alone now; the man who had sat opposite her earlier was now gone, and the dim and sparse lamps that lit the library were flickering slightly in a breeze she could not feel. The wind continued to howl at the windows, and far into the shadows she heard the whistle as the breeze cackled through cracks and passageways she could not see. She felt dirty. She glanced up at the closed book on the table and felt her stomach tighten as she considered reading more. The song that had been playing when he came to her was stuck in her head. She recognised it as the song from her dream when she last slept. It crawled around inside her head, over and over.

Pulling herself up off the floor, she decided that she couldn't face any more of her past yet. What she had just remembered was too much for her. She needed to get it out of her head for a while, so she speedily returned the book to its place on the shelves and headed towards the exit, lamp in hand. As she reached the door, she sensed sudden movement somewhere behind her. She turned in time to see a figure retreat into the shadows. Fear bolted up her spine as a low sinister laugh crawled out of the dark. She did not have it in her to face this now, locked away in a huge shadowy library with a rapist. Who would help her if he set upon her? It was a split second before she was on the other side of the door and running down the dark musty hallway. Cockroaches crunched underfoot and hands brushed against her as she sprinted away from the invisible spectator's laughter and mockery.

As soon as the dim light of the Lobby came into view she felt a surge of relief. She arrived by the front desk, shaking, the lamp clenched so tight in her hand that her knuckles were white, as the flame flickered violently, oil sloshing about inside its metal body.

"I think we need to speak for a moment," said a voice.

Dakota jumped and her head snapped around to see Ariel beside her.

"I-I-I..." she managed, before Ariel placed her hand over hers and took the lamp from her. Dakota calmed slightly, her eyes still surveying the room to see who was watching her. Ariel guided her around the reception desk into a small room that lay beyond. Once inside, Dakota sat down on one of the large armchairs by the fire, and Ariel joined her by sitting herself opposite in the other chair.

"So you found the library?" asked Ariel, handing her guest a cup of tea from nowhere. Dakota was shocked, having seen no other drinks apart from alcohol since she arrived at the hotel.

"What's this? How come you have tea? I thought we only got whisky or vodka."

"It's to soothe you. You are allowed soothing drinks occasionally, if they deem you deserve it," replied the blonde-haired lady.

"How did you know I had found the library?" Dakota said, sipping at the tea, which tasted Heavenly to her.

"They know everything you do. I expected you would be in some distress afterwards. Didn't get past the first time with Jackson, then?" Ariel said sympathetically.

"Huh... I had a feeling it wouldn't be a one off," Dakota muttered, the images flooding back as tears pricked her eyes.

"I know it's hard, but you have to remember it all. It's part of your journey, you must be made to relive it."

"But why doesn't anyone else go there? I only saw one person there... well two. Surely if the library is part of the 'Journey,' wouldn't they all be there, remembering?"

"You overestimate your colleagues." Ariel laughed softly. "Everyone knows about the Library, but not many have the courage to relive their lives. These people have all done terrible things, but they cannot bear to see it all again, so they do not go there. They prolong their sentence here, through fear and guilt. But I can guarantee that there are more than two other people there – you just haven't seen them all. It's a big place, with many dimensions."

"But most people remember what they did wrong! I don't remember anything. If they already remember, how can reading it make any difference?"

"You did it, Dakota, you should know! To remember is one thing, but to re-experience everything is more traumatic than any memory. There are many very... unhinged residents here, and half of that is from the knowledge of what they did. Guilt is a terrible emotion; it can drive you mad. But everyone knows that to attempt to gain entry to Heaven, you must relive your transgressions, and that can drive you mad, too. People cannot cope with what they have done wrong, and they punish themselves further by not making an effort to get out of here."

"This place is all about trickery, Danny told me that, and how is a person supposed to get to Heaven if it is made so damn hard!" Dakota was growing angry again.

"Whoever told you it was easy to get to Heaven?"

Dakota stared back at Ariel, finally understanding. "This is Hell, isn't it?" she muttered.

"Hell is a Christian concept, but I think you get what it really is now?"

"If you have been bad, you have to fight to get into Heaven?"

"Yes, in a way. But the tasks that are set to you are not told to you, and every effort is made to keep you here. Hell is the absence of God, Dakota. And God has no place here."

Dakota felt sick. She wanted to cry and scream and smash things. Maybe this was the closest thing to what Hell was perceived to be: no fire and brimstone, but despair and trickery, evil people suffering the guilt for what they had done; and their proximity to Heaven was dependant on whether they could do everything required of them, without even knowing what it was that was required of them. She was suddenly afraid, that this might be the closest she would ever get to Heaven.

"So where is Satan then? Does he have a room?" she asked half laughing.

"He's here." Ariel nodded as she moved in her chair.

"Where?"

"There," she replied, pointing directly at Dakota's chest, where her now dead heart sat silently.

"What?"

"He is in everyone. He is not a person – he is not even a He – but it's easier to say that. When God created you, she relinquished control over you, just the same as every other human being. She gave you free will, and in accordance with the Eternal Balance of things, she gave each person duality, two very different sides to their personality. Every Human has the ability to be like God, and every human has the ability to be Evil. There is no explanation for why one person is evil and another is good. In history the balance has always been fairly good, but if you can have Mother Theresa, you must also have Hitler.

"It was unavoidable. God created you to be free and develop, evolve as a planet without her intervention. In doing so she ensured that there would always be a balance. Evil is necessary, and exists in every single human being."

"So because there are do-gooders in the world, we have to have murderers?"

"Yes, that's one way of describing it. But God never intended for anyone to be as evil as some of those that have come to be. Another problem is the influence the dead can have on the living,"

"What do you mean?"

"Well in the past some residents of this hotel have managed to get to the living, enough to make them evil, too. Some of the world's most prolific serial killers are a result of possession by the dead. Unfortunately also, past life can encroach on present life. Some of the most evil people have returned to Earth in a new body and the evil was unleashed again. In a way, it is correct to see Evil as the Devil or Satan. It is an opposing force to God, and it is the one thing she cannot control. It started somewhere, with just one person, but now it is self-perpetuating and it is growing like a cancer on earth. Evil grows in one person, it rubs off on those around it, and when the body dies it returns again in a new one. Why do you think you get children who commit murder?"

"They are a reincarnation of a murderer?" Dakota shook her head, almost dizzy with the revelations. Ariel nodded.

"Sometimes things break through from the last life. This is worst when all that can break through is evil. There is nothing we can do but exist as we do. I am here to help people get to God. But I guess some people don't want to get there." Ariel shook her head sadly.

"I still don't understand what I'm doing here. I was murdered. I was sexually abused by my sister's boyfriend when I was twelve! I am the victim. Why am I here?" Dakota was weeping now, so upset that the brief bliss the cup of tea had afforded her was now long gone. She had used the word 'abused' because she knew that's how it would be seen from the outside. But the minute she had said it she knew that it wasn't right. Yes, he should have stopped her, but she remembered how insistent she was.

"You are here because of something you did wrong, in your last life or one of your previous lives – something you did not pay for by the time you died in your life as Dakota Crow. It may be that your crime was only committed in your last life, and that is why you are here, but to really understand you must look back to your other lives as well."

"That could take me years to read all my lives. Isn't there a York Notes edition or something?" she asked in despair.

"No." Ariel laughed. "You will be here for as long as it takes. Use your time wisely, Dakota." And she got up and opened the door, signalling for Dakota to leave.

Residents milled around in the lobby, distressed and disturbed. Dakota looked over them and felt despair growing in her again. It felt as though it was in the air and with every absent breath she lost a little more hope and gained a little more sadness.

She moved out of the lobby and stood outside the Bar, feeling lost and unsure of what she should do next. Deep down she knew the only thing she could do was return to the library and continue reading, but where was she to start? Should she be reading about her past lives or about her last life? She decided suddenly that she needed help; she needed someone to read her other lives whilst she read her last one.

The Bar was as dim as ever as she walked through the tables. Danny was sitting beside the bar talking to another man who was wearing a hooded coat pulled up over his head.

"I need to talk to you, Danny, if you've got a minute," she asked as she came within a few metres of him. The man who was sitting with Danny got up without a word and moved away into the shadows before Dakota could get a look at him.

"What is it?" he asked, casting his eyes past her to the retreating figure.

"Who was that? Did I interrupt something?"

"No, he was just going anyway. What can I do for you?"

"I need you to come to the Library with me, and help me read up on myself. I can't get through all my lives on my own. I need to know what I'm doing here."

"I can't, Dakota. I can't leave the Bar. Who would serve everyone?" he replied with a nervous laugh.

"Can't someone else do it?" she asked desperately.

"No, I told you before I can't leave. Sorry I can't help you." He got up and made to walk away but Dakota put her hand onto his chest to stop him.

"You can leave, you can go to the library, anyone can. Or don't you want to help me?"

"I can't go there..."

"Yes, you can! Ariel told me anyone can go there!" She was raising her voice now, and other residents were looking over at them. Danny's eyes flicked around nervously as he pulled her hand off him.

"No, I can't! I'm busy!" he replied brusquely.

"You mean you won't! You fucking chicken, too scared to face up to what you did! I need your help. I'm not asking you to read your own life, just mine!"

"No! I won't go there, now leave me alone! I'm not interested!" he shouted at her finally before pushing past her and disappearing behind the bar.

The people sitting in the Bar all murmured among themselves, sniggering and sneering at her as she stormed out.

Dakota was furious with him. Any respect she had for him was now gone and she was sure now he was trying to hinder her progress. Anger was her only emotion as she set off back towards the Library and considered that her only other friend in this place was not likely to want to go there either. Betty would rather hide away in her room than traipse down here, Dakota thought. She was so angry that all fear had left her. She stomped down the dark corridor, slapping away any hand that reached for her, shouting expletives at anything that got in her way. She felt ready to take on Woods, too, if he was still hanging about in the shadows, but she didn't encounter him on the way or even after she entered the Library.

Further down into the shadows she could see a person or two sitting reading or crouching on the floor with books in hand, but any desire she had to communicate with other people was gone. She just wanted to carry on reading and remember everything, no matter how awful it was. Nausea gripped her stomach briefly as she sat down and opened the book at the last words written – the song lyrics that began to gnaw at her insides again. But she swallowed hard and turned to the next page as the words began to appear before her.

FOURTEEN: The Morning After

The morning after Jackson's visit, Dakota could not eat her toast. Her body ached and she had found blood in her knickers as she rose to dress that morning. It was the first day of the summer holidays and she did not know what to do with herself. Lula would be out at work as would Jackson.

She felt strange, as though her body was new. She was not a virgin anymore; the great mystery of sex had been unravelled in her by her sister's boyfriend late in a hot summer night with the sound of music in the air.

She couldn't look at Lula because she remembered the words Jackson had said as he made ready to leave her room when it was over.

"You know what would happen if Lula found out, don't you?"

"Yes," she had replied, knowing she could not see her sister's dream of Jackson shatter. Lula had enough heartaches. It would surely kill her if she knew, so Dakota could never tell her anything about it. There was a threat to Lula, but Dakota also felt there was a threat to her in what he said. She did not know this man very well, and something in his eyes scared her and said he could really hurt her if he wanted to.

Jackson looked at her across the breakfast table as Lula fluttered about behind him fixing his food.

"Are you OK?" he asked. When she looked up she saw concern in his eyes and she almost cried. What had happened was wrong, she knew that. She shouldn't have kissed him, he shouldn't have let her. But it had happened and she had enjoyed it. It was her own guilt that weighed heavy on her that morning. She had seduced her sister's boyfriend just so that she could not feel alone anymore. And she didn't even regret it.

She was aware, and had been for a long time, that there was a place in her heart that was empty. She felt it late at night, a lonely echoey room in her heart, with high ceilings and no windows; the wind whistled through it, accentuating its emptiness.

That hot July night, Dakota had felt that space was filled. And in the morning, she could still feel it. Jackson's presence filled her stomach and chest like a multitude of startled butterflies. The touch of his hand on her skin was a proximity she had felt with no man, not even her father. He had loved her, she knew, but he had rarely hugged her, never put his hands on her for more than a second. But Jackson had put his hands all over her, had seen into her soul with his bright blue eyes and made her feel, for the first time since her parents died, that she existed. Even when her parents were alive, a lot of their attention was devoted to Lula and her mental problems. Since that fateful night, Lula had done her best to play mum, but her medicated state and her busyness with work meant she had put Dakota after Jackson in her affections. Lula needed Jackson more, to make her feel safe and chase away the demons in her head.

Dakota knew Lula loved her, but she didn't always feel it.

She also knew that she should never have let Jackson touch her, and that what they had done was dirty.

But deep down a tiny voice said it didn't matter, that Jackson loved her and would always make her feel good and needed. Half-sickened, half-yearning, she returned to her room and poured the contents of her mind into her diary.

The following night, Dakota sat in her room, lights out, by the open window again. Lula had gone to bed an hour earlier and since then Jackson had been downstairs.

She had been listening to his music trailing up the stairs for the last hour when it stopped abruptly in the middle of a song. Then, a new song began.

"There's a devil waiting outside your door..."

She heard a faint creak on the stairs and her stomach

twisted with anticipation as a shadow fell across the beam of light that seeped under her door.

"He's bucking and braying and pawing at the floor,
Well he's howling with pain and crawling up the walls,
There's a devil waiting outside your door,
He's weak with evil and broken by the world
He's shouting your name and he's asking for more..."

Dakota got up and moved over to the bed, her entire body trembling and an odd feeling growing beneath her belly button.

"Loverman! Since the world began!"

The door opened suddenly and the silhouette with long hair and a strong body was briefly visible before the door closed again and she could hear him moving towards her. When he reached her, he placed his hand softly on the side of her face for a moment before bringing her toward him for a kiss. His tongue slipped into her mouth and she responded hungrily before her guilt kicked in and she struggled against him for a moment. But as his hand slipped down her body into her knickers, she began to go limp in his arms, giving in, knowing that no matter how wrong it was, it would feel good.

Tears pricked her eyes as he entered her sore body. She'd had no time to recover from the previous night and he hurt her no matter how gentle his thrusts were. Yet through the pain another orgasm wracked her small body.

"Loverman! Here I stand for ever Amen
Cause I am what I am what I am what I am
Forgive me baby, my hands are bound
And I got no choice, no, I got no choice at all..."

"Are you OK?" he asked, hearing her sniffling in the darkness.

"It hurt a bit," she replied.

"Sorry, I didn't mean to. I don't want to hurt you, D," he said softly and held her small hand, weaving his long fingers through hers.

They lay together. He pulled her into his arms for an

embrace and she laid her head on his chest, remembering again the night her parents had died and how he had wrapped her up in his coat and wordlessly soothed her.

Downstairs the CD played on, a mixture of highs and lows with a deep melancholy threaded through.

She expected him to get up and leave as he had the night before, but he stayed with her, lay in the dark, breeze-stirred room. They smoked cigarettes and Dakota thought it was like in the movies when two people made love then lay together smoking.

As the CD drew to a close downstairs, the singer's voice asked sadly, over and over, half-pleading, if they were loved. And she wondered, too, for a moment, did he love her?

From that night on, everything slipped into a kind of routine. Jackson came to her nearly every night, and the nights he did not come creeping into her room, she would lie awake and alone, wondering what kept him from coming.

Some nights he stayed and read to her, passages from 'Wuthering Heights' and 'Lolita,' and she never asked him to do it even though she secretly hoped every night that he would take up a book from her bedside table and begin to say those words that spoke of great yet obsessive love. The nights he did not come to her, she would read them alone, remembering how the words sounded when they came from his mouth. She took down her religious pictures and turned the pictures of her parents to the wall before climbing into bed at night, feeling that they could no longer see what went on in her life if she hid it from their faces.

And while his occasional absence was a relief to her, she also found that she missed him.

Lula remained unaware of what happened in the house when she fell into her drug-induced slumber, and Jackson and Dakota continued to communicate briefly and civilly when in Lula's company. Lula continued to try as hard as she could to communicate with Dakota, and Dakota returned the attention knowing that Lula's mind was often on other things. Throughout the whole summer holiday, Dakota spent every day on her own, either walking in the nearby woods, or reading quietly in the house. Her diary filled up with her feelings about what went on at night, when the dark-haired man would crawl up the stairs, whisky on his breath, cigarette smoking in his fingers and a strength growing in his jeans.

Dakota often thought about what would happen if she told Lula. Would she slap her? Collapse? Scream? She felt she would call her a liar and say she was jealous of her and Jackson. Maybe she would kick her out, or Jackson. Or would she go insane and finally kill herself?

Dakota knew there was no way she could ever tell her.

She couldn't tell anyone how she felt, so she wrote it all down.

One afternoon while she was at home alone, she found herself wandering around, picking up Jackson's things, his CDs, his books, turning them over in her hands as though they would bring her some sort of understanding of how he was feeling.

He never said anything, nothing of his own. There was a part of her that needed to know why he was doing it all. She needed something, some ammunition to make it easier for her to hate him. Suddenly she was rummaging feverishly through his belongings, looking for his notebooks, the red and black notebooks he was always scribbling in but that he never left lying about to be read. What was he writing?

She stood on the sofa and looked at the bookshelves higher up that she couldn't normally reach and noticed that one section of books was standing out further than the others. Behind a bunch of her dad's old books was Jackson's book.

Once she had it in her hands she began to shake. Guilt took over her even before she began to open the pages. She was breaking in to Jackson's brain, she was snooping. And even though she knew he was miles away at work, she felt like he was there, breathing down her neck.

She began to leaf through the pages, some entries dated, but all the pages were different, some filled with drawings, others with poems and most with straightforward prose, almost like a diary. She felt some sort of peace reading his words, like the words proved he was human, not some figment of her imagination. Not knowing how long she had, she opened the first page and read.

Today I met the love of my life. I never thought it would happen but it has. The strangest thing. When our eyes met it was like we had known each other forever, something inside of us that we didn't have to say out loud. That's it. You can stop looking now because I'm here. I'm here. But I can't have her. I'm not crazy, I know it's her, it's like I know her soul, but I can't be with her. She's too young. Too young.

Dakota smiled to herself to see he was so passionate even when he used his own words. She flipped forward through poems about trees and love until she found a dated entry from the night after he first came to her room.

I'm sitting down here and I know she is awake up there. God, how can I stand it? I just wanted to be in the same room as her, sitting in silence with someone else who understands loneliness. Every night she sits up there awake and I sit down here. And then suddenly she was kissing me. I tried to hold her off but once I had felt her lips it was harder not to let her kiss me again and again. I've never felt that before. Like our lips meeting created something I had no control over. It was wrong, so so wrong. But she made me feel.... I don't even know what words to use. All my poems and fancy prose are useless to me now. She made me feel something I can't even find the words for. I want to be beside her so much my heart hurts. Just to feel that calm again. Every day since I met her has been the same, I feel equal parts blessed and damned, like she is my saviour and yet still the end of me. I always knew from the first time I laid eyes on her that she was important. I just didn't know why. When I looked at her this morning I couldn't even see her like I used to, I see endless lifetimes receding into the trees, I see eternity.

"Hello?" A voice in the hallway broke her from her trance. It was Lula. Dakota snapped into action, climbing back up the bookshelf to stuff the book back into its hiding place.

Even while she was hugging Lula to say hello she was thinking that she wanted more of his words. She felt so much love in her heart, she thought it might burst.

One year after the first time, almost to the day, Dakota's nightmares began.

After the first, they came irregularly, once or twice a week, and she woke every time soaked in sweat, grabbing blindly for the light to make sure that the sticky, wet residue covering her body was not blood.

The dream varied but was basically the same every time.

It was always night-time. She was either in a house she did not recognise, a forest, a cemetery or by a river. Wherever it was, she was always crying angry, hot tears, and Jackson was always there, screaming back at her.

"You said you loved me! You can't finish this!"

"It's wrong; it's always been wrong!"

"No, we are meant to be together and you know it! You just can't accept that you are as dirty as me, and that you love the way I make you feel. You're just a coward!"

"Just go, leave me alone. This ends now! Tonight! It had to end sometime. Did you really think that it could go on forever? You knew it would end someday."

Suddenly he stepped forward, grabbed her by her shoulders and began kissing her passionately. She, unable to resist him, reciprocated through her tears.

"And you should know by now," he whispered, "this is never over!"

A sharp burning pain in her ribs came first, then stumbling back in the rainy graveyard, thumping into a tomb as she looked down at the blood pouring down her. In his hands the knife glittered red, rain diluting it over his fingers. And in the moments before darkness swam into her eyes, he began to sob, his face streaming with rain.

In similar dreams, he strangled her in a house – the beautiful and glamorous home of a wealthy person, the moon at the window peering in. The last sight she saw, the last sound she heard, was his weeping.

In the woods, he gave her no warning as he stove her skull in with a rock, sobbing wildly against the sounds of the animals flickering in the undergrowth.

Then, in the shadow of trees by a rushing river, he held her head beneath the torrent until all faded into black.

The location and method of murder differed but his last words to her never changed.

"You should know by now, this is never over!"

The dreams were so vivid that they always left her shaken. Panic continued in her waking as she searched for the knife wound, the garrotte or the blood pouring from her broken skull. Sometimes she awoke unable to breathe, trying to cough up river water that moments before had been swilling around in her lungs.

Then, as reality dawned, and the light revealed a sweat-soaked nightdress, Dakota would collapse back into her bed, weak and tired from her struggle to survive.

Her dreams made her feel slightly more nervous around Jackson and she recognised more than ever that sharp edge to his eyes that had frightened her when she first met him. One morning, after a particularly bloody episode in the rain-drenched cemetery, Jackson touched her mischievously behind Lula's back, but the contact made her jump so much that she cut her finger open with the bread knife she was holding.

"What's wrong with you?" asked Jackson as Lula switched the tap on for her bloody-handed sister.

"Did you slip?" she asked Dakota, who looked pale and sweaty. "You feeling under the weather?" Lula touched her sister's clammy forehead.

"Yeah, a bit. I didn't sleep too well, might be coming down with something," offered Dakota weakly as the blood disappeared in the cold water.

Lula left the room to fetch a plaster, and Dakota found she could not meet Jackson's gaze.

"You trying to make her suspicious or something? What's wrong with you? Why won't you look at me?"

"Sorry, you made me jump," she answered, staring down at her hand.

"You've been like this for a month now. Every time I come near you, you act weird. What's changed?" he asked, pushing his fingers through her dark hair as upstairs, Lula turned the bathroom upside down.

Dakota had become accustomed to her relationship with Jackson over the year. It made her feel more wanted than she ever had. Despite all the wrong she knew happened between them, she trusted him.

For this reason, she told him about her dreams. He laughed slightly and whispered, "You know, I probably would kill you if you tried to leave me, but I know you won't so don't worry, they are only dreams." And his eyes became soft suddenly as she looked into them.

Lula bustled back into the kitchen and stood between them to apply the plaster to Dakota's bleeding finger.

As she sat down to breakfast, Dakota realised that Jackson was telling the truth. He probably would kill her if she tried to leave, but she knew she never would, even though something about him disturbed her.

After that day, she felt her feelings for him change. She knew that she was in love with Jackson. She welcomed him into her bed and cherished how he made her feel – like a woman, not a thirteen-year-old school girl. She belonged to him.

The dreams continued to wake her up, long after Jackson had sloped off to her sister's bed, and after a time, the thought of dying in his big hands became strangely erotic. Her deep fear of him became an aphrodisiac and her fantasies took a dark turn. Their lovemaking often incorporated the threat of him killing her, and she discovered things about herself, she found hard to even tell her diary. What she and Jackson got up to late at night was becoming something she felt she could never discuss with anyone, even if it had been acceptable for her to be with him at all. Everything about their relationship was dangerous, and it was this, she told her diary, which kept her wanting more.

It no longer crossed her mind that she was betraying her sister, or that she was too young to be having an active sex life with a twenty-eight-year-old man. She slogged her way through her normal life of school and homework. She ignored every bitchy comment thrown her way by school bullies, acting innocent when her school colleagues talked about their own sex lives, and looked forward to her late-night meeting with her lover.

She was living a double life, and one life made it possible for her to cope with the other.

FIFTEEN: Another Secret

Dakota sat back in her chair as the wind howled fiercely at the library windows. She put her head in her hands and felt that at last she might understand what had happened to her. Recalling the nightmares she had had about Jackson murdering her had put forth images she had not long ago seen with her own dead eyes. The dream where she was murdered in the woods had been in exactly the place she had seen her own dead body when she had returned to her death scene. It was beginning to look like she had been having premonitions of her own death back when she was thirteen years old. She had somehow known that one night deep in the future, she would die in a rain soaked forest at the hands of the man who had taken advantage of her for years.

Yet as much as she tried to tell herself he was her abuser, she knew that she had become dependent on him, and had loved him so deeply she couldn't think straight. Something told her that the obsession that had clearly driven Jackson to kill her had been in her own heart, too. And it seemed that she had been aware of the danger all along, and yet had done nothing to stop seeing him. There were still many years to cover, though, before her inevitable demise, and she wished it would all become clear sooner; but she knew that she would have to go on reading before she would understand anything any better.

Movement somewhere behind her made her jump up, ready to defend herself, but the person who stepped forth from the shadows meant her no harm.

"Betty? What are you doing here? What are you doing out of your room?"

"I was looking for you, Ariel told me you were here. Are

you OK? I haven't seen you in ages, feels like weeks." Betty pulled up a chair beside Dakota, glancing briefly around her. Dakota suspected that she was still expecting her ex-husbands to leap screaming from the shadows.

"I'm sorry, I wanted to come and see you but I ended up here instead."

Dakota began telling Betty everything that she had been through, from seeing her own dead body, up to discovering who probably put her there.

"I think they call that Stockholm Syndrome," said Betty, lighting another cigarette between her thin wrinkled lips.

"What's that?"

"It's when victims of abuse or kidnap victims fall in love with their abusers. It sounds like that's what happened to you."

"It's so weird. I know that they were my feelings, cos I remember having them, and yet I also feel like I must have been sick in the head to be the one who started it. Why didn't I care that he was so much older than me? Why did I feel so much... love for him... missing him when he didn't come up?" Dakota shook her head, confusion clouding her mind: the remembrances of her feelings for him, half-fearing, half-loving, and now the thought that what was happening was so wrong she couldn't believe she had never seen it before. "How could I have thought I loved him when he was doing that to me? I was so young!"

"That's what I mean. You developed a dependency on him. You cherished every soft hand on you, every tender word because it made all the other stuff seem bearable. He made you feel needed!"

"How do you know all this?"

"Oh, I read a lot of books. One of the ones I read had a character who had Stockholm Syndrome. I guess it stuck in my head because they say it's what makes battered wives stay with their husbands. That and fear. I figured that must have been what was wrong with me... putting up with that bastard so long. I don't know if it's that – a syndrome, something with a name. I think it's just fear, a genuine fear that you will be murdered, that one day the abuse will take a different path and he won't let up… won't stop… till you are quiet." A tiny flame of anger burnt in Betty's eyes for a moment, taken over suddenly by memories, her brain taking her away from what Dakota had been to and sending her off, back into a time in the past where every day was full of that fear for herself.

Pushing her own past away, Betty looked around the dusty library. "That still wouldn't explain why you ended up here, though."

"What – in the library?"

"No, in Purgatory Hotel! You still don't know what you did wrong?"

"Ariel said it could be something from my other lives. I am going to have to read them, too, by the looks of it. Could be years before I get out of here!"

Betty laughed, as did a few other disembodied voices.

"You will be lucky if you ever do anyway, like Ariel says, there are many tasks, and you don't even know what they are,"

"I know, but it will be a start if I can just know what went on to put me here… Will you help me, Betty?" Dakota asked, putting her hand on Betty's.

"What do you want me to do?" She smiled back, patting Dakota's hand affectionately. For a moment, Dakota wondered how this lovely woman could possibly have murdered two men.

Dakota explained how the Library worked and that there were books for every life of every person. She needed Betty to start reading her past lives while she got on with the last one. With a daunted look at the endless rows of books that scratched out lives incessantly, Betty nodded.

They located the book entitled Miriam Diana Page, and it, too, seemed less dusty than some of the other books.

"Someone been reading about you, do you think?" asked Betty, carrying the book back to the table. "This one's got finger marks on it and they aren't mine."

Dakota inspected the book briefly and paused for a

moment to consider the fact that this book contained details of a life she had no recollection of. She looked up and smiled warmly at Betty as she sat down and readied herself for a spell of reading.

"Good job I like reading, eh? Does the fact that I can speed read help at all?" Betty chuckled. "Let's just hope I can read the last page of this one!"

The two women settled back into their chairs and began to read silently, as storms fretted at the windows.

The following year she turned fourteen, and as always it was a non-event; a card and a small present was all Lula could manage along with a tearful hug and best wishes, before the visit to the graveyard to lay flowers for their parents.

That night, after Lula had gone to bed, Dakota made her way upstairs, glancing briefly at Jackson as he lit a cigarette in front of the TV.

The small lamp beside her bed cast soft light across her room, her walls now covered in posters of her favourite rock bands and artwork by pre-Raphaelite painters. As she lit a cigarette and threw the dead match out of the window, she noticed a small package on her bed. Sitting down she picked up the note that lay folded on top of it, and read it. In a large blocky script, were the words:

'*L is for LOVE baby*
O is for O yes I do
V is for VIRTUE, so I ain't gonna hurt you
E is for EVEN if you want me to
R is for RENDER unto me baby
M is for that which is MINE
A is for ANY old how, darling
N is for ANY old time...'

She recognised the verse from the song he always played her and smiled at the words that rose out of the paper. Reaching across she picked up the package and tore away the wrapping paper to find a CD. It was an album called 'Let Love In' by a band called Nick Cave and the Bad Seeds. It was the album he had always played at night when he came to her, and he had actually given her her own copy. After all these years he had given her it as a gift and she was unsure of what he meant by it. She sat in the dim light, smoking, and read the lyrics to the songs even though she already knew them by heart.

At a little after midnight she put the CD into her stereo and hit the play button. Jackson had been silent downstairs that night; He played no music and she even wondered if he had fallen asleep, but as the first notes of the first song vibrated out of her speakers, she heard him begin to mount the stairs.

As he entered the room, he smiled at her and said, "You called?" and she understood what he meant. After years of him coming up to her, never a choice of hers, he was giving her the power to call him. She knew at that moment that she could no longer blame him, that he would no longer come unless she played that music and called him to her. And she knew she always would.

Stepping forward, he tore her shirt off and made love to her right there on the floor.

It was a couple of weeks later when she began to panic. Dakota had begun her period when she was thirteen, and since that time, Jackson always used condoms when he came to her room, but over the past few months there had been a couple of occasions where there had been no time for condoms. There had been a few incidences where Lula had popped out and Jackson had used the opportunity to have sex with Dakota in different parts of the house. For both of them the risk involved and the break from their routine had sent them into a sexual frenzy, thus the thought of condoms was far at the back of their minds.

It was the first day of August and Dakota had missed her last period. She had not discussed it with Jackson yet but knew she would have to go out and buy a pregnancy test to make sure before she said anything to him.

On a hot afternoon, while Lula and Jackson were at work, Dakota discovered that at just fourteen she was pregnant by her sister's twenty-nine-year-old boyfriend.

She threw up twice before she managed to leave the bathroom and dragged herself off to her bed where she lay until late that night when she played her Nick Cave CD to call Jackson up to her.

When he came in, he made ready to remove her clothes but she stopped him, her head bowed.

"What's wrong?" he asked, letting go of her. When she did not answer, he put his hands on her shoulders and gently asked again.

"I'm pregnant," she muttered and sat back down on the bed, steadying herself for what she thought might be a blaze of anger from Jackson.

But he said nothing. He just sat down beside her on the bed and put his head in his hands.

She made no effort to force him to react. She just sat back on the bed and lit another cigarette.

Nick Cave sang on in the background, his mood unwavering. Sometimes she felt he was there in the room, singing to her from the shadows, singing about her life somehow.

"You been to the doctors yet?" he asked quietly lighting a cigarette himself, his hands steady as rocks. Dakota noticed and looked down at her own quivering fingers.

"No, just did the test today," she replied.

"Well, you need to see the doctor soon as you can, get the test confirmed, and then you'll have to arrange a termination..." He spoke steadily, as though he were reading from a script.

"You knew this might happen someday, didn't you?"

"There was always the possibility since you started your period. I have been careful mostly, but there's been a few times... when I haven't. It's my fault," he declared, looking across and into her eyes. She felt odd, and afraid. She knew she couldn't have a baby, but she was afraid of the word itself... 'termination.'

"I'm scared, Jackson," she said quietly, tears forming in her eyes, ready to break free over her hot cheeks.

"There's no need for that. It's simple; no one will even know."

"But Lula will want to know why I went to the doctors, and what about when I have the termination... how will I hide that I have to go to hospital?"

"Leave it all to me. Give me time to think and I'll sort it out. But you have to go to the doctors soon as you can. They will be discreet, I am sure. Lula need never know. If they need to speak to your guardian, give them my work number, OK?"

Dakota was numbing now and the tears were drying up.

She felt too young to have ever even considered what she would do if she fell pregnant. It was all rather new and confusing, and she wasn't even sure how she was supposed to feel about possibly aborting a baby.

Jackson stayed with her for another hour before going back downstairs, even though they barely spoke as was usual. He had his own mind to sort out now, and all thoughts of touching Dakota had gone out of the window into the summer night. So she sat alone in her bed, thinking of him sitting alone downstairs, and all night long she lay there feeling suddenly more alone than she had in years. Nick Cave sang 'Nobody's Baby Now,' and she wanted to laugh, or maybe it was just more tears; she wasn't sure.

She told herself it was just another secret in a long line of secrets. The past three years had been full of secrets... she could easily handle one more.

After two weeks and several visits to the doctors, Dakota prepared to go to hospital for the abortion.

She knew that for the rest of her life she would never feel as uncomfortable as she had the day she told her doctor that she was pregnant and wanted an abortion. She had known Dr Owens for her whole life – this woman had known her mother, and she looked almost as disappointed as Dakota believed her mother would have.

After the lecture and the desperate attempt to talk her out of it, Dr Owens agreed to make the appointment for her, putting the results of the pregnancy test to one side.

"Lula can never know, though. Do you understand?" Dakota said seriously as the doctor made notes on her computer.

"Well, by my doctor patient rule I can't tell anyone, Dakota, but you have to be sure it's what you want. It will be a big secret to keep from her, and I'm sure if you spoke to her she would be supportive."

"I doubt it. You know her mental health history. Dead babies aren't exactly her favourite subject," replied Dakota caustically. Dr Owens looked mildly embarrassed and turned away again, nodding faintly.

Jackson gave her the money for a taxi and had invented a friend of Dakota's for Lula's benefit. Dakota would be off spending the day with her friend Mary, and Jackson would be going to pick her up that evening.

Lonelier than ever, longing for Jackson to be there to hold her hand, Dakota silently underwent the procedure, all the while trying not to give any human qualities to the child waiting in her belly.

Just before they came to take her down to theatre, Dakota put her hand over the belly she had spent the last few weeks ignoring and whispered low, "I'm sorry, but I'm not ready for you yet. Come back another time and I promise I'll be good to you..."

On the way home in Jackson's car, she stared quietly out of the window as he smoked nervously asking how it went. When they pulled up outside the house, he reached out and put his hand on hers. It was the first time she had looked at him since he had picked her up. She stared deeply into his eyes, trying to show all her pain and fears without speaking, and behind his blue eyes she saw that he was sorry, so sorry for everything she had been through because of him. There in silence, in the dark car, with a wind tapping at the windows, they stared into each other's hearts and were relieved to find themselves in the other. As tears brimmed up in their eyes, a soft smile of reassurance appeared on Dakota's lips. It was OK, she silently told him, she still wanted him as much as before; she still could not live without him.

At the quiet arrival home, Jackson explained to Lula how Dakota had been very ill at her friend's house. She must have caught a stomach bug, he said, and was not up to much other than bed. Lula flapped and fussed, helping her sister up to bed and remarking on her pale face. She offered hot milk or hot chocolate and a hot water bottle, but all Dakota wanted was some painkillers and sleep.

Lula stroked her sister's head and sat on her bed, saying how good it was of Jackson to be so concerned about her.

Dakota smiled briefly before pretending to fall asleep just so Lula would leave her alone. Guilt was settling in her stomach for the first time in years. She knew how desperately Lula wanted a baby, and here she was unknowingly comforting her after she had just aborted a child. A child of the only man Lula had ever loved. And the only man Dakota had ever loved.

The world had been turned over for her. There was nothing she could do but lie down and be still while the dust settled again. All she wanted was sleep. So she slept.

She stayed in bed for a couple of days, enjoying the fuss and attention that Lula was paying her. It seemed to be the most time she had spent around her in years, and she didn't want to waste it, even though, deep down, she wondered if Lula would be so nice if she knew what was really wrong with her.

Late at night, after Lula had gone to bed, Jackson came up and got into bed with her, just so they could cuddle and smoke and listen to low, soft music. Dakota saw a softer side to him in those few days, and knew that he must really love her. It all felt so much like love, she thought; it all felt so right. Their words were as sparse as ever; no declarations ever passed his lips. They had no deep discussions, but he would often sing to her or read poems aloud to her. She once realised that most of the words he spoke to her were usually the words of someone else: Nick Cave or Baudelaire, Edgar

Allen Poe or Yeats. It was as though he could only speak to her using someone else's language, someone else's feelings from decades gone, and she would be left to wonder which feelings were really Jackson's, which words did he really mean? He had always recited one poem to her in French and she never knew what it meant, but she loved the sound of it as the words left his mouth and reached her ears.

He wanted her to feel safe and comforted, so he spent most of the night with her, only leaving when the first light began to tint the sky. All of this meant love to her, but she could not risk telling him that. She feared that if she said the words, he might vanish in a puff of smoke or that she would suddenly wake up and find it had all been a dream and that he had never come to her room.

SIXTEEN: The Other Life

They never spoke of the abortion again. Life just continued as normal. Dakota went back to school in the September and her secret life with Jackson continued under the nose of her sister.

Following the abortion, Dakota began to notice she was losing her appetite. Her sleeplessness had grown, so that she now only slept an hour a night at best. Instead of sleeping, she would lie in bed after Jackson left her and read poetry and whatever books Jackson had lent her that week. He would always bring books home from the library for her and Lula thought it was so sweet that they had something in common. Dakota could see that look in her sister's eyes. It said, 'I'm so pleased you two are close because I love you both so much.' And she hated it. She wanted her to not make such a fuss whenever Jackson showed her some affection in front of Lula. But it always happened. Each time Jackson handed over the books he had borrowed for her, Lula would be at her side, looking to see what he had brought her, cooing and saying things like, "Aw Jackson, do you remember when we read that together?" or "Oh, Jackson read that one to me years ago."

Eventually Dakota asked Jackson to just put the books in her room, so that Lula wouldn't see them. He used to slip little notes in between the pages of the books, or place a book mark on a poem he wanted her to read. It was a secret language that he used, borrowing another person's words again to charm her and make her feel wanted. He always called her 'D' at the top of a letter, but when he was sending her words of a sexual nature he used to call her 'Lo' after the young girl in Nabokov's book 'Lolita.'

He did these things to make her feel special and desirable. And it worked. But she had begun to feel the space between them more and more. When she was younger and had only been growing accustomed to Jackson's desires she did not notice: she focused more on when he was there. Now, as she found herself depending on him more, she had begun to focus on the time he did not spend with her. And her focus on that empty place in her life began to make her feel angry and depressed. Part of her wanted to demand that he leave Lula for her, but she knew she could not ask that, so instead she decided she wanted someone else, too.

School had always been an unhappy experience for Dakota, who had never fitted in a primary school and went on to secondary school with the same problems. Her parents had died not long after she started at St Mary's High School, and she had taken time off school for a while to help Lula get herself back together in some way. She knew that she would be put back a year but she had no friends to miss anyway.

By the time she had returned, the other pupils looked on her as an even bigger freak who had somehow wangled a year off school. The fact that her parents had died didn't matter, in the minds of the crowd; she was probably a bit mental now her parents were dead, and the music she listened to meant only one thing: she was totally weird.

There were of course a few other kids who liked the same music as her, but they were all a lot older than her so they didn't really hang around together.

The girls of the school hated her for how different she was and how unafraid she was of their taunting, so she kept her distance from them and often hung around with a group of boys, feeling more at ease with them than with girls. Girls were far often too bitchy and spiteful for her to trust any of them. Instead she kept it simple by hanging out as 'one of the lads' and they accepted her. Two of the boys she was friends with lived locally, so they often met up at weekends to sit in the park and smoke cigarettes. One day she went over to her friend Jimmy's house for an afternoon of computer games. When she got there, the door was answered by a tall handsome boy of around eighteen. He had short spiky blond hair and an angular face, similar to Jackson's, only younger and somehow softer.

"Umm is Jimmy home?" she asked after a few seconds of silence.

"Yeah, you're Jimmy's girlfriend?" asked the boy, a look of disbelief on his face.

"Uh no!" She almost laughed. "I'm his friend. We're just friends."

"Oh sorry, come in," he said stepping aside. As she walked in past him she looked up into his eyes and he winked fiendishly. He laughed as she shut the door behind her.

"I'm Charlie. What's your name, gorgeous?"

"Dakota." She smiled back at him.

She found that out of her years of silence and sexual secrecy, she had developed a sudden desire to flirt.

It only took a few more visits to Jimmy's house before Dakota managed to get into bed with Charlie, or rather into a car with him. She did not want Jackson to know about him yet, and Charlie did not want anyone to know he fancied a fourteen-year-old. But when they finally got down to business, he was shocked to find she was more sexually experienced than him. She refused to answer any of his questions on how she had come to know so much at her young age, and instead told him that he could come over to her house one night and they could have sex there instead of in his car all the time.

Dakota began to fill up with loathing every time she had sex with Charlie. She had no real feelings for him, and she just wanted to use him, to make Jackson jealous. She also hated it because she knew she meant nothing to Charlie. He used her as much as she was using him, and it made her feel like a whore.

But she gained some satisfaction from it. Though it made her feel disgusted with herself, she felt she was taking something out of life for herself, something she could shove in Jackson's face as if to say, "I can do this on my own!" She wanted Jackson to be as jealous of her as she was growing of him.

One night she invited Charlie over when she knew that Jackson and Lula would be at home.

"Hello love, who is this?" asked Lula when Charlie arrived.

"Oh, this is my boyfriend, Charlie," replied Dakota loudly enough to make Jackson come storming out of the lounge.

"D, I didn't know you had a boyfriend," Lula replied, smiling falsely at the obviously much older boy standing beside her sister.

"Well, I kind of kept him a secret – y'know, like you did with Jackson?" replied Dakota, feeling a wriggle of pleasure as she saw Lula's expression change and almost heard the words 'that means I can't tell her off' flash through Lula's eyes.

"How old are you?" Jackson asked Charlie brusquely.

"Eighteen, and I know Dakota is younger than me, but she is very mature," Charlie said, trying to quell any kind of argument.

Dakota watched Jackson's expression turn from interest to anger.

"Well, Dakota isn't allowed friends over on a school night so you'll have to go,"

"Shouldn't we discuss this first, Jackson?" said Lula, quietly turning to her boyfriend who by now was visibly enraged but was keeping it harnessed.

"No, Dakota knows the rules: no guests on a school night... Oh yeah, and no eighteen-year-old boyfriends, so just bugger off, OK?" Jackson's voice rose slightly and Lula looked embarrassed, while Dakota was almost physically wriggling with pleasure.

"Look mate, it's all right—" began Charlie, but before he could say another word, Jackson was frog-marching him out of the front door, whispering in his ear, loud enough for Dakota to hear, "Come near her again and I'll call the police."

The door slammed shut and Dakota began to feign disgust.

"Lula, he can't do that – he's not my dad. I can see whoever I want."

"You are a bit too young to be dating an eighteen-year-old, sweetie," replied Lula, softly.

"I might not be your dad, but I look after you and I don't want you messing around with stupid teenagers under this roof," Jackson said, growling.

"It's not your flamin' house. Our parents left us this; it's ours. I can do what I like," she snapped back, loving every second of his rage.

"Yes, but I pay the bills, and I put food on the table, so as long as I do that I think I have some say in how this house works."

"He is right, sweetie. You should respect his wishes. Now go and do your homework, and we don't want you seeing that boy anymore, OK? Wait till you're a bit older for all that relationship stuff." Lula spoke softly and touched her sister's hair briefly.

"Bit fucking late for all that," snapped Dakota and shot an angry glance at Jackson, her own rage simmering again.

That night, after Lula had gone to sleep, Dakota got into bed and deliberately didn't play her Nick Cave CD. She already knew he would come storming up the stairs at any moment, ready for a fight.

Sure enough, just after 1am, he stormed into her room smelling of whisky, his eyes wild with anger.

"What the fuck are you playing at?" he growled, his voice low and terrible.

"What?"

"That prick you invited here. What are you doing with him?"

"Nothing that you didn't teach me." She smiled and giggled. His rage boiled over and he flew across the room grabbing her throat with his large hands, the force of his anger pinning her against the wall.

"And who said you could share that with anyone else? That's what I am here for. How dare you go fucking around behind my back!"

"Well, you fuck her all the time. Why can't I get some elsewhere?" She struggled to get the words out under his grip.

"You are mine! I never said you could go elsewhere. We are together and that means you don't get to go around letting any old bloke stick his dick in you. You get it?" He was still speaking low so as not to wake Lula but he wanted to shout. Dakota could feel the rage in his body. He was shaking, and while she had never seen him like this, she had felt his strength before, all the times that she played at submission. It wasn't the first time he had used this force with her, and although she could feel fear thumping wildly in her chest, each word he spoke with anger and jealousy made her want him more.

Her little experiment had worked. She had reduced Jackson to an angry wreck by letting him imagine her with another man. She knew that she had some power over him then. She knew he was so obsessed with her he couldn't stand the thought of her being anyone else's lover. She knew that she owned him as much as he owned her, and that if she wanted to, she could hurt him.

After that, it became a game between them. He would start touching Lula and being intimate with her in front of Dakota. Sometimes he even left his bedroom door open when he and Lula were having sex, just so that Dakota could hear them.

In return, Dakota would write little notes to Jackson, describing sexual encounters she had had with Charlie in great detail, hiding the notes in his trouser pocket so he would find them while he was at work. Or she would say goodbye to Charlie, with a passionate kiss on the doorstep in full view of Jackson. Jackson would always chase Charlie off, or threaten to call the police, but he never did. Dakota knew his temper was dangerous. It often boiled over, leaving Dakota with bruises she had to hide. At one point she had to wear a neck scarf for a whole week to hide the huge bruises his hands had left on her throat. She was realising more and more that she had a reason to be afraid of him, but she could not stop provoking him. She felt like a child with a new toy – a very dangerous and volatile toy whose unpredictable nature kept her wanting more and more.

And every night that followed a jealousy-invoking encounter, they had angry, violent sex together, laying claim on each other all over again.

It was five years since her parents had died in a car accident one summer night. A few months had passed since that particular anniversary, and Dakota was back at the cemetery to wish her mother happy birthday. She had stopped by the church that day. Even though she clung to the religious icons her mother adored, Dakota had stopped attending Mass on a Sunday. And since her relationship with Jackson had begun, she had felt too ashamed to even set foot in the church. But that day it felt right.

The church was small and cold. Her footsteps on the wooden floor echoed around the walls and ceiling, and she eventually stopped to sit down on one of the pews. The faint smell of incense still lingered, as her eyes travelled around the Stations of the Cross wood carvings that hung evenly spaced around the church walls. Her childhood returned to her in a series of religious memories: saying the Creed in Latin every Sunday, the taste of the wafer bread and how it often stuck to the roof of her mouth. She remembered Easter and its long church services, the black sooty mark of Ash Wednesday on her forehead and not being allowed to wash it off, the feel of palm leaves and the long walk up to the alter to kiss the feet of the crucified Christ. She remembered reading the Bible at home during Lent, Mum and Dad and Lula and her, sitting in the lounge taking turns to read sections from the gospels. Dakota always loved reading the parts in red ink, because only Jesus's dialogue was printed in red.

There had always been comfort in going to church when she was a little girl, but as she sat there now, she noticed that everything seemed creepier than before. The shroud that sat ghostly over the tabernacle, the long empty aisle to the alter, the staring dead eyes of the statues, blood frozen over the holes in Jesus's hands, and the closed doors that led to places she would never see, their mystery frightening her in the dark cold church, its wooden echoes reminding her more and more of a huge coffin.

It was a cold afternoon in early November outside, and she was alone at the graves as Lula had visited earlier that day. Dakota stared down at the huge bunch of flowers her sister had laid and was pleased she had waited until twilight to come by herself.

Hannah and Jack Crow lay beside the tiny graves of their lost children. She had not visited since July, whereas Lula came by whenever one of her dead siblings had a birthday. Dakota felt less inclined to do so, as she never knew any of them. She also worried that visiting the grave left her more vulnerable to her parents' discovery of her relationship with Jackson. She knew it was silly, that they probably visited the house all the time to keep a ghostly watch on her misdeeds, but she felt easier in the belief that they had no idea about her life now… unless *he* visited the grave and informed them of it.

Had there been fewer clouds she could have watched the sunset, but instead she stared at the cold grey headstones, feeling half-angry at her parents for leaving her when she was so young, and feeling half-grateful.

What would her life be like now if they were still alive? Jackson would never have moved in nor had the opportunity to take her virginity. Perhaps she would have had a boyfriend of her own by now, one that she did not have to share. Or would he have found a way anyway? Was it her destiny to belong to him?

It made her so angry that she had to keep quiet about Jackson, that she had to deal with losing her virginity and having an abortion all alone. The few girls who didn't pick on her at school always talked about their own exploits, and she had to lie over and over and only admit to her relationship with Charlie. She could never tell anyone, no matter how much she trusted them. And every night she had to let her lover walk away down the hall and climb into bed with his girlfriend. All her pain and confusion dealt with alone, and in silence. She knew the consequences if she ever told Lula: their pretend-perfect world would shatter, and she would lose Lula and Jackson forever. Her life wouldn't be worth living. As far as she was concerned, the only real and permanent things in her life were Lula and Jackson. If she didn't have them, she would have nothing left, not a friend or relative to be there for her. And above all things, she feared being alone.

The chill winds of autumn whipped her hair around her face. Leaves scuttled around her feet like scarabs and she wished that the gravesite was more sheltered. Skies overhead took on the twilight grey of a promised storm as the first spots of rain darkened tiny circles on the concrete headstones of her dead family.

"Thought I'd find you here," said a voice behind her. She turned to see Jackson, his hair tousled and blown across his face, his blue eyes accentuated by the black hair that semi-shielded them.

"What are you doing here?" she asked frostily, turning back to her parents' grave.

"I wanted to see you alone, somewhere other than your room." He smiled briefly and brought a lit cigarette up to his cold lips.

"Why? What do you want? I just want to visit my parents alone!" She heard anger in her voice. Somewhere in her head she was afraid that her parents were there, reading the body language between them, putting two and two together. She was afraid that they would be angry with her, shouting in disgust somewhere beyond her hearing.

"They aren't here, D," he said as though he had been reading her mind. She turned her green eyes to him, surprised. "You think they'd be hanging around this place?" He laughed. "They've probably been reincarnated by now. Their souls could be in Africa or Russia, living new lives, unable to remember the life they had with you."

She wanted to be angry with him for ruining her

graveside ritual, but she tended to agree with him. She believed in reincarnation, but she had never put that belief into action where her parents were concerned. She had never imagined her parents being born again somewhere else, starting a new life far from her. And those few words spoken by Jackson had made her feel altogether stupid for standing staring at lumps of stone and marble.

"Seems so silly, really," she began, not looking at him, "to come here every year just to stare at stones and flowers, just to let the dead know we haven't forgotten them, that we remember the significance of the day, that we will always remember them and we will always miss them. But they aren't even here, not my parents, or my brothers and sisters. Not any of these people. All there is is stones, words, bones... and regret..."

Rain was falling more heavily now, and her hands felt cold. Realising that she had been speaking aloud, she turned back to look at Jackson. His face was intense, as though he wanted to shout or scream. But instead he reached out and put his hand on her face, his fingers wet, his hair moving less, now it was heavy with rain.

"I love you so much," he whispered, and a tear broke from his jewel blue eyes.

Dakota suddenly filled with emotion. Her stomach surged and her heart flew up into her throat. Tears brimmed over in her eyes and she turned her cold face into his hand, smelling his skin, feeling the smoothness of his fingers.

Without a word, he took her hand and led her away from the grave, further into the thicket of tombs and headstones. In moments, they were sheltering inside a large tomb, rain clicking at the stained glass window, and he was kissing her, his hands raking through her wet hair, his lips roaming wildly about her face and neck.

Dakota realised where they were when she saw the name 'Boncoeur' on the sepulchre. He had taken her to the place where he had taken her sister's virginity many years before. She had heard the story from her sister's lips a hundred times and now she was there, in the same tomb with the same man.

She had never been here with Jackson before and yet it all seemed strangely like déjà vu.

"No wait," he said, pulling away from her. Again she wondered if he had read her mind. "Not here, come on, let's go to the woods."

Before she could speak he was pulling her back out into the rain and leading her off to the woods that lay beside the cemetery. Behind the cemetery wall, the fields rolled on for miles, rippling in the rain and wind. She knew Pan's Wood well, for she had taken walks there all her life. As a small child, she'd joined the whole family for Sunday walks and picnics there, and as she grew older she used to take walks alone with Lula.

She had never been there with Jackson.

They seemed more foreboding than ever before in the quickening dark. Rain fell like sheets of cold glass and the urgency in Jackson's footsteps grew as the forest closed in over their heads. He led her deeper and deeper into the trees, darkness growing as they travelled further from daylight, the deep gloom of the trees thickening. If she had been wandering there alone, a deep sadness would have taken her. The time-worn path disappeared as he led her away into untrodden foliage. Her clothes snagged on branches and thorns and tiny cuts sprang up threads of blood as the soft ferns gave way to the brambles and thorny bushes that closed in around her.

Jackson led her to a concealed clearing. It stood in a grove of tall trees that hid all else from their view. The floor was covered with thick moss and was just wide enough for two people to lie down side by side. She would never have known the place existed if he hadn't shown it to her. She could hear her mother's voice warning her, "Don't stray off those paths, Dakota Grace. If you got lost, no one would be able to find you in those trees."

But she knew she had been lost for some time and no one was going to rescue her.

The rain and wind whispered somewhere overhead in the tall branches of the tired trees, as she lay herself down and gave herself up under Jackson's rain of kisses. And there in the chattering gloom and whispering breezes, she felt for the first time in years that Jackson really loved her. There was no pain or games, or fear of his wrath. There was only tenderness and desire.

"Did you really mean it?" she asked afterwards, as he lay back beside her, resting his dark head on a tree stump.

"What?" he asked, through the cigarette hanging from his lips. Dakota zipped up her trousers and sat up to light her own cigarette.

"When you said you loved me."

"Of course I meant it. I've told you often enough!" he replied.

"You've never said it before, Jackson."

"All the notes I sent you, the poems I read you. You couldn't take it from that?"

"It's the words, I've never heard you say them, not even to Lula," she replied warily, afraid she had overstepped her mark by talking about his relationship with Lula. He often told her to mind her own business if she asked about it.

"Because I don't really love her," he said, the smoke from his mouth rising gently before a breeze whipped it away. Dakota felt suddenly confused.

"But why have you been with her so long then? You have always seemed so together. I... I am a bit jealous of the way you are together," she admitted, blushing slightly. In all the years they had been sleeping together, they rarely spoke about Lula.

"It's a habit really, plus I get to be with you without anyone suspecting."

Wind whispered somewhere; squirrels twitched in the undergrowth.

"Oh," she managed. Looking down at her hands, she wanted to look anywhere but at him. She always knew that what she was doing was wrong, but she tried to ignore it. She dreamed that people would accept her and Jackson as lovers, but she knew that what they had been doing for the last four years was not only morally wrong, it was illegal.

He would be labelled a pervert, a deviant, a paedophile, and she would be his confused and naïve victim. Lula would never forgive herself for bringing a sexual deviant into her family home. She would blame herself entirely for the years of sexual abuse and rape Dakota had suffered.

Nobody would believe that Jackson and Dakota were in love. No one would accept that she had invited Jackson into her bed, that there were several times when he would not come to her room and she would go downstairs to where he sat, lost in dark melodies and a cloud of cigarette smoke, and beg him to make her feel good again.

Who would believe that the music that he played to warn her of his approach, would be the music she would eventually play to call him up to her room.

She had come to realise that nobody would ever understand what was going on between her and Jackson. No one would ever believe that she allowed him to do all the things he did. No one would believe she could no longer live without him.

She hated it when reality slipped into her life with him. She had learnt not to feel guilt about the fact that she was sleeping with her sister's boyfriend. She had learnt never to show any affection for him around other people.

But when it came to the fact that she may never have Jackson all to herself, she switched off before the thought drove her insane. Deep in her heart, she dreamt of a time when she would not have to share him, when she could be alone with him all the time and not have to hide her desire for him.

"OK, we'd better get home. Lula will be worried," she said suddenly and stood up. Jackson looked up at her from the moss-drenched floor. His blue eyes showed the understanding that reality was with them again.

It was getting darker and colder. In the distance beyond the trees, the rain had stopped and all that they could hear was the whispering sky above them. When Jackson had led her back to the path, she had paused and looked back to where the clearing was hidden. She found herself standing in front of the 'Witch Tree.' It was a huge dead tree that resembled a wild-haired woman with her arms raised to the sky. Knots in the wood gave the impression of a tormented facial expression. She had been told as a child that the tree was where a witch had been executed in the olden days, and her spirit had gone into the tree and killed it. She had never seen it before because it was so far off the beaten path; she had often thought it was just a mythical tree. Spooky stories that Lula told her said that at night you could hear the witch screaming to be released from her prison of a tree.

Dakota shuddered.

Jackson and Dakota walked home in silence. She was unsure if knowing he loved her made her feel better or worse. While it was a wonderful affirmation, knowing that her love was reciprocated, the thought that Lula was the one who got to be public with him made her angry. But she and Jackson knew that the only way they could continue to be together was if he stayed with Lula.

Dakota was comforted by the fact that Jackson and Lula rarely had sex, and even more rarely slept in the same bed. Her sister's dependency on strong sedatives always meant their nightly meetings went undiscovered.

As much as she longed for things to be different, the years had let her slip into an acceptance of how things had to be.

By the time they reached home, Lula was sitting in front of the television with a bottle of wine and a cigarette.

"You were right, she was at the cemetery," said Jackson, sitting down and giving Lula a brief kiss on the cheek.

"You were gone a while. I put the dinner in the oven," she replied indifferently.

"Well, you know D. She wanted to sit awhile by the grave, so I wandered off and waited for her. Didn't want her walking back in the dark alone," he said, taking a cigarette from Lula's packet.

"Did you tell her about the job?"

"What job?" interrupted Dakota from the doorway.

"Well, Jackson has managed to get you a job at the library, just on Saturdays and holidays," explained Lula excitedly.

"Oh right. Weren't you going to ask if I wanted a job?"

"No. You need a job – you're sixteen now. I can't afford to keep buying you things. You need to be earning so you can buy your own clothes and things. Anyway, it will stop you spending all your spare time moping around the house," Lula quipped at her. "Say thank you to Jackson, then!"

"Thank you to Jackson!" she mimicked in a high-pitched voice.

She hated that Lula had gone over her head, but she was quite pleased that she would get to be a part of Jackson's life that Lula had no part in.

She remained standing in the doorway as Jackson and Lula cuddled up on the sofa. She grimaced slightly and turned away to notice a man standing on the other side of the road. His features were hidden in shadow as the amber streetlight poured evenly down over his head. She could tell he was fairly old, as his hair was thinning. He had the look of a vagrant or wandering drunk person as he brought the can of beer up to his invisible mouth and continued to look directly into the lounge at Dakota. For a few moments, she stared back at the spectator. Then she began to feel a bit nervous; she could feel his eyes burning into her, and the fact that she could not see his face began to unnerve her even more.

"Uh, there's someone out there, staring right into the house," she muttered, moving slightly towards the window. Lula and Jackson stood up together and made their way past her to get a closer look.

"Oh shit," muttered Jackson, and quickly made his way out of the house into the street.

"Come on, want some food?" asked Lula, physically removing her sister from the lounge.

"Do you know who that was?"

"No, Jackson's gone to see him off. Just some drunk, probably. Come on, your dinner will still be hot," and before she could do anything, Dakota had been made to sit down at the dinner table and was being watched as she started to eat.

A few moments later she heard Jackson come back in through the front door. Lula made a quick exit, pulling the kitchen door half closed as she went out to meet Jackson. Even though they were whispering, Dakota could still make out their conversation.

"What the fuck was he doing out there?" muttered Lula, sounding furious.

"You know what he's like. He just wanted to see how we were doing. He won't come back," Jackson replied.

"I don't want him anywhere near D, OK? If I see him out there again, I am calling the police!"

"Calm down for god's sake, he's gone all right!"

Dakota finished her dinner off and went up to her room in silence. Later on, when Jackson came in, she asked him almost immediately, "Who was that man outside?"

"My dad. And don't ask me anything else cos I won't answer you," he replied. And that was the end of the matter.

SEVENTEEN: L is for Love

Dakota was wandering the corridors of Purgatory. Darkness was pervasive as ever, yet she strolled unafraid, but with a feeling that she was looking for something. It seemed hers was the only soul in Purgatory. Everyone else was gone, leaving the feeling of entering a long empty house.

Shadows swayed about her and lights flickered in the gloomy distance.

A voice was singing somewhere ahead of her, words she could not yet make out although she recognised the tune. It was as though they were beckoning her, taking form, a man in the blackness calling her onwards with his long-fingered hands. The voice was distant and hollow, as though the owner was singing through a tin can, but Dakota began to make out the words:

"*L is for love baby*
O is for only you that I do..."

She followed the disembodied voice, out of the maze of corridors until she was in the deserted hotel lobby. No dim creatures lurked in the corners, no breezes disturbed the cobwebs as she moved through and out of the front door, out into the night. There was no rain and above there were stars, a wind was whispering somewhere and the voice continued to call her on, to lure her into the endless night, onwards into the bleak trees.

She paused a moment, considering whether to continue her pursuit, but a second later when the voice resumed its song, she moved forward, into the wall of trees.

"*R is for rape me*
M is for murder me..."

She felt no fear of the woods; it was as though she really

belonged there, as though she felt safer amongst the trees than in the hotel. The dead trees rubbed their dry fingers together as she looked up at the branched sky, and she felt her heart beating again in her chest. Joy filled her as she put her hand over her chest and felt life within, and then she felt another movement in her.

A gentle kick in her womb.

Tears filled her eyes as she clasped her swollen stomach, the joy of being given another chance to have her child. And she continued to walk, the breeze carrying the tinny voice of the shape in the distance, a figure up ahead moving through the trees. And no matter how fast she ran, she could not catch up with the person up ahead; they remained elusive and clothed in sinister shadows, always just out of reach.

"I'll be your lover man, til the bitter end,
while empires burn down
Forever and ever and ever and ever Amen..."

There was something familiar about the woods to her. The smells grew more familiar and the path formed ahead to show her the way. She knew these woods; she had been here before.

The figure ahead was gone and she began to run, only to collapse in agony as a searing pain shot through her torso. She screamed against the grim trees as blood covered her hands and her swollen stomach shrank back into her body. The moonlight broke through the trees to illuminate her hands, slicked with dark blood.

"My baby!" she screamed, her heart suddenly silent in her chest. And as the pain ebbed away she looked up to see a tree, in the shape of a screaming woman, with wild hair and her dry arms raised to the sky. She had been here before.

At the base of the tree, where the bark bunched to form a shape like the top of a woman's thighs, stood two men, still and silent. No one moved until the old man Woods opened his mouth and began to sing again to her:

"L is for love baby..."

As the lyrics led down to the words 'rape' and 'murder', Jackson joined in. The voices trailed around her like smoke, then crawled inside her head and circled around, unending and hypnotic. The two men moved towards her, hands outstretched, and she sat frozen on the ground, blood dripping from her fingers as she attempted to scream. Hands closed over her mouth as the blackness swarmed into her eyes.

Awake, Dakota was thrashing her arms about her, still unable to scream, but Betty was there trying to hold her down into her chair.

"It was a dream. You are awake, OK? It was a dream!" repeated Betty, over and over until Dakota sat still again.

"What happened? I was reading... I thought it was happening, or had happened." Dakota wiped tears from her face, a hand pausing over the quietness in her chest.

"You dozed off a while ago. I just left you and carried on reading. What did you see? You were singing, you know!" She half laughed, offering Dakota a cigarette as she lit her own. Dakota took it without thinking and didn't enjoy it one bit as she went through the motions of smoking it.

"What was I singing?"

"Couldn't make it all out; sounded like you were spelling something out. I remember you saying 'L is for Love' but the rest was a bit mumbled. What was going on in your head, darling?"

"It was horrible; I don't want to think about it anymore. Uh, have you read much?"

"Well yeah, I just skimmed most of it really, to get the gist, you know, and then skipped to the ending!" She giggled. "It was fab. I got to read the end of a story!"

"So who was I?"

"Well, Miriam!" said Betty enthusiastically. "You led a mainly boring life, born in the mid-1950s. You were rich, you married a rich man while you were quite young and did things that rich people did in those days." She faked a yawn. "But... you became a bit naughty when you met a servant called George Whatley. He was working in your house and you got involved with him, only two days after he started working for you! I won't go into details, but it was steamy to say the least!"

Dakota giggled slightly as Betty raised her eyebrows and shook a finger at her.

"My my, how very interesting!" She laughed, ignoring grunts from other patrons of the Library who lurked behind the shelves.

"Anyway... he got a bit obsessed with you and vice versa, but after a while you realised you would lose everything if you were caught out, so you sacked George and ended the affair. Needless to say, he didn't take it well, and he... well he murdered you one night after forcing you to meet him to talk about things. That was in 1975, just before you were reborn as Dakota, I'd say."

Dakota looked silently at her. The news that she had been murdered in her previous life was a shock to her.

"Where did I go to meet him?" she asked quietly.

"Ummm..." Betty thumbed back through the book and located the beginning of Miriam Page's last meeting with her lover. "Uh, you met him by a river on the edge of your estate, in the early hours of the morning. You argued for a while – he had threatened to tell your husband – and you told him you would lie and say he was stalking you, have him arrested. So he lost his temper, hit you a few times, then drowned you in the river."

"Betty, is it possible for two souls to meet up in more than one life?"

"Don't see why not. We all have a few lives, don't we? What's to say the same souls don't meet up in every life we live? Why do you ask?"

"Betty, I think that I was murdered by Jackson, in my last life, and now I think he may have killed me in the life previous to that. Does that sound crazy?"

"When you are here in this place, nothing seems crazy anymore! Why would you think that he was George Whatley?"

"The way he killed me. In my last life, I had nightmares all the time that Jackson murdered me. In the dreams, he always killed me, but in different places and with different methods. One of them was to drown me in a river," she explained, her mind racing suddenly with the possibilities. She stood up suddenly and put her hand to her forehead.

"I am so stupid! All this time, I have been going through the horror of remembering my whole life, when all I had to do was look at Jackson's book!" She shot off past Betty, disappearing into the dusty shadows of the library. Her eyes strained in the dim light to find the right bookcase, as Betty appeared beside her.

"What name are we looking for, then?" she asked, puffing smoke all over Dakota.

"Jackson Shade. It should be along here somewhere," Dakota replied, frantic with desperation to find him, as though she would actually meet him there in the gloom of the library, with his long dark hair and his eyes like a sad dream.

"I think I found where it should be," began Betty from the shadowy distance. Dakota followed Betty's voice and raced over to where she stood, her hand resting on a gap in the books.

"What? It's not here?"

"No, love. Looks like someone else is interested in him, too!" Dakota felt lost suddenly. What should she do now? Run through the library asking anyone she met if they had Jackson's book?

"Problem is, sweetie, you can't just go and demand everyone hands over their book. You might just have to come back another time. Besides, it would probably take you all week to search every corner of this place for everybody who's in here." Dakota felt deflated suddenly, as though she had been let down at the last minute. She would have to keep trolling through her past for more evidence, more clues to help her solve the elusive mystery of her death. In her mind, she was completely convinced that Jackson had killed her, but she needed to know. She needed to see it happen.

"Hang on... I'm so stupid! You can read the end of my book for me! Save me reading it all, you can read it!" Dakota half yelled excitedly. She picked up her book and thrust it towards Betty who had a slightly less excited look on her face.

"I don't know, love, it seems like cheating... I wouldn't ask you to read mine."

"But you are reading my past life. Why not my last one?"

"It's different... it's the one that matters most, isn't it? Your last chance to get it right? And you didn't get it right for some reason, so... maybe you should be reading it?" Betty replied uncomfortably.

Dakota looked disappointedly at the book and then back at Betty.

"Could you just look and see if you can see the last page?" Dakota pleaded. Betty leant forward and flicked to the last page silently. Then she laughed.

"No, love, it won't let me," Betty said, shaking her head.

"Why'd you laugh then?"

"It said... 'Perhaps you should be reading your own last page, Betty.'"

"This place is stupid. You can read that book but not this one? This place is just so fucked up it's not even funny!" Dakota threw a brief tantrum and then sat down to realise that this place had its own rules and they changed whenever they saw fit.

"I think I'll go home, Betty. If I go back, I will know. There might be some clue as to what happened. Lula might still be living with him. I need to warn her!" She filled with panic again.

"Do you think he would hurt her, too?" Betty asked. "Sorry, but it seemed to me that you were an obsession that he could only end by one of you dying! He might never hurt another thing as long as he lives! But if you want to go back, you go. I'll stay here and read more of your lives. If they're as racy as the last one I read, I might just have to read 'em all!" She giggled.

"OK, if I don't get anything, I'll come back here and carry on reading, myself," she said and smiled weakly. Betty patted her arm affectionately and turned back to the reading table.

"You be careful going back home, dear. Last time you went took it out of you; you need to be strong," said Betty, wagging a motherly finger at her as she turned for a moment in the dark of the library.

On her way out, Dakota paused at the door to the Bar. Through the frosted glass on the door, she saw the dim glow of the table lamps and the brighter glow of the bar area. She thought of Danny being stuck in there for all eternity, forced forever to serve alcohol to the dregs of humanity, listening to their woes and seeing the horror in their eyes as they recalled past transgressions, never able to partake in the mind-numbing, deepening blankets of drunkenness.

She pushed the door open slightly and peered through the soft-edged gloom of the Bar, past the tables and chairs and through the layer of cigarette smoke to the silhouetted figures by the shiny-topped wooden bar. She recognised Danny's shape sitting on a bar stool, his head resting on his hand holding a cigarette, smoke curling up into the dark air. He was listening intently to a person sitting beside him, whose back was turned to her. She decided she had nothing to say to Danny right then. She felt bad that she had lost her temper with him before, but she didn't have it in her to apologise, so she decided to leave him with his companion. But just before she closed the door, he looked across at her in time to catch a smile on her lips, a smile he half returned, with a look of surprise in his eyes.

EIGHTEEN: Down Amongst the Living

It was early evening. The last remnants of the day were slipping lower beyond the houses she could see through the window. Cars passed by, oblivious to anything but their own worlds, each car, a life that was a secret from her.

Dakota wandered down the hall and paused in front of the photo her father had taken of the Dakota Badlands before she was born. She had that feeling again, of wilderness and wide-open spaces, of endless dark and unforgiving terrain. She felt so alone among the living; it accentuated the feelings of eternity and separation. She was dead. She was dead and nothing would ever bring her back – nothing to jolt her physical body back into motion. Her dead eyes were closed forever while the eyes death had given her could never shut again. No amount of sleep would relieve her of the burdens of eternity. Nothing would ever be good again.

Somewhere in the twilight house she could hear her sister's voice, talking through tears.

She was on the telephone in the lounge, her head resting on a hand full of soggy tissues, her bloodshot eyes staring through her sister's ghost.

Dakota felt a lump rise in her throat. To see Lula now, knowing what she had done to her in life, made her feel more sadness than she had felt so far since waking up in Purgatory. Poor Lula, alone again, no brothers or sisters or parents to help her through her grief, no hope that there might be a replacement for her dead sister. Dakota was just another baby she couldn't save. But she guessed that her body hadn't been found yet, and that poor Lula was still thinking her little sister was alive somewhere, not dead and alone out in the woods.

She wanted so badly to tell Lula it wasn't her fault – that she could never have known what Jackson was like. She wondered if Lula knew yet. Had Jackson confessed to years of secrecy with Dakota? Had he confessed out of guilt and used that excuse to leave her?

Dakota wished that it had all come back to her, that at some point, in a rush, she would remember it all clearly. Yet nothing came to her unless she was staring into the pages of her life, unfolding out in front of her, metamorphosing into the hideous monster her life became in the end.

Dakota could tell Jackson wasn't in the house. She could feel all the empty spaces in the house, closing in on themselves and whispering of all they had seen.

Lula was discussing Dakota's disappearance with whoever was on the other end of the phone call.

"I know her; she will write at some point. She's just done her 'running away' trick again." ... "No, I'm not worried – she'll be in touch." ... "No... no, I'll be OK. I'll see you tomorrow." ... "Goodnight," she said and hung up the receiver.

Dakota looked sadly at her sister as she got up and trudged off into the kitchen to flick the kettle switch on. She could tell that Lula must have snapped at some point, as some of the pictures she used to have on the walls and mantelpieces were gone, no doubt smashed up in a fit of grief. The pictures of Lula and her as children that used to line the lounge wall were gone, leaving pale squares like ghosts of the pictures on the wallpaper.

Even the pictures of Jackson were gone. All that remained were empty spaces in the dust, sad reminders of a life that Lula had once had. Dakota guessed that her sister could not look upon the faces of her parents anymore, angry at them for leaving her alone.

Perhaps Lula knew about Jackson and that was why he wasn't there with her. He might already have been kicked out by her, or run away. Wherever he was, she felt he hadn't been in the house for a while, and she was relieved that she did not have to warn her sister that she was living with a murderer.

He was gone and Lula was safe.

Dakota wandered around the house, looking into rooms and trying to breathe in the memories that lingered there.

At last she came to her own bedroom and paused before entering. The door was locked but the key still sat in the lock. She found for the first time she had the ability to move objects, allowing her to turn the key and open the door. She stood for a moment prodding at the door, amused that she did not pass through objects like the ghosts she had seen on the TV.

For a moment, she thought something had moved in her bedroom, a brief shadow that was gone the moment she pushed the door open.

Her room looked different to the way she remembered it looking when she was fifteen. The religious pictures that had belonged to her mother were now gone, replaced by posters of bands like the Smiths and The Doors. Above her bed was a huge poster of Nick Cave, and for a moment it startled her in the waning light. Just for that second she thought it was Jackson staring out at her from the wall, but it was just the man he modelled his looks on. The same long black hair, the same smart suits. She shook her head as the music she now remembered playing in that very room echoed faintly around her head.

Her books were still there, worn and battered from overuse, and her music collection still sat on the table beside her stereo. It felt odd to be back there. She wasn't comfortable there, and the memories of what had happened in that room were beginning to rise up in her. She could almost see it again, the movement of the man in the dark, coming towards the bed. She turned back to the doorway from where she stood by the bed, and almost felt that tiny twinge of fear and excitement in her stomach. The sound of their rhythmic movements on the bed, the smell of the sex assailing her senses; it was getting too much, as though the volume on the stereo was rising uncontrollably, and she unable to stop the noise and the smells. She was trying to cover her ears, close her eyes to the tidal wave of emotion and memory that was attacking her from every angle. She had not even heard Lula climb the stairs, but she heard her when she started screaming.

Dakota's eyes flicked open to the sight of her sister, eyes bulging and red, fear bursting in her larynx as she stared directly at her.

"You can see me!" cried Dakota, but Lula was hysterical. She seemed to be staring from the poster of Nick Cave to her and back again. "It's OK! It's me!"

The moment was becoming more and more frightening. The sight of her sister screaming at her as if she were a hideous monster, and the sound in her dead ears. Her sight began to blur, and she managed to make out Lula slamming the door shut and the click of the key locking the door again just as darkness swarmed into her eyes.

Dakota woke on the lobby floor again. She was looking straight up at the ceiling when Ariel's face came into view.

"That little visit to the living was a bit more than you could take in your still fragile condition. Did you mean to show yourself or did it happen by accident?"

"Uh... I don't know why she saw me. I wasn't trying to be seen. I didn't know that I could be," she managed as Ariel reached down and began helping her to sit up.

"You got upset, didn't you?"

"I guess I did. I was in my old room and I was remembering... stuff."

"Stuff that upset you? That's when they can see you if they are sensitive enough. If you get emotional you can become visible to certain people, especially family. You have to try and keep a hold of yourself if you go back. I don't think you should go back for a while." Dakota felt as though she was being scolded. She propped herself up and tried to put the sound of her sister's screams out of her mind.

"Oh god, poor Lula! She didn't even know I was dead; she must do now, at any rate."

"Hmmmm... well, it's a bit of a shock if they don't even know you have passed on," said Ariel, pulling Dakota onto her feet. Dakota wobbled uncertainly until she leant against the wall. She closed her eyes again, trying to will away the pain in her head.

"I went back to find something out, but I didn't get enough time. Can I go back quickly?"

"No! You need a break from visits for a while. No, you will have to stay away from the living until you learn to control yourself."

Ariel walked away, back to the room behind reception, leaving Dakota to try and steady herself alone.

NINETEEN: A Meeting in the Woods

Her head was still throbbing as she looked up into the dim light of the lobby. Residents glanced across at her, blowing smoke about their faces and sniggering at her. She trudged back through towards the Bar and muttered, "Oh fuck off!" as she passed a group of snickering old men and women.

She was about to walk past the bar when Danny popped his head out and pulled her into the dark room.

"What's wrong?" she asked, slightly perturbed by his actions.

"Nothing, I just wanted to know how you are... you doing, OK my love?" he asked, offering a glass of clear liquid she suspected was neat vodka.

"No, I've been back again. I went back to my house to see my sister," she muttered and surprised herself by taking the drink and necking it as Danny guided her towards the barstools.

"Oh dear, how did it go? Not too well, I gather, if you ended up looking as shaken as you do!" He laughed slightly as he lit a cigarette for her.

"No, not well at all. She saw me and freaked out, so they won't let me go back now." She sighed and smoked another cigarette, wondering if she'd smoked this much when she was alive.

"Oh dear, no they don't like that when you get seen. Got upset, did you? Remembering stuff, I suppose?" he asked.

"Yes, I was in my old bedroom, and I was... well, remembering. I guess I did get upset and she saw me. She screamed so much, but then again, she didn't even know I was dead! Guess they still haven't found my body yet."

Danny ignored her last comment and poured another

drink for her.

"Well I guess that's it for your investigating, then? You'll have to wait a bit before you remember, I expect."

"No. I'll just have to keep reading until I remember it all." She sighed and paused a moment. "I just really hoped that if I went back, I would remember everything suddenly, like my brain would suddenly switch back on and everything would be back in my brain again instead of in that book."

"Oh... you have been in the library, then?" He seemed disappointed at the hint of the library.

"What's your problem with the library, Danny? Why are you so against me going there?" She felt suddenly annoyed at him again.

"Nothing, I just wonder if you might be better off not remembering? You know, just getting by here like I do..."

"You mean just give up and stay here for all eternity? Why would I want to do that? I want to make amends! I want to get out of here and go to Heaven! I lived who knows how many lifetimes and I want to have a happier eternity! As far as I can tell my lives weren't that great." She was becoming irate now and her voice was getting louder, attracting the attention of the other patrons.

"All right love, calm down..."

"No! I am fed up with you trying to silence me! I want to know why I am here so I can say sorry! Just you are too fucking scared to face up to whatever you did! And what did you do, Danny? You are dreadfully quiet about that, aren't you?"

"Get out before I have you removed!" he snapped, standing up. She had never seen him angry before and it caught her off guard. But in a moment her anger returned and she stormed out of the Bar yelling, "Fine! Fuck you, too!" knocking people's drinks over so that a few of them lurched after her, ready to thump her.

Fury raged in her as she stormed down the corridor towards the Library. If anyone had tried to speak to her she felt she might beat them to a pulp. When she saw a figure up ahead, half-concealed in shadows, the tiny glow of a cigarette letting her know where his mouth was, she stuck two fingers up and spat out, "Got nothing better to do, you wanker?" before stomping into the library.

She didn't know why Danny made her so angry, but she couldn't help it. She had felt so much trust towards him since meeting him. He was one of only two allies and it made her upset that he was trying to hold her back.

He had lied when she arrived, saying he was never allowed to leave the Bar, and that was the excuse he used for never making an effort to make amends. She knew he had been out of the Bar because he had told her he had visited earth once and had taken ages to recover. What had he done? What was his crime and what had happened to him when he returned to earth?

These were all questions she ranted off to Betty when she found her sitting in the same place she had left her, dozing over a large book.

"Not being funny, love, but don't you think you should be concentrating on yourself? Whatever Danny has done or won't do isn't going to help you. You can't force him to face up to his crimes; that's up to him. What I am doing here won't help me. But in the long run it might. And it's my choice. You can't help Danny. He's been here a long time, and he will do whatever he wants. You need to focus on getting your head straight and your memory back."

Dakota felt she had been scolded by her mother, but smiled at Betty. She knew she was right. Placing her attentions on Danny was only slowing her own progress out of Purgatory, perhaps another trick by the Powers that Be.

"I'm sorry, what have you been reading then?"

"I'll tell you after you tell me what happened to you. I went to Ariel when you were gone so long." She tutted and lit another cigarette.

Dakota filled her in on her unhappy return home, and how she had been advised against going back for a while.

"Well according to the Miriam Page book, you were once known as Maud Pope and you lived in London in the 1940s.

This time you were lower class and worked as a house maid. It was all very basic... rich people, poor people, upstairs downstairs antics." Betty laughed behind her cigarette smoke and continued. "After a year's service, the man of the house, a wealthy gentleman called Harry Blake, took a shine to you and began having sex with you in secret. No one in the house knew and you were too afraid of losing your job to tell anyone. So you let him have sex with you whenever he wanted to. He was a cruel man but always saw that you had a little more in your wages than others, which was also a secret. It didn't continue for too long, only a year before he murdered you for no apparent reason in his drawing room in the early hours of the morning."

"He strangled me, didn't he?"

"Yes, how did you know?"

"The nightmares I used to have. He strangled me in a house I didn't recognise... a posh house." Betty shook her head in disbelief.

"And you were only eighteen! So... that was a short book." She laughed, trying to lighten the mood, but the discovery that she had been murdered in three of her lives was disturbing to both of them.

"Christ, I haven't had much luck with men, have I?" Dakota laughed though tears had begun to stain her cheeks. Betty didn't know what to say, so she told her there was another life under the name 'Brigid Murphy' and she was off to locate that volume.

Dakota thought of all the nightmares she had suffered in her last life and felt for certain she had deep down knowledge of her former lives. She felt that somehow she had always known that Jackson would kill her one day. And had she made no effort to stop it happening? With dread in her dead, cold heart, she turned her face to the book that lay open on the table before her.

Dakota began working on Saturdays at the library a week later. She feigned boredom and disapproval of Lula's decision that she should start work, but when she was there, she stole brief, dangerous moments with Jackson, as usual the fear of being caught heightening the pleasure.

For the last few weeks they had had to stop their almost nightly meetings as Lula's medication was no longer working and she had begun to wake up occasionally, going downstairs to look for Jackson.

The first night it happened, Dakota had stopped Jackson's rhythmic movements after hearing a door open somewhere in the house; they lay frozen in panic, listening to Lula shuffling down the corridor and down the stairs whispering 'Jackson' to the darkened house. He had quickly jumped up and put on his trousers and crept out, following Lula, explaining that he had been in the bathroom.

After that night, they had to stay away from each other. Dakota lay awake all night, unable to relax without him there, unsure why jealousy of her sister had begun to creep into her troubled mind. She had become too accustomed to his ways with her, and though she sometimes felt she should stop it all, his absence left her lost and in despair. For the past four years he had made her feel special and necessary – the most important thing in his world, which went some way to cancel out the upset she felt at being excluded from everyone else's world. He had made her feel she mattered and that was all she wanted.

Lula was soon put on new medication, but it was a whole month before she dragged herself off to pick up the prescription.

In the meantime, Jackson had to find another way to have Dakota on her own. For several weeks in a row, he had told Lula that they were working late, but instead they had been driving out to the woods to return to the secret grove they had visited so often before.

It was late December, a few days before New Year's Eve. The forest floor was blanketed by a thick layer of leaves, dead and dry underfoot, their dreary colours imperceptible in the darkness. The torch that Jackson kept in the car was all they had to light their way through the bleak forest of chattering trees.

Just as they reached the grove, Jackson could no longer wait and began to kiss her passionately, his hands reaching desperately for the fastening of her coat, hungry to feel her skin against his again. They were half into the clearing when a muffled cry made them pull apart.

Jackson turned the torch into the grove, the bright beam framing an intimate moment neither of them wanted to see.

The little girl was no more than eight or nine, and tears streaked her tiny face, blonde hair fell in strands from her disturbed ponytails as she struggled to pull her knickers up.

Then the man who knelt before her stood and turned, flicking his long grey hair impatiently out of his eyes, his grip on the little girl's mouth and arm not releasing as he swung her round in front of him.

As a semi-toothless grin broke across his lined face, Dakota recognised him.

Back in the library Dakota was gagging and closing her eyes, turning desperately away from the book as though the images would go away. But for all her gasping and eye-shielding, the face remained.

It was the man she knew as Woods.

He may have been a few years younger, but it was definitely him. The same man, who had been creeping around after her here in the afterlife, had known her in life. She didn't want to go on reading, but Betty calmed her and said she had to go on and find out the whole story.

Jackson shone the torch in the man's face and whispered.

"Mr Goldman? What the fuck are you doing?"

Dakota's eyes flicked from the little girl to the man who had been her next-door neighbour for the last twelve years. She felt sick as her mind raced. All this time, she thought, he has been messing around with little girls, probably enjoying all the times she and her sister had played out in the back garden, in the summer when they wore bathing suits to play in the paddling pool. All those years he could have been planning to do the same to her.

"Might ask you the same, Mr Shade," replied the grey-haired man, with a sickly smile, ignoring the tears of the little girl in his grasp.

"Dakota and I were taking a walk," Jackson explained.

"Oh yeah? Can't get away with it in the house anymore, then? Thought it had been a bit quiet for a while."

"What? What do you mean?" Jackson snapped.

"Walls like paper you know." His grin widened as his eyes fell on Dakota. "Very willing, isn't she?"

Jackson darted forward and grabbed Goldman by his lapels.

"Watch your mouth, pervert!"

"Hehe, takes one to know one, eh?" The man laughed, appearing and disappearing as the torch in Jackson's hand wiggled around.

"Right, I am calling the police." He let Goldman go and shoved the torch into Dakota's shaking hands. She could hear Jackson fumbling through his pockets for his mobile phone, but she couldn't take her eyes off the man and the small girl, framed in a circle of shivering light in front of her. The girl moved quickly as though to run away, but Goldman slammed his big hand over her face, holding her still and muffling her squeals.

"Oh yeah? You going to explain what you were doing out here with your girlfriend's sixteen-year-old sister?"

"Taking a walk!" hissed Jackson.

"In the dark... to a secret grove... kissing?" All the while the smirk never left Goldman's face. He looked so calm, and Jackson looked so angry.

"You can't prove anything, you shit! You think they would believe you over me? That is a child in your hands, and I don't think they would believe you were taking a walk with someone else's little girl in a dark wood with only the best intentions!"

"And legally, Mr.Shade, she was only a child when you started your relationship," Goldman replied, pointing at Dakota, who was shaking the torch light violently as her mind reeled with images of what Lula would do if she saw this situation. "Oh and I have photos too..."

"You what?" asked Jackson incredulously, his phone back in his pocket.

"Oh, I have an extensive private collection of pictures. Quite a few of them feature you and your young lady here over the last few years, getting up to all sorts of mischief." Goldman sniggered like a dirty teenage boy, licking his cracked lips. "You might get me done, but you would be coming down with me, Mr Shade. Believe me, I could have you carted off any time I liked. How would your dear Lula feel about that, I wonder?"

Silence fell over the cold gathering in the black woods. The ring of light trembled like a frightened star in the darkness, as winds shook the empty overhead branches into chattering conversations with themselves. Distant rustles in the undergrowth let them all know they did not belong in this lightless world, and the little girl continued to sniffle and occasionally try to wriggle out of Mr Goldman's vicelike grip on her tiny face.

"You fucking bastard," whispered Jackson almost inaudibly.

"Jackson, we can't do this... Lula can't know!" Dakota began to rattle off words nervously at his side.

"Shut up," he whispered not looking up at her.

"Well pretty, unless you want everyone to know that he's been shagging you since you were twelve, I'd bugger off and leave me alone."

"I don't believe you've got photos!" she half yelled, a light wind alerting her to the tears on her cheeks, a mild rage burning beyond all her fear.

"Don't you, Pretty?" He turned his full attention to her. "Try sitting in the tree at the end of my garden. Great view, straight into your curtainless bedroom. I only watch in the summer. This time of year, I just listen." He winked at her.

"Jesus Christ, you bastard. You sick bastard!"

Goldman responded with a cackle.

"I can copy 'em if you like? Got me own darkroom, you see. Bet you'd like to see what I see..."

Dakota lost control and launched herself at him, clawing at his face and hitting him with the torch, the light jiggling and bouncing off the dead branches above them. He laughed, turning away as Jackson pulled her off.

"Leave it, we're going!" growled Jackson.

"We can't leave her with him!" she cried as he began dragging her away. She looked back at the little girl, who was wide eyed; her sobbing had ebbed away, replaced by silent tears. Her big blue eyes were the last thing Dakota saw as she was pulled away from the grove and the low sound of Goldman's laughter.

TWENTY: Consequences

"This isn't right, Jackson! We should have made him let her go!" she whimpered as she followed him back to the car.

"Dakota, shut up! He has got me by the balls, and I am making the decisions here. I am telling you to forget about tonight; it never happened, OK? God help me, I'll murder you if you get me put in prison by running your mouth off."

"But I—"

Jackson cut her short when he turned and grabbed her by the throat. "I mean it, D. Shut it now! Forget tonight, OK?" he half shouted, not releasing his grip until she managed to nod her head.

When they got home, Dakota went straight up to her room, hearing Jackson say to Lula, "Oh, she hasn't been feeling well all day – got her period or something. Just let her rest."

"Oh, shall I get her some hot chocolate?"

"No Lula, leave her alone, OK?" he snapped.

"OK baby, OK. Can I get you anything?"

Dakota slammed her bedroom door. She hated hearing Lula being sycophantic to Jackson. He treated her like dirt most of the time, and when he was nice to her, Lula acted like it was Christmas.

She stayed in bed all night and didn't leave her room until midday the next day.

Wandering downstairs, she found Jackson sitting in front of the television.

"Where's Lula?" she asked without looking at him.

"Gone to get the Sunday papers. Feeling any better?" he asked as though she really had been ill. She couldn't even bear to look his way, so she immersed herself in the news as it began.

She had lain awake all night rationalising their actions, and had even told herself that James Goldman had let the little girl go right after their meeting in the woods. It would all blow over and she would ignore him if she ever saw him again. He was a very quiet and reclusive neighbour; she didn't even know if he had a job. But she did know she would never acknowledge him again.

She allowed the news to take over her thoughts and did her best to put the previous night out of her mind.

"Tonight, parents of a nine-year-old girl are appealing for any witnesses to help with locating their daughter who disappeared yesterday afternoon in Little Mort. Michelle Taybury was last seen going to the shops at around 3.30pm. It is a five-minute walk to the shops from her home, but her parents fear she may have taken a short cut through some alleyways…"

The photo that appeared on screen was a school portrait of a pretty girl in her uniform. Her blonde hair was in plaits that fell down her shoulders, past pink cheeks and a wide smile. The only reason Dakota recognised her was because of her eyes.

"Oh shit, Jackson!"

"I know. Shut up." Both of them were on the edges of their seats, throats dry, frozen, eyes frantic.

The last time they had seen Michelle Taybury, she didn't look as pretty. She had been dishevelled and streaked with tears, leaves clinging to her clothes and hair.

"Jesus Christ, has he still got her?" At that moment, Lula came in through the front door and Dakota got up, bolting out of the house, pausing only to slip her trainers on.

She could hear Lula call her name out after her but she kept running down the road, straight to the woods. It was a cold and grey Sunday as she raced through the cemetery to take the quickest route to the grove, her chest burning with a racing heart.

Last night's rainfall still sat in tiny pools on fallen leaves.

Within minutes her trainers and the bottoms of her jeans were soaked through. There was no sun yet, just dull dirty clouds that gathered over the empty branches like nosy neighbours. A light breeze set the leaves cackling around her and she began to wish she had stayed at home. For the first time in her life, she felt afraid of the woods. She had been walking there her whole life, and never been afraid, but now she felt that a thousand eyes were watching her trudge through pathways she was not invited to tread. She passed across the clearing that lay out before the Witch tree and headed past the screaming woman into the dense undergrowth towards the secret grove that lay beyond anybody's vision.

She paused for a moment. An unseen breeze encircled her, lifting her hair up off her shoulders and making it float around her face for an instant, and goose bumps broke out over her entire body.

She stepped slowly into the grove.

Wind had blown leaves across her. Her pink sweater bore brown mud stains, one of which looked like a handprint, Dakota noticed.

The girl's blonde hair streamed across her cheek like a skeletal hand reaching from her scalp. Her flesh was pale, her lips blue under the strands of hair.

Dakota's first instinct was to pull the little girl's skirt back down, but she knew she could not touch anything. What bothered her most was that little Michelle Taybury appeared to be staring at her with the same pleading in her eyes as when she had encountered her in these woods the night before. Dakota couldn't help thinking that she had been alive only hours before but now she was still, never to move again.

She could almost hear her voice pleading 'help me' but it was only the wind murmuring through the dead trees. Dakota felt sure she would collapse but her body was rigid, frozen, staring at the dead girl's eyes. As she noticed the burst veins around her eyes, the words 'petechial haemorrhaging' and 'asphyxiation' sailed through her mind along with other phrases she had read in books about murder. All the books she had read about true crimes suddenly sprang into her mind and she remembered how she had often wondered what a dead body looked like.

It was as though the girl's glassy gaze was all that was holding her up.

"I'm sorry," she whispered.

Suddenly she was on the floor, wet leaves in her hair and soaking through her jumper.

James Goldman was on top of her, fumbling at the fastening on her jeans. Fear had turned her mind rigid under his frantic body; her mind seemed to float away to where the dead girl lay.

Just as she felt her trousers being pulled down, she snapped into action, bending her knees and bringing her feet up into his face. He flew back, blood spurting from his nose as she leapt up pulling her trousers back up.

"You don't get to fuck me, too, you prick! That's not part of the bargain. They'll catch you even if I don't tell them about you!"

He laughed through the blood running over his lips.

"Your poor sister might just kill herself if she found out about you, don't you think?" Dakota stepped forward and kicked him in the head as he tried to stem the blood flow with a handkerchief from his pocket. "You can kick me all you like! But you can't tell anyone about me! Still, that shouldn't be hard for you; you kept Jackson a secret all these years, didn't you?"

"That's none of your fucking business!"

"Heh, kinda became my business when I first heard your moans, little one. You and your Loverman have provided me with lots of entertainment over the years... missed it when you had to stop. What was it, Lula's medication not working?"

"What are you still doing here?" she asked, ignoring what he had just said for fear she might start screaming at him.

"Liked to be here with her when she is quiet. It's easier when they aren't wriggling and trying to scream." He winked again, turning Dakota's stomach over. "Wondered if guilt might bring you back here and I might get a go of you, too."

"Fuck you!"

"That's what I had in mind." He grinned.

"She was on the news; they are looking for her now. Her poor parents..." she broke off as she looked back at the little body on the bed of leaves. But she didn't look for long before she was running away, desperate to be away from him and Michelle's pleading gaze.

At the top of her road was a phone box, and there she stood for a few moments. She was staring through the glass door at the receiver as though concentrated thought alone would do what she knew she had to.

She paused a moment longer, considering the consequences of calling the police, then she snapped into action, briefly glancing around for any possible witnesses. But the roads were empty, shrouded in a clinging mist of rain. She felt as though she was the only person alive on the earth. All there was in the world was her and the dead girl who lay staring into dead trees a mile away.

In seconds, she was calling 999 and was put through to a disembodied voice.

"There's a body in Pan's Wood, Little Mort... a girl."

"I'm sorry, could you repeat that, Miss?"

"I said there's a girl's body in Pan's Wood," Dakota repeated nervously, looking around.

"Can you give me your name?" asked the lady on the other end of the line.

"No, I'm not getting involved; I'm just telling you she is there, in a grove behind the Witch Tree."

The voice on the other end began to speak again, but Dakota hung up the receiver, pausing a moment to wipe her hand prints from it. Her mind reeled with scenes from TV crime dramas. She began wiping down every surface she had touched with the sleeve of her sweater, believing that, somehow, they would track the call to the phone box and get her fingerprints. Her mind wasn't rational enough to realise there would be thousands of different prints in there.

"You OK, sweetie?" asked Lula as Dakota came in the front door. Her face dropped when she looked at her sister's clothes. "Christ D, what happened to you?"

"Uh... oh, I just went for a run and slipped over in the woods." She laughed pathetically.

"You went for a run? Your nuts, D. You sure you weren't meeting a fella for a bit of a snog?" Lula giggled like a schoolgirl. "You look like you were rolling around!"

"Don't be stupid, I just fell over," Dakota replied weakly and wandered off into the kitchen.

A moment or two later, Jackson appeared beside her where she was steadying herself on the kitchen sink. The tap running on full washing away the liquids she had just regurgitated.

"What is wrong with you?" he whispered urgently.

"She is dead, Jackson. I found her in the grove," she managed in a low voice.

"Oh Christ! Why did you go there? What if someone had seen you?"

"Someone did. Mr Goldman was there." She stopped as she gagged again, her empty stomach twisting in her belly. She filled up a glass with water, drinking it down to rid the taste of bile from her mouth.

"What happened?"

"Well he tried to rape me and warned me off telling anyone again."

"Jackson!" called Lula from the lounge making them both jump. "I changed my mind. I will have a cup of tea."

"OK," he called back. Turning back to Dakota he returned to a whisper: "Did he hurt you? Are you all right?"

"No, I am so fucking far from being all right!" she snapped, raising her voice slightly.

"Shut up! You have to keep your head together. If anything happens I am the one who goes to jail, not you! I'll be a paedophile. What would happen to Lula?"

"Yeah, I know. You don't have to pile the pressure on, too. I know what I am doing." Rage boiled over in her and the glass in her hand shattered, throwing shards of bloodied glass into the sink.

"What was that?" called Lula.

"Oh nothing, I knocked a glass over!" Jackson shouted back. Dakota stared numbly at the cuts in her fingers and the blood dripping into the white ceramic sink. She felt she was snapping, losing a grip on her sanity. Everything was slipping away; the life she had grown to accept was changing again. She wasn't sure if she could take another big change, another big secret.

And what a dirty secret it was, she told herself. At such a young age, the only secrets she had were of sex and murder. Would she have to take them to her grave? She could not forget the dead girl's eyes, looking into her, pleading to be rescued, begging to be saved.

"I called the police," she muttered as Jackson threw the broken glass in the bin.

"What? Are you nuts? They'll..."

"Don't worry I made an anonymous tip-off. No names. I just didn't want her lying out there in the woods to be eaten by wild animals. They'll catch him eventually..."

TWENTY-ONE: The Ghost of Michelle Taybury

"I feel so sick, I am disgusted with myself." Dakota sighed, her head in her hands. Betty slipped a lit cigarette in between her fingers and patted her shoulder comfortingly.

"You were too young to be making decisions like that! What would anyone else have done in your position? You might have ended up with no one, Jackson in prison and Lula in the morgue."

"That's terrible... as though it was better that little girl died than my sister? That's so wrong. I made a decision and a little girl died because of it."

"No, Jackson made that choice. He would've probably beaten you black and blue rather than let you go back and free that girl. Anyway, it was her time." Betty sniffed back some tears and puffed away at her cigarette.

"Her time? How can it be her time to be raped and murdered in a cold forest? That's not fate." Dakota wanted to shout out the injustice, but tears caught in her throat.

"Yes, dear, it is! There is no such thing as an accidental death or dying before your time. Everyone dies precisely when they are supposed to and that's it. They have a plan for us all and we cannot stop it from happening."

"So, you really can't cheat death?"

"Nope! These books you hear scratching away all around us? The endings are already written when you actually die. They keep apace with you most of your life, but in the end they go on ahead and finish the story before you get there. Little Michelle Taybury was already dead when she entered that forest. She just had to act out the final scenes."

Betty fell silent and they both sat and listened to the low roar of lives being written all around them. Dakota thought about how, sometimes, not so long ago in earth time, she was waiting to die. Here in Purgatory her book had already fallen silent on the shelf of the library. Here she was already dead, her fate decided by invisible fingers. But back on earth, had she felt it? That moment when the ink stopped forming on the page, the moment when God had decided she was going to die, had she felt it in her heart somewhere? In the dark chambers of her heart, in the dusty corridors of her brain, had she known that her time was almost done? That soon she would cease to be and her body would give up on her?

She wished she could remember.

"Have you been to see Ariel?" asked Dakota.

"Oh yes, I went to see her once and we talked for quite some time. She explained everything to me there and then; I guess she is able to answer most of the questions God could," she mused.

"How come I never had it all explained to me? I have just learnt bits from different people."

"Did you ever ask her all the right questions?" Betty asked, a wisp of smoke escaping her lips.

"No, I guess not. She answered the questions I did ask. I suppose I just didn't think to ask everything." Dakota stubbed her cigarette out in the ashtray, trying to think of all the relevant questions. Why do we die when we do? Why am I here? What is life all about?

They were questions she had pondered when she was alive. After her parents died she had thought of every conceivable question she would ask God when she met him. Only then she did not know she might never meet him.

Dakota retreated to the bathroom where she stripped off all her clothes and scrubbed her body with hot water until she was red. No matter how much she washed, she still felt dirty, as though James Goldman's fingerprints were a permanent mark on her. Looking at herself in the mirror she felt dirty, despicable, akin to the monster next door.

She felt so sick that all she wanted to do was sleep; it seemed the only way to get the day's events out of her head. Occasionally Lula let her have a glass of wine with her in the evenings; at that moment, she felt sure it was the only way she could relax and get some sleep. Something to blur the images in her head, make it unreal.

By the time she could bear to be around other people, it was early evening. Winter darkness had already taken over the streets, and the smell of Lula's shepherd's pie was wafting up the stairs, reminding her she couldn't recall when she last ate.

Dakota joined Lula and Jackson at the table, desperate for something normal, and ate dinner with them, using all her energy to act as though she was normal and happy and actually enjoying the food, not just forcing herself to go through the motions.

Jackson went out after dinner with a sour look on his face, murmuring something about the pub and leaving Lula to clear up on her own.

Dakota felt sad when she saw the disappointed look in her sister's eyes. Lula wasn't angry with Jackson for not helping her clear up, nor was she angry that he had abandoned them in favour of the pub. She was just sad, it seemed, and lost without her prince, left alone to do the housewife thing and wait at home for him to return smelling of beer and cigarettes, by which time she would have already fallen asleep on the couch, an empty wine bottle on the table, its contents causing her medication to deepen her sleep.

Dakota noticed that it happened rather a lot lately. When Jackson came to her room, he would tell her that there was no way Lula was going to wake up that night. It may have been this sort of behaviour that had stopped Lula's medication working in the first place. The tablets were just not strong enough anymore to keep Lula in that safe cotton wool world of sleep and dream.

"So, did you get your new medication?" asked Dakota, standing up to help her sister with the dishes.

"Yeah, started them last night, worked like a charm." She

smiled, gratitude in her eyes.

"Think I might need some of them! Can't seem to sleep properly at all these days."

"Worried about something? Sometimes that's all it is, too much on your mind. Is it that Charlie bloke?"

"Oh no, we don't really see each other anymore." Dakota thought briefly about him and realised she had used him terribly but it was no different to how he treated her.

"Ah well, best thing really, he was probably too old for you. With your exams coming up, you need to focus more on that. You don't need those sorts of distractions, eh?" Lula smiled warmly and for a moment looked so like her mother it jarred Dakota. She felt she had stood here a dozen times, wiping up wet dishes with her mother, and her mother throwing in the odd word of wisdom. In that false light, by the soap-filled sink, Lula in an apron damp with dishwater and yellow marigolds on her hands, she could have been her mother, slightly weary around the eyes, but still so ready to love.

"Can I have a drink with you tonight?" asked Dakota, her heart full of pain and regret for her sister and all the lies she had told her over the years. She wanted more than anything for things to be normal. She wanted to get drunk with her sister and watch a girlie movie and eat too many crisps, laugh and remember old times. She wanted her sister back after the many years since their parents' late night departure changed their relationship. Lula had been trying so hard to be a mother figure, and all Dakota had done was hide from her and lie, that terrible dark secret expanding the void between them.

She wanted those sisterly chats back, when they would lie awake in their darkened bedroom, with the lights of passing cars slanting across the ceiling, and the day's events and Lula's secrets unfolding amidst wonder and giggles. She wanted to share everything with her, all her feeling about life and sex and boys, and laugh about when they were children and the games they would play.

But Dakota couldn't do any of that, for a great secret like

a disease had infected their relationship and no matter what happened she would never be able to share anything personal with her again, and everything that would ever happen to her in her life would always lead back to Jackson and what he had made her into with his late night music and his driven hands.

"Yeah OK, let's have a bottle of wine and watch an old movie. Jackson won't be back till late now so sod him!" Lula giggled and threw her washing-up gloves down.

"Who does he go out drinking with? I never knew he had friends." Dakota laughed.

"No one! He just goes and sits in the pub, probably doesn't even speak to the barman. I guess he just needs to get away from us sometimes. I wonder if he regrets moving in here with us. He must feel like a father to you now, and I don't think he ever wanted children," Lula went on as she carried the wine and glasses off into the lounge.

"Oh, I don't think he regrets it at all, Lula. He has everything he wants right here."

"Yeah, I know, he does love me. He just has a hard time showing me is all." She smiled as though someone had lit a fire within her, filling her with renewed warmth and feelings of security. As guilt began to weigh on Dakota like a stone on her chest, she felt the only solution was to get drunk and forget everything. So she did, and that night she fell asleep on the couch with Lula, having the best night's sleep she'd had in years.

She awoke the next morning in her bed. A small note written in her sister's hand told her that Jackson had carried her up to bed when he got home. Instinctively, her hands went down to check she still had her knickers on and she was relieved to discover they were still in place.

She trudged downstairs in the weary eleven o'clock morning light. Rain was tapping the windows all through the house like small voices in every room. Her head ached from drinking too much wine, but it felt good to her – something physical she could moan about, something she could lay all anger and ill feeling onto.

Through her mildly blurred gaze, she noticed a pile of letters on the doormat and picked them up, throwing them on the side table. Just as she turned to walk into the kitchen, her own name in bold black letters caught her eye.

A large brown envelope bearing her name was mingled with the bills and junk mail she had just picked up. As she reached out to touch it, fear jabbed at her stomach. Like a premonition, she knew that whatever was in that envelope was not good. Sudden heat in her body transformed into cold sweat and by the time she was pulling the envelope open she was shuddering like a naked child in the rain.

The first seven pictures were of her and Jackson in various positions and stages of a sexual act. From the lighting and the clothing she could tell each was taken at a different time, some when Lula was out of the house, others when Lula was asleep and Jackson had come to Dakota's dimly-lit bedroom late at night. Some were years old now, proof that they had been having sex since she was well under age. Her mind, though racing, still managed to wonder what kind of zoom lens he must have been using to get such close-up shots. It felt odd to see herself naked in a picture, in all those poses and positions.

Then the last picture was of Michelle Taybury.

It must have been taken at first light, as it was quite a dark photo but light enough for everything to be clear. She was dead. But her eyes were still staring.

Seconds later Dakota was vomiting violently into the kitchen sink, the photographs still clutched in her white-knuckled hands.

She felt as though she had had her stomach ripped out. She had truly doubted that Mr Goldman had any real proof of her and Jackson's affair, a hope that she had clung to despite everything else. But now she knew he had proof, and most probably quite a lot of it.

She also knew that his inclusion of a picture of the dead child was a warning to her and her alone. The photos were a threat to Jackson, a little message to say, 'don't even think about turning me in!' But the photo of Michelle with her blue lips and staring glassy eyes was a threat to Dakota. He was saying that he would have no qualms about doing the same to her as he had to Michelle. Perhaps she would be one in a long line of dead girls, all of them lost to the woods and dead leaves, their skirts ruffled and their knickers missing forever.

She had always been aware of what the consequences of her relationship with Jackson could be; she just never thought it would ever come to that. But seeing the act through someone else's eyes made her feel sick and dirty. Her tiny body entangled with his much older body in a dark seedy room where the pictures of Jesus and Mary were long buried in her sock drawer, their pitying eyes turned away from her.

For the first time in years she wanted to never see him again. Never hear that song again, hear him climb the stairs, see him slink across the dark room towards her.

TWENTY-TWO: Choices

The months that followed were the hardest she had yet faced; her exams loomed ahead of her and beyond that was college and the possibility of university, but all she wanted was to disappear and get a job in a quiet town where no one knew her and she could forget the first sixteen years of her life. She even wanted to forget her parents, for their existence led to their death and the arrival of Jackson in her life. She wanted it all gone.

But she also felt that she wanted her life to be better one day, to have a good job and a world where none of this mattered. So, with every ounce of her determination, she decided to take her exams then leave afterwards, perhaps to Ireland to live with an aunt or something, somewhere far away from Jackson and Mr Goldman.

But these plans she kept to herself, managing to dissuade Jackson from visiting her quite so often and let her revise for her exams. He would not always be told, though, and would force his way in late at night while she was trying desperately to sleep. She even resorted to stealing her sister's tablets to be sure that she would be in an impenetrable sleep by the time he crept into her bed.

After a few months, he became angry with her.

"But I have been really tired, Jackson. I have to revise so much. I need to pass my exams," she whimpered.

"You have been making excuses and trying to put me off ever since he sent you those pictures," he snapped, throwing a used match out of the window.

"Hey, I think about that little girl every day, OK? I can't forget that she died because of us!"

"No, D. She died because of that freak next door!"

"Why won't you do something about him then? He could do it again! They found other bones in those woods when they found Michelle. He could have done it loads of times!"

"We don't know that. It's a wood, a great place to dump a body if you don't want it to be found for ages!"

"Given it some thought, have you?"

"Oh shut up, D! If he gets arrested he will tell the police about me and I will be in prison, too!"

A little part of her wanted to say that it wouldn't be such a bad thing, but her priority was Lula. Lula would fall apart if she ever found out. And if she was being honest, she wasn't sure how she would survive herself without the love Jackson provided her with.

So, she gave in and let him back into her bed, back into her body. She knew she would only ever be able to resist him if she was not around him, and she would have to wait until summer before she could get away from him.

She refused to go back to the woods, instead using the quietest parts of the cemetery when they needed an outdoor venue. She swore to him that no matter what, she would never set foot in those woods again.

Mr Goldman kept as low a profile as ever, moving unnoticed through the changed world, but Dakota often saw his curtains flicker when she passed by his house, and she could feel him there, beyond his yellowing net curtains, baring a semi-toothless grin at her discomfort, wishing he could pass a remark at the fact she had put curtains up in her bedroom.

The murder of Michelle Taybury was now old news. It always featured in the local paper, but no longer on the front page. It had shocked the village, and posters of the smiling little girl still hung fading in shop windows asking for any help people could give about her last movements the day she died. Nobody saw her again when she entered an alleyway down the road from her house. Nobody saw her journey from there to the woods which lay a mile away. It was as though she had become a ghost the moment she entered that alleyway in the fading light, a ghost passing into fog.

When her body was found, the streets all around the woods became a mass of police cars and white tents. Police men and women knocked on every door including her own, asking questions and showing a recent photo of Michelle in hopes of jogging the memories of any possible witnesses. When asked if she had seen her, she lied under Jackson's staring eyes. When he asked her later if it was hard to lie, she replied, "I'm used to it."

The fine toothcomb search of the woods led to the discovery of the remains of six other bodies, all of which were so decomposed they were unidentifiable. All the police could say was they were all young girls aged from ten to fourteen years old. Eventually they would be identified by their dental records.

The village became a hotbed of media activity, press people harassing locals for information and the face of Michelle Taybury appearing everywhere like a vengeful spirit reminding Dakota of the choice she had made.

The killer had been dubbed two names, depending on what paper you read: The Pan's Wood Murderer or the Babes in the Wood Killer. But the police had no evidence of the killer and no leads, and eventually a known nutter from the next town turned himself in for her murder and the Police seemed satisfied with his confession. Jackson muttered about how the police were desperate to pin the murder on someone and would have charged Mickey Mouse if he had been in the area at the time.

Dakota went to the local library to use the Internet and looked up 'The Babes in the Woods Killer' to try and read up more about the case. She had read everything the local papers had to say and had watched every news bulletin. She had even been caught reading the national newspapers by Lula who thought it was odd that she was suddenly interested in reading newspapers. Dakota knew the best way to find out about how the case was going was to look it up on the Internet.

During her research, she came across several other

murders that had been dubbed 'The Babes in The Wood Murders.' The first was one in Brighton, thirteen years ago, where two little girls were found murdered, the case was unsolved. And there were four more dating back as far as the early 1800's. All involved the murders of small girls whose bodies were found in wooded areas. Something clicked in Dakota's mind as she realised that Goldman had moved in next door twelve years previously, and her mother had said he had moved up from the coast. Was it possible that Goldman had done this before?

Back in the Library, Dakota snapped back into herself. The possibility that Goldman had murdered before was interesting to her, as was the possibility that he had committed similar crimes in previous lives. Could he be that bad, through and through, as to have been a murderer in all his lives?

Making her brief explanation to Betty, she dashed off in search of the life of James Goldman wherever it lay on its shelf in the shadowed room. She finally found it after having to flick through the lives of several other James Goldmans; she recognised him from a single page – the pages she opened it on, the page where he strangled a small blonde-haired girl in the woods. She didn't want to read anymore; she just wanted his name from his previous life, and when he had been born as James Goldman. It appeared he was younger than she thought having been born in 1953; he looked about sixty years old, but could only be in his early fifties. The name he went by in his previous incarnation was Alexander Autaud.

By flicking through Alexander's book, and reading pieces here and there, she was able to ascertain that he was a French Canadian, living in Vancouver in the early part of the twentieth century, born in 1925. She passed over much of his life, his basically non-eventful life, until she reached the year she was looking for: 1953. During her research on the Internet she had read about the unsolved murder of two children in Vancouver in 1953. It appeared that Alexander

Autaud was the perpetrator, but as coincidence would have it, he was hit by a bus just days after he had committed his first murder.

Returning to the book entitled James Goldman, she began flicking through his life, half-annoyed that she wasn't allowed to pick and choose whatever pages she wanted to read in her own book.

James Goldman had killed for the first time when he was just nine years old.

It turned out that he had taken a shine to a girl of his age and wanted to play with her on his own. He tricked her into joining him on a trip to the local woods by telling her that he had discovered a family of foxes. The young girl's love of animals was to be the end of her.

Not long after they had entered the woods, little James Goldman told her he wanted her to take her dress off. When she refused, he strangled her and pushed her into a brook where she was found a week later. He was never a suspect and was never caught, and this was what made him realise he could do it again.

Dakota closed the book, a nausea rising in her dead stomach.

She had a hunch that if she searched back through each of this man's previous lives, she would find the murderer in a string of unsolved child murders that spanned across centuries.

Something that Ariel had said sat up in her head. Something about children committing murders because they had been murderers in their previous lives. Could it be that simple? That there were only a certain number of killers in the universe but that they just kept coming back? The Babes in the Woods Murders were repeatedly given that label because of their similarities with other murders. There was no copycat at work here; it was just the same every time, because the same person was committing them, the same soul returning time after time.

In some ways it seemed hard to believe, and in other ways it seemed the most logical explanation. Centuries of serial murders, and perhaps there were only a handful of souls responsible for the likes of Ted Bundy and Dennis Nilson. Perhaps it was something so deep in those souls that it could never be escaped, something as deep as her love for Jackson. It was all they knew how to do, and there was no cure for it.

Dakota returned to her own life, and waved her hand at Betty's questions. She didn't want to talk about it, nor even think about it. All the poor little girls that had been murdered throughout time, their souls passing on to a better life, while their murderer kept coming back to do it again, somewhere else in the world, over and over again, stealing lives and innocence. It seemed like innocence was something James Goldman never had, something he wasn't even born with.

Even though the guilt was tearing her apart inside, Dakota threw herself into her studies and grew more and more confident that she could pass her exams.

As soon as they were over and the waiting for results began, Dakota began to plan in her head how she would tell Lula that she wanted to go to Ireland and get a job for a while. And then, after a while over in Ireland when she was settled, she would tell Lula she wasn't coming back and she would be free of Jackson.

It was late June when she finally got a chance to be alone with Lula and tell her of her plans.

"What? You want to move to Ireland?" Lula turned away from the dirty dishes in the sink.

"Well, just for a while so I could get a job and stuff, you know, spend some time with the family."

"Bollocks, D, you hate most of the family. Besides, you haven't even been to college yet! I'd understand if you wanted a year out before university, but you need to take your 'A' levels before that." The despair in Lula's voice was clear as the glasses she had just washed.

"But I thought I could skip all that, get a job instead."

"No, you can't do that, D. I am sorry but no." Lula turned back to her washing up and began scrubbing a plate so hard

Dakota thought she might bore through the glaze.

"Why not? I don't want to do all that!"

"D, Mum and Dad wanted you to go to university. You're clever and you shouldn't waste yourself. You'll end up like me, working in a shop for your whole life. You are worth more. They knew you would be a success." She spoke, not turning back to look at her sister, but with a determined edge to her voice. She wasn't going to back down.

"Mum and Dad didn't care what I did. You are making that up," Dakota snapped like a spoilt child.

"Really? So why did they leave money to you and stipulate it was to be used for you to go to university?" Lula turned, one hand on her hip, soap suds trailing down her leg.

Dakota fell silent, staring at her sister. How could she not follow what her parents wanted? Or what Lula wanted? After all she had done to Lula, she felt she owed her something – not that going to college would make up for any of it, but it would keep her happy.

"Well, can I go after my 'A' levels?"

"Yes, of course. Loads of people take a year out to travel; it would do you good. But I know Mum and Dad wanted you to get a chance to be properly educated. I blew all their hopes for that while they were still here. Please say you won't let them down, too?"

Dakota felt that one more piece of pressure would make her snap, but she nodded dumbly, enjoying for a moment the broad smile that spread across Lula's face.

Dakota felt utterly deflated when she returned to her bedroom. All her plans that she had laid out in her head were shot to pieces; she would have to stay for another two years while she took her 'A' levels. Two more years of Jackson and lying, two more years of Goldman next door to her watching and listening to her every move. Two more years of forcing strength into her body to go out and act like life was normal and happy.

Suddenly, her heart seemed to stop. The thought of making it through another week with all the secrets she had to bear seemed suddenly impossible. The ghost of Michelle

Taybury everywhere she went, the spectre of Goldman beyond his yellow net curtains and the late-night hauntings of Jackson, the tortuous guilt she felt for needing him and not being able to resist him over and over again. She was suddenly distraught, air left her lungs and she began to gasp as she pulled herself along the passage to her bedroom. She wanted to scream, smash windows, run away to where there was nobody and nothing. Her panic attack caused her to faint just as she closed her bedroom door behind her.

When she came to, the horror of her mind capsized. She had to get out; she couldn't spend one more day in that house with all those lies wriggling around in her brain. In a split second, she made the decision to run away, and it all made sense. She got her hold-all down from the top of her wardrobe and calmly began packing away her most worn clothes. She made sure she packed jumpers, even though it was summer; she knew she would be cold at night most probably lying down on park benches, so she packed her waterproof jacket as well. As soon as Lula had settled in front of the TV, she would go downstairs and take as much food from the cupboards as she could before anyone noticed. Then, as soon as Lula had dozed off or gone to bed she would creep down the drainpipe by her window and head off before Jackson began to make his way to her room.

Sometimes in the summer, Jackson would tell Dakota to sneak out of the window and meet him down the road so they could go to the woods and make love. He liked being outdoors on summer nights and she did, too, but they hadn't been back to the woods since that night with Goldman. She never wanted to enter those woods again; she didn't even want to pass by them. She hoped after that night that she would never have to do so again.

She spent the remaining hours writing in her diary, pouring out all her feelings and fears, and the absolute certainty she had that another night in that house would surely kill her.

As the sun began to get lower in the sky, she put her diary into her bag along with her pen and finally, the picture of her mother and father she had laid flat on its front every night for the last five years. The sixth anniversary of their death was a week away, as was her seventeenth birthday. She felt sad that she would not be able to visit her parents' grave on their day, but she had a feeling they would be with her wherever she went.

It was an achingly beautiful summer evening; the sky so clear and blue, darkening slowly but its edges still so bright, the trees still swaying gently in the warm breeze. She knew the pavement would still be warm and the grass would be cool in the garden. On nights like this, she would lie on the lawn waiting for stars to arrive, bright and promising only the dark. She would breathe in the cooling summer air and dream of warm beaches and palm trees somewhere a thousand miles away, perhaps in California.

The tarmac on the roads would still be humming with traffic long gone and swallows would be chirping through the impossible skies.

It was some time after eleven o'clock when she slid soundlessly down the drainpipe, leaving a short note of apology to Lula, not mentioning Jackson's name once, but knew he would notice she had taken the photo of herself, Lula and Jackson that had stood out on the landing by the top of the stairs. As much as she hated him, she couldn't help loving him. Knowing she could never live with him, she knew now she would have to learn to live without him. He had been her demon-lover, the man she was most afraid of, the man she loved more than anything in the world.

She headed off on foot towards the main road; she knew if she followed it, she would get to the next village within an hour and then she could go on from there. She wasn't entirely sure where she would end up, but knew that she could not get any money until the bank opened the following day, so with her account passbook and ten pounds in cash, she set off to nowhere.

She stopped by the grave briefly to leave some flowers she had stolen from a garden, and carried on past the woods, saying a silent farewell to her parents and her brothers and sisters. Passing by the woods that night, she wondered if the ghosts of the graveyard wandered through, unseen by all eyes, trapped in their own afterlife of trees. Lula had always told her stories when she was little about ghosts in the woods. She said that there was a ghost for every tree, and they all came out at night when no one was around. Dakota never really believed her, but she liked to hear Lula tell stories.

The roads were quiet, just as they were whenever she had visited the woods at night. It was a quiet village and no one was out at this time of night, except the occasional dog-walker or couple on their way back from a night out.

Dakota got as far as the next village before Jackson tracked her down and dragged her into the car.

TWENTY-THREE: An Ordinary Life

The drive home was unusually silent. Jackson didn't shout at her, but only asked her one question:

Was she all right?

When they reached the house, Lula wailed at her, tears on her face, a trail of unintelligible words coming from her contorted mouth. Dakota could only make out the odd word and just wanted to crawl into her bed and stay there until her sister had gained her composure.

Jackson led her into the kitchen and sat her at the table, putting his arm around Lula and pushing her down into a chair. In moments, he had poured them all a glass of wine and put lit cigarettes in everyone's hands. Dakota was amazed at his composure but still couldn't bring herself to look into his eyes.

"OK, you need to tell me why you left," managed Lula, finally. "If it's because I wouldn't let you go to Ireland I won't believe you. I want to know why you wanted to leave in the first place." Silence fell over the kitchen.

Dakota's eyes flicked across to meet Jackson's, and for a second, she thought she saw fire behind them.

"What? You don't like Jackson?" Lula half shouted, having seen the exchange between her sister and her boyfriend. "I thought you two got on all right now?"

"I think we just rub each other up the wrong way," Jackson replied in place of Dakota.

"I don't want this to be a problem, D. I thought we could all live together; we have been doing OK, haven't we? I mean, you haven't had any big arguments, have you? Is there something I don't know?" Desperation echoed in her voice as she sucked away on her cigarette, seeking strength in the wine.

"No, there's nothing you don't know. We just don't really get on, and I wanted some space, that's all," Dakota lied brilliantly, sad that her plans of freedom were dashed and that she would have to go on with life as it was. She half feared that Jackson would beat her later for trying to leave him; after all, he had once said that he would kill her if she left him. By now he would know that she had asked to go away to Ireland, and would want to know why she was trying to get away from him.

And throughout the heart-to-heart Lula was trying to have with her, all she could think of was what Jackson would do to her when he got her alone.

She was surprised to discover that Jackson had nothing up his sleeve, no sudden attack once Lula had calmed and fallen asleep at around two in the morning. He didn't even come into her room that night; she heard his insomniac hours of solitude all night long as she lay awake waiting his approach. But he never came.

He stayed down in the lounge all night, listening to Nick Cave albums. She could see him in her mind's eye, Jackson sitting alone smoking endless cigarettes, a magical tumbler of whisky that was never empty and a musty old copy of some poetry book in his hands, Blake or Baudelaire.

She did not know why he had left her alone, but he did so for a few days after. The most contact she had with him was one stolen moment when he held her face in his hands and looked deep into her eyes, as though he was looking for something.

She felt tears in her eyes as she looked back at him, her heart so confused with what was right and wrong. All she knew was that she had such deep feelings for Jackson that she almost never wanted to see him again.

One evening, a week or so later, Lula announced she was going out for the evening, which was most unusual as she rarely went out without Jackson.

"Where are you going?" Dakota asked.

"Oh, just over to Linda's house for a few drinks. I'll be gone a few hours," she explained and her eyes flicked across to where Jackson was sitting. "Why don't you two watch a movie together?"

"What?" Dakota felt shock washing over her; Lula had never been like this before. Then she realised Lula was expecting Jackson and her to have a 'bonding session' while she was away.

"It'll be nice for you to spend an evening together. You both like the same movies... you can even have a bit of wine if you like." Lula smiled excitedly and went into the hallway to put her coat on.

"Why are you doing this, Lula?" Dakota raced out after her and spoke in whispers.

"I don't want you two to be at odds... I love you both and I want you to get on. You just need to spend more time together, talk about all the things you have in common. You like all the same books; he used to make such an effort with you by bringing books home from the library for you, didn't he?"

Dakota smiled weakly and hugged her sister back when she gave her a kiss goodbye.

"Have a nice night, you two," Lula called, smiling like an excited teenager.

"Yeah, you have fun," Dakota replied.

As the door shut, silence descended over the house, cars passed outside and she could hear people laughing somewhere up the road.

Dakota turned and walked into the lounge.

Jackson was sitting in his chair looking at her.

"So, Lula wants us to get closer. Do you think we should do as she says?" he said, a wry grin on his face.

"If only she knew, Jackson, she'd kill us." Dakota sparked up a cigarette and threw herself into the sofa.

"I'm sorry, you know," he said.

"For what?"

"For whatever I did that made you run away. Please don't

do that again. You belong here with us."

"I can't bear the lies, Jackson. So much has happened that Lula doesn't know and I have no one to turn to."

"You have me! Or don't I count?" he snapped.

"I used to be so close to her – we always told each other everything... It's hard to not have a female friend anymore." Dakota felt sadness welling in her.

"You don't need anyone else when you have me. I am everything you will ever need and you know that," he said, his voice softer now. She felt herself weakening, her defences melting in her tiredness.

"I just want an ordinary life, normal life... a normal boyfriend, a family and friends. I can never have it now, but don't stop me from trying," she said, half-angry, wiping a tear from her cheek. He stood up and slowly walked across to where she sat. In a few movements they were lying cuddled together on the sofa, and Dakota was lost to him again. All the resistance she managed when he wasn't near her fell away and she was safe and warm again, just like that night in the hospital when he had been her only comforter.

"Can we try to look like we like each other in a platonic way from now on? I mean, can we act like we like each other but not too much? I'd rather Lula thought we liked each other than hated each other." Jackson faced her in the still lounge, the muted TV mouthing soundless words in the background.

"I'll try... If only she knew that I was trying to leave cos I liked you too much... maybe she would rather I left," Dakota muttered.

"You'll always be my girl, D, always," he whispered into her dark hair.

And so the act continued. The great play that was her life went on unhindered and she knew that Lula believed that she and Jackson had worked their differences out. And in a way they had. Dakota knew that as long as she lived in that house, he would never leave her alone, and she didn't want him to, but no matter how much she desired him, she knew that one day she would have to get away from him, and if it took two years before Lula would let her go, then she would keep on going till then.

Dakota had dozed off again in the library, but woke sharply when a crack of thunder shook the windows.

Betty was asleep, too, but the empty bottle of vodka indicated that it would take more than thunder to wake her up.

Dakota stood up and felt she needed a break, a walk, anything to get her away from the books for a while. With one of the ink quills on the table she left a note for Betty telling her she had gone to get her another bottle of vodka and would return soon.

The scratching of lives rose and fell behind the thunder as she made her way out to the hallway, with one of the table lamps in her hand; in the distant shadows of the library, souls moved, moaned and wept quietly amidst the tall shelves of secrets.

Dakota decided she would give nearly anything to have a moment without hers or someone else's despair. But she knew that there was not a single cobweb in Purgatory that wasn't saturated in sadness.

As she stepped out into the dark corridor she thought of the young boy she had met earlier who had run off deep into the hotel. His laughter had taken a long time to fade into nothing and it made her wonder how much further this corridor went.

The familiar whispers and sniggers came from the direction that led to the lobby, but in the opposite direction there seemed to be only silence.

"I'll just take a look; it won't take a second," she muttered to herself and headed deeper into the darkness of the hotel.

The wall lamps continued to fade and swell in the distance and she was glad of the steady light from her lamp. The further she went the quieter it got. She felt that not even the crazies came this far in, and she began to wonder whether it was a good idea to go on.

Then, as one of the lamps up ahead reached full brightness, she noticed another door.

TWENTY-FOUR: The Chapel

Dakota saw that the door had been opened recently as there were no cobwebs draped across its peeling front. Silence beyond the door made her unsure of whether that was a good sign or a bad sign, but she knew that she wanted to take a look, so she did.

The door creaked in a suitably Hammer-Horror way as she entered what appeared to be some kind of temple. The one window on the far wall allowed lightning to elaborate on the details of the room that the weak lamps could not pick out.

It was very cobwebbed and dusty, but she could see by the floor that at least one other person had visited this room recently. There were a few seats but the walls were completely covered in religious imagery from nearly every religion she could think of and perhaps a few more she hadn't heard of. Buddhas, pentagrams and crucifixes were just a few symbols she recognised.

Great gold leaf paintings of various gods and goddesses spread themselves out across the huge walls. The room was almost as big as a church, she realised as she wandered further in.

At first, she wondered what this sort of room was doing here in Purgatory. Then she realised that it was most probably there for the same reasons as the Library was: to aid in everybody's journey to repentance. But like the library, this place was fairly disused, a sad reminder that people here just weren't any good deep down, that no one there really wanted to get out because they didn't even know how to be sorry for whatever they had done.

Dakota couldn't even remember what she had done to get

there, but she knew she was sorry nonetheless. She almost wanted to say it out loud, 'I am sorry really, I'm not like all the others, I'm good deep down, and really I am!' But the sad-faced gods looked down on her and she felt unworthy of them.

Movement somewhere deep in the shadows stirred her, and she turned frantic to the source of the noise.

"Did you know you've got a stalker?" said David, stepping forward from the row of chairs.

"Christ! Why do you always have to creep around like that?" She relaxed slightly when she noticed his wrists weren't bleeding anymore.

"Sorry, didn't mean to scare you. Not used to seeing anyone else in here,"

"No, I guess not. This place seems a bit derelict. How come you're here?" Dakota asked, sitting down.

"I like it here. It's safe, and peaceful. There's nowhere else in this dump I'd rather be."

"Why did you say I had a stalker?" she asked warily, recalling his opening sentence.

"I keep seeing someone behind you or waiting by the library for you. Never see a face or nothing, just a silhouette, smoking a cigarette. Whoever it is often walks this corridor. I always find the lights dim down when he goes past, like I am not allowed to see his face or something."

"Oh, it's just Woods; he follows me around… I knew him, you see, in life," she said uncomfortably, as though revealing a difficult secret.

"Oh, guess it was him, then. Don't think I know him," David replied.

Silence sat with them a while, wind moaning above their heads through some unseen crack in the high window. Lightning lit up the face of a golden Buddha and Dakota wondered, "So what religion are you?"

"Me?" he asked, somewhat surprised at the question. She nodded with a faint smile. "Oh, I don't know. I think I believe in them all; they are all basically the same thing after all – a higher power that created us and now watches over us, god or goddess, doesn't really matter, does it?" he said, his sad eyes falling on an image of the Virgin Mary.

"I was a Catholic, had a picture like that in my bedroom," she said softly in the dark room, motioning towards the beautiful woman on the wall.

"I like the idea that God is a woman, you know. Seems all the men I met in my life were so brutal. Perhaps the devil is a man," he mused, his mind recalling the violence of his father.

"Yeah, I like that idea, but where is the devil in all of this? There is no hell as such, so where does he live if God is in Heaven?"

"He's probably here, lurking down the hall somewhere... your stalker probably!" He laughed slightly but jumped as thunder rattled at the windows.

"So why do you stay here?"

"Well, I think it's my best way out, you know, to stay here and pray, hope He will forgive me and let me into Heaven. I've been here a long time now, and I've stayed out of trouble. I was hoping that God might understand in some way that I only killed myself cos I was so unhappy. I just think if I show how sorry I am, he might..."

"Have you been to the library?" Dakota asked as her mind skipped back to what she should be doing.

"Yeah, I did all that. It's amazing how much you forget, all those things from childhood. My father loved me once, I think. He used to be nice to me sometimes when I was a baby. Don't know why he stopped..." He paused, his thoughts going to places that Dakota couldn't follow. "Anyway, yes, I did that. I just have to hope now that prayers might help."

Dakota stared at David and his skinny body, wondering if he was right. Was religion and prayer the best way out of this replacement for Hell? But she couldn't even begin that process until she had worked out what she had done to get here in the first place.

She wanted to stay here, in the peaceful safe air of the Chapel, but she knew she couldn't stay. She had work to do.

"I'd better go, but I will come back. I just have to keep

going in the library till I know why I am here. Then I'll come back and pray with you," she said, standing up.

"Really? Will you pray with me? I'd love that... Come back soon, OK?" He seemed moved to tears by her words and reached out to touch her hand.

"I promise I'll come back, see you later, OK?" She smiled and moved off towards the door to the corridor.

As she stepped out into the corridor, she listened. There were distant shufflings further down towards the Lobby, which meant she would have to fight her way through the shadowy occupants. She sighed and stepped further out, closing the chapel door. As she turned back to the hallway, she jumped back as she came face to face with Goldman.

He was smiling his gruesome grin at her, his proximity to her making her skin crawl, and all the while Dakota kept repeating a phrase over and over in her head: 'Don't show him you're scared of him.' Even so, his cruel smile led her to believe she wasn't doing too well at hiding her fear.

"Nice to see you, pretty." He smiled, leaning up against the wall, blocking her exit.

"Wish I could say the same. What do you prefer to be called now? Woods or Goldman?" she replied, aware of a shake in her voice.

"I'd actually prefer you to call me Daddy." He licked his lips at her and she felt her dead stomach roll over into knots.

"Forgive me if I don't. I think I'm a bit too old for you, aren't I?" she snapped, trying to accentuate the defiance in her tone.

"I'd always make an exception for you, pretty. Been waiting to get my hands on you since you were the right age; I'd just have to use my imagination a bit, that's all." He chuckled, reaching out to touch her hair.

"So you still don't have anything better to do with your time, eh? I guess dying didn't teach you any lessons."

"I'm starting to think you aren't happy to see such a familiar face here – thought we could use the time wisely... you know, get to know each other better..." He was creeping closer to her, her back pushing up against the wall, wishing she could just vanish. "After all, pretty, we do have all the time in the world now, don't we?"

He managed to get within inches of her face, his body beginning to press on her lower half before she snapped into action and shoved him away with all her strength, making a run for it.

After a brief tussle with the crazies down past the Library, Dakota made her way back into the Bar to get some more vodka. She actually felt she needed some now, and she even craved a cigarette. In her pocket she found one last cigarette, slightly battered but not split, and she lit it in the dim light by the Bar door, her hands shaking almost uncontrollably. Her close encounter with Goldman had left her nervous; she feared that she might not have the strength to fight him off next time.

Inside, the usual suspects sat in the dim shadows and anger burnt low like a fire reduced to embers. She could feel it in the air, mixed with the softer, weaker emotions of pity and despair.

She recalled the last time she had been in the Bar, the fight with Danny still clear in her crowded mind. She felt bad suddenly, as though she could forget everything and tell him it wasn't worth it – that they had to stick together in this place and be friends.

As low music murmured in the background, muffled by thunder, she saw Danny, sitting at the end of the bar again, head in hand, a burnt-out cigarette still clinging to a column of ash sitting between his fingers. He was asleep and hunched over, his grip on his one pleasure continuing through sleep.

Dakota reached out and lifted the dead cigarette from his finger, dropping the cold ash across the bar. The movement woke Danny suddenly, and she reached out her hand to his arm to calm him. But instead, his eyes showed horror at the sight of her. He fell back, off his chair, muttering and crying, as though he was terrified of her.

His actions startled Dakota at first, but she still knelt

down beside him to try and calm him. "It's OK, it's me, Dakota. You were dreaming. Calm down," she whispered. In seconds, the look of fear melted and he stared at her like she was a new species of plant.

"Dakota? Oh, it's you... you looked like..." He continued to mutter inaudibly as she helped him back onto his stool.

"Who did I look like?" She laughed slightly. "You'd think you'd seen a ghost!"

"Nothing... no one. I was dreaming, as you said." He was visibly shaken and looked more than ever like he needed a drink.

"Can't you have just one drink? Will they notice?" she whispered, pouring out a shot of vodka. Danny looked sadly at the glass for a moment before reaching out and dragging it down the bar towards him.

The liquid in the glass caught the candle-light for a moment as he lifted it to his mouth, but in a second it was gone.

"What happened?" she said, staring at the empty glass that sat against his closed lips. Danny held the glass in front of his eyes and stared at it with more sadness in his eyes than she had ever seen in him before.

"They took it away. I told you I can't drink. It happens every time I try. I can hold a glass of it in my hand for hours, but as soon as it goes near my mouth, it disappears, evaporates," he said sadly. Dakota took the glass and ran her finger around the inside. Despite the fact that she had filled it with vodka a few moments before, it was bone dry, as though it had been sitting on the shelf for ages.

"Sorry, I thought they might let you have one occasionally," she said.

"What are you doing here?" he said, rubbing his tired eyes.

"Came for more supplies. Betty needs more booze and I need more cigarettes, this reading business is thirsty work, obviously. She has got through a few bottles already! Plus, I just had a close encounter with a rapist so I think I could do with a stiff drink myself." She laughed, despite feeling that her levity was out of place.

"Ahh, OK, let me fix you up with some then." He got up and shuffled behind the bar to get her requests.

"I wanted to say sorry, too… for when I was last here. I was angry. I didn't mean to be nasty," she offered, slightly afraid one of the nearby punters might break into laughter.

"I'm sorry, too. What you do is up to you. I can't expect you to give up like I have. You are young; eternity must seem longer to you…" he replied, not looking up at her. She sensed he was reluctant to talk to her, and she didn't blame him; all she seemed to do was fight with him.

"Well, I'd better get back. I'll come by again soon, fill you in on what I have learnt, you know?" she said hopefully. Danny said nothing but smiled and turned his back to do some unnecessary cleaning.

TWENTY-FIVE: A New Life

Betty was still asleep but, much to Dakota's amusement, the clink of vodka bottles woke her more easily than thunder.

"Ohhh lovely... hair of the dog, eh?" Betty repositioned herself in her chair, putting the book down on the table to make drinking easier for her.

"Well, I might just join you for a drink, dear, but I have to press on with this. I have to get started with this whole repentance thing." She smiled, lighting a cigarette.

"Someone's been reading that!" exclaimed Betty, pointing at Dakota's book. Dakota looked down to see the blank pages near the end of the book were on show to her. It felt like they were mocking her, saying, 'Wouldn't you love to know what is written here?'

Dakota turned back to the last page with writing on it and watched as the sentences began to grow across the page.

"Perhaps it was just the wind blew the pages across," Dakota replied, unconvinced but not wanting to think of anyone snooping around her life.

Dakota settled back into the tome that was her recently extinct life. The years that followed her escape attempt were much the same; the routine she had known for the past five years slipped back into play. Even though she found a steady boyfriend at college, Jackson continued to act as though she was his possession and he hers. Her boyfriend, Simon, was allowed to stay over at weekends, and this new part of the routine allowed Dakota three nights' respite from the attentions of her secret lover.

It seemed the older she got the more she accepted her role in life but still allowed herself to have some other kind of life just as Jackson did. He continued to play the dutiful boyfriend to Lula, even taking her away on holiday a few times, and all the while Lula looked at Jackson as though she had only just met him, a look that was always mixed with a remote sadness that Dakota suspected was borne out of her desire to be married and have a child of her own.

But Jackson still avoided marriage as much as he avoided the possibility of a baby.

Dakota had her own life, too, in which she was a normal college girl who did college girl things: having friends, going out, getting drunk and having a boyfriend that she had no plans to marry or settle down with.

Before Simon, there was a string of bad relationships with boys of her own age. She would go out drinking with her female friends, and as she had grown older, she had become quite beautiful, and very popular. In her mind, the process of going out to the pub or a club was very much like donning a mask and putting on a show, but she became dependent on this escapism from her real life. Wherever she went, she would turn heads. Men of all ages found Dakota attractive and they all wanted to be with her. Their attentions made her feel good, but they also made her think less of the men themselves; the more they vied for her attention, the less she liked them. She gave them her best smiles and her cutest winks and always took time to talk to them but always left them high and dry as she walked away from them at the end of the night.

Every Saturday and Sunday morning she would wake up with a hangover, her clothes stinking of cigarettes and her eye make-up smudged across her face. But worse than all of this was the come-down from her previous night's acting. She would wake up alone and feel like a bitch from playing games around men she didn't really fancy or find interesting. She could still see the disappointment in their eyes as she dropped them at the end of the night, refusing their offers to take her home, or worse still, letting them walk her home then not inviting them in.

There were some that she would agree to date, but it was

all a game to her, and when she did actually date someone, she would end up building them up and then dropping them from the height she had brought them to.

Dakota hated herself for doing it, but no matter how hard she tried to be good and have a meaningful relationship, she always ended up resenting them for worshipping her. She realised she would trade all their doting for one harsh look from Jackson.

She never brought any of these brief lovers home. She would hint at the existence of a new boyfriend but never parade them in front of Lula or Jackson, because she feared he would see through her, and laugh at her weakness for him.

Simon was the one she settled on because he was just as elusive as she was. He was mad about her, but was keen to keep it from her, and this made her like him more than any of the others.

Simon was wonderful to her and he was a great distraction from her other life, but all the time she knew that as soon as college was finished she would have to leave and go to Ireland. And when she did, she would not look back or spare a thought for Simon – because he was, after all, just as expendable as the rest – in one last attempt to have a completely ordinary life.

A life without Jackson.

Sometimes the thought of never seeing him again frightened her. She felt a deep sea of panic rising in her whenever she realised she wouldn't see him every day – perhaps only once a year if she went to visit Lula. Yet as much as the prospect of Jackson not being in her life caused fear to lurch in her, she knew that she had to get away from him one day, before Lula ever found out.

Dakota still managed to keep Jackson a secret from her friends and everyone else. Her only sounding board was her diary where she could pour out all her feelings and know that no one was going to slap her and call her a slut. The only people who knew were her, her diary, Jackson and Mr Goldman. Goldman had kept his end of the bargain; he had left them alone and not sent any more photos in the mail.

And she had kept her end.

Even though the ghost of Michelle Taybury seemed to be there all the time, Dakota had not spoken her name out loud since the day after she was murdered. She had promised Jackson and she intended to keep that promise for the rest of her life.

Life moved on and, after two years, Lula kept her promise and allowed Dakota to go to Ireland to live with relatives. The plan was that she would go and live with her cousin in Dublin and get herself a job for a year or so, and then return and go to university.

That was Lula's plan.

Dakota's plan was to stay with her cousin and get a job so she could afford to rent her own flat. And she would never return to the house she grew up in, the house where she remembered her parents, the house where she had first heard they were dead, and the house where Jackson had changed her life forever.

So, one summer day, Jackson and Lula took her to the airport and said their goodbyes. Lula sobbed like a baby and said she had to call all the time and write every day.

Jackson had said his good byes the night before. In the early hours, he had crawled into her bed and held her so tight she thought she would suffocate. He whispered to her over and over how much he loved her and how he would miss her every day and that he would write to her all the time.

"You will come back to me one day, I know it," he said in the dark lonely hours. He pushed his own copy of Baudelaire into her bag along with the Nick Cave CD he had bought her. "Listen to this and think of me, won't you?"

She felt sad to be leaving him, as though she was about to die and they would never see each other again. But for all her deep sadness and fear, she knew she had to go and that it was the best thing for everyone, especially Lula.

The dreams of Jackson murdering her still came in those few hours of night that she managed to sleep, and the years had taught her that it could easily happen. Perhaps by leaving him she was saving them both: saving her own life and saving Lula from the heartbreak of losing Jackson to prison.

Dakota had found a million excuses to leave but she knew that beneath every reason was Jackson, no matter how much she said it would be a great opportunity to meet new people in a new country, she knew that it would always come down to him and why she had to leave him.

Her life in Ireland began quietly. Though she lived in the city, the only friends she had were her cousins, so it took a while before she began to socialise. But once she started she didn't stop. Every night she was out with her cousins and their friends, and soon she made new friends of her own. The freedom she felt was a new and shattering gift. She could meet new men and not stop herself by thinking: how will Jackson react? She was a free single young woman and before long, the confidence and personality that lay buried beneath years of Jackson's authority began to surface.

She found a job in the local record store on the High Street and spent her days listening to music and seeing and talking to dozens of different new people. Her life in England seemed like ancient history, and even though she knew Jackson had tainted her, perhaps forever, she no longer let him interfere with her everyday life.

His letters arrived every few days at first, and after the first few, she stopped opening them but instead buried them at the bottom of her wardrobe, unable to understand why she could not simply put them in the bin. Perhaps she might need them one day, when loneliness or feeling unloved overtook her. She could open them all and read how much someone had wanted her once. She hoped that day would never come, but the unpredictability of life never escaped her mind and so she chose to keep the letters as a safety net.

Dakota felt as though she had spent the first eighteen years of her life in prison. Now she was living with one of her cousins who never nagged her or asked where she was going and who with. She had a job and was earning her own money without being under the watchful gaze of Jackson, and she was free to date anyone she wanted without it being a reason to annoy Jackson.

She found she was popular and liked by nearly everyone she met. In short, her life in Dublin was Heavenly to her.

After a few months of 'seeing' various men, she settled on one. His name was Aiden and she met him in a pub in Temple Bar one Friday night. It was halfway through the evening and she had decided to have another cigarette, only to find her lighter was no longer in her pocket, so she turned to the nearest person for a light and there he was.

With black hair and green eyes, he could have been a relative, but the second she saw him she knew she wanted him. After a few meetings in pubs they started a relationship and Dakota felt finally she was free of all Jackson's influence. Aiden provided her with everything she needed from a man and had never really had. Though she always believed Jackson loved her, there was an oppressive nature to that love, something about it that meant pain would always be a large part of her life. With Aiden she felt different, a different kind of love that was light and uncomplicated.

The months passed and her friends told her she had placed all her eggs in one basket perhaps too soon, but her need for Aiden was almost adolescent. She found herself becoming paranoid and afraid he would leave her, calling him on his mobile phone whenever he was out with his friends just to check he was really with them.

Dakota was not ready for a relationship with anyone, and the result of this was devastating to her.

It was just over two years since she had left home when Aiden left her for another girl. It seemed to confirm everything Jackson had ever said about 'other boys' and she was heartbroken. The first relationship she had ever had that she had actually put her heart and soul into was over and for the first time in her life, even after everything she had been through, she felt as though she could not carry on living. She was only a month shy of her twenty-first birthday, but was afraid she wouldn't make it that far.

She slipped easily into drunkenness every night and her friends could do nothing for her. The way Dakota saw it, she had left England to prove that a normal happy life was possible for her, and in as little as two years she had discovered that it wasn't.

And it was on one of those lonely, rain-soaked drunken nights that she crawled to the bottom of her wardrobe and pulled out the letters that Jackson had written her.

There were literally hundreds from the first year and a half of her life in Dublin, but in the last six months after she had finally written to Lula and said she was happy and in love he had stopped writing.

Deep down, she had almost missed the sight of his handwriting on the envelope as it lay on her hallway floor, but she knew it was a good thing he had stopped writing.

She had written to Lula regularly and through the letters she felt that they had finally resumed the friendship they had shared all those years before as young girls. They shared girly gossip and spoke deeply about their feelings for their respective partners, and for the first time in years Dakota didn't have to write in her diary in order to let her feelings out. What she had to say was suitable for public consumption, everything before Ireland was a ghastly secret that was hidden away in the pages of those diaries, their covers scuffed and worn but held together by sellotape and glue.

Dakota never read old entries in her diary and had often considered burning them, but had always held on to them finally, perhaps for the same reason she had held on to all those unopened letters from her one-time lover.

So on that deep lonesome night, she dug out the Nick Cave CD she had not played since before she left England and turned up the volume to drown out the sound of the rain and wind at her window.

All at once those dark nights in her old bedroom were alive again, and she thought that he would creep through her door at any moment to take her again, burying her in kisses and crazed love. But he did not come singing low through that door, so she ripped the envelope off the first letter and began to read.

All night long, she drank and read Jackson's pleading words, his unread promises and tears pouring off the pages to the sound of that music he played for her when he was her Loverman.

There was page after page of stolen words – Baudelaire, Yeats, Cummings and Byron – the words he had stolen before to try and explain his love for her. And in the passages she could barely read for the pain in her heart, were words from Wuthering Heights, heady declarations of love as old as the earth and as powerful as the storms.

By the time morning came she was washed out, drunk and crying still as though she had only just lost Jackson and she was dying with the pain, as if a limb had been removed or, worse still, her heart.

She realised that reading Jackson's words hurt more than knowing that Aiden was gone, and in this truth lay the fact that she did love Jackson and that he was right all along: she couldn't live without him and she would come back to him one day.

That day had come.

She was going home and suddenly Lula no longer mattered. It was Jackson and her and that was all. No one mattered anymore.

Within hours she had packed her belongings and was on her way to the airport, leaving a note for her cousin to say she was going back home and didn't know when she would be back.

It seemed that the sudden fire within her had burned off any possibility of a hangover and though she was chain-smoking until the minute she got on the plane, she felt half-calm and assured of what she was doing. After all these years she was choosing Jackson. It wasn't about abuse or rape anymore; it never had been. It had always been there but she had been too young and stupid to see it: Jackson was her destiny, the only man for her, and that was all she needed to understand.

TWENTY-SIX: Haunting

"Well, I finished that one, too, now," said Betty, prodding Dakota away from her old life.

"Huh?"

"The second life you had. I finished it. Not much different to the others really! You had a dodgy affair, it all went wrong, he killed you, heheh." Betty laughed as she clutched the cigarette between her lips, long enough to light it.

"Well there's a surprise, let me guess, I was stabbed in a cemetery?"

"Yup, I take it that was your other nightmare?"

"Yes, which means I was having past life flashbacks and also seeing my future death. Shit, I wish I had known! I did have a hunch." She giggled as she lit a cigarette herself.

Just as the cigarette glowed into life, a huge flash of lightning lit the shadowy library, revealing a tall figure standing only a few feet away from them between the bookcases. A split second later a second flash lit up the same area to reveal the figure was gone.

"Jesus fucking Christ!" exclaimed Dakota, and a small drama ensued as her fallen cigarette burnt a hole in her trousers.

"What is wrong with you?" Betty laughed.

"Did you see that?"

"What?"

"Is this place haunted?"

Betty laughed incredulously for a moment, wondering whether she was joking. "Jesus, Dakota, you're in Purgatory. This place is full of dead people!"

"Can you appear and disappear whenever you like?"

Betty stopped laughing when she realised Dakota was

visibly shaken. "What did you see?"

"Well, I saw a fucking ghost, Betty!"

Rain began to crash into the windows again after a brief respite, and Betty stared from Dakota to the place that Dakota was staring at. Lightning lit up the shadows again but the shape was still gone.

"Well shit love, I think you need some sleep." Betty laughed nervously.

"Have you ever seen anything like that?"

"Seen weird people and lurkers but nobody ever disappeared in front of me before!"

Silence passed between them and all there was in the air was the persistent scratching away of lives in their separate volumes, and Dakota realised that somewhere, light years from here, life was continuing. All the people she had known were still there, carrying on without her, and for the first time since she had died she wondered… was she missed?

"Perhaps we should go back to our rooms and get some shut-eye? We been in here for what feels like days and these chairs aren't comfy to sleep in." Betty shifted her ample bottom slightly in her chair with a grumble.

"No, I can't stop now, I am nearly there. I'm about to turn twenty-one and that means I'll be dead soon," she explained as the rain smashed its tiny, angry fists against the glass.

"Well… will you be OK on your own? I need to sleep on something half-comfy!"

"Yeah, I'll be fine, you go on up for a rest." Dakota smiled warmly and put her hand on Betty's. "And I am really grateful for your help, thank you so much."

Betty smiled back and held on to Dakota's small hand for a moment longer before patting it affectionately.

"There is another life of course, your first one, but I suppose there's no point reading that – I already know the ending, hehe,"

"Seriously though, thank you, Betty."

"It was fun; I got to read a book with an ending." She laughed and winked before taking one of the bottles of vodka and shuffling away into the shadows of the library.

Dakota felt suddenly lonely again. The long and dense shadows breathed in and out as the lamp flames flickered in a draught from the old windows, and even though she was aware of other souls shifting about beyond the rows of book cases, they were not her friends and they did not care.

Taking another swig of vodka for Dutch courage, Dakota returned to the day she came back into Jackson Shade's life.

TWENTY-SEVEN: Home Again

Dakota turned the key in the front door at around two in the afternoon, and was surprised to find that Lula was home.

"Oh my god, what are you doing here!" cried Lula throwing her arms around her sister and then holding her away from her to get a better look.

"Well, I just felt I needed to come back, so I might stay if that's all right?"

"Of course it is! Did you get the invite, then? I only posted it yesterday." Lula took her sister's suitcase from her and began carrying it up to her old bedroom.

"No, what invite?" she asked, following her upstairs.

"Oh, Jackson and I are getting married!" Lula scrunched up her face with delight and pushed the bedroom door open.

Shock passed through Dakota as the words registered in her brain. They were getting married.

"Well? Aren't you happy, D? Oh, please say you are. God knows it's taken him long enough to propose!"

"He proposed?"

"Yes… well, no, actually I did! I know it's weird but I asked loads of times before and he always said no, but this time he said yes!" She was talking like a schoolgirl who had just asked her big crush to the school disco and got a positive response.

"Well, that's great Lula. I am really happy for you both," she managed half-heartedly.

"We should celebrate your return. Shall I cook something special for dinner tonight?"

"Yeah, that would be great. I just need to unpack and freshen up and stuff, if that's OK?"

"You take your time and get settled back in." Tears filled

Lula's eyes and she hugged her little sister again. "I am so happy to see you, you have no idea how much I missed you." With that, Lula said she'd go make her a sandwich and disappeared off downstairs.

Dakota flopped on the bed and looked around. It was like a shrine to her youth in that room; everything was just as she had left it. Nick Cave and Doors posters still on the walls, the books she didn't need to read all the time still sat on her shelf gathering dust and her CD collection sat unlistened to by her quiet stereo.

The only thing Dakota could do was dig out her diary and pour out her immediate feelings on the news she had just received. Shock was still coursing through her as feelings of despair began. Did this mean Jackson didn't need her anymore? Or had he just given up hope that she would return to him? She decided swiftly it was the latter and set about unpacking before soaking in the bath and making sure she looked pretty for when Jackson came through the door.

At 6.10pm, Dakota started the CD and Nick Cave's voice began to crawl out of the speakers. A few minutes later she heard a key in the front door as she made her way out to the top of the stairs.

The few seconds that followed were something she thought she would never forget.

As Jackson came through the front door, he was initially stuck in his nightly routine. He came in, shut the door, dropped his keys on the hall table and started to remove his shoes. But suddenly, just as he was kicking off his right shoe, he froze.

The music from the bedroom upstairs had finally reached his ears, and he looked as though someone had thrown a bucket of ice water over him. Very slowly he stood up straight and stepped back a few paces to look upstairs. The second he saw her she could see tears in his eyes, and all they could do was stare at each other.

It had only been two years since she last laid eyes on him, yet it felt like it had been an age, but he was as beautiful as ever, his black hair still swept away from his face and down to his collar, and his eyes were still as blue and deep as ever. He was the answer to all her questions, and the only thing she felt she had ever really needed in her life, and after two years of him creeping into her dreams and her constant attempts to push him aside and out of her life, she accepted that he had always been right; they belonged together.

The moment she had seen him, her stomach seemed to leap up into her throat and as much as she wanted to run down the stairs and throw her arms around him, she was frozen to the spot, as though every emotion she had ever felt had just revisited her and temporarily paralysed her.

"D?" he whispered in the dim light of the hallway, staring at her as if she were a ghost.

"Oh Jackson, guess who's come to stay? You'll never guess!" cried Lula,

running out from the kitchen, hands flapping in the air like an overexcited six-year-old. Jackson still couldn't manage any words, and neither he nor she could tear their eyes away from one another.

"Oh! Damn, you spoiled my surprise!" Lula laughed, wagging her finger up at Dakota. "She just arrived a couple of hours ago. Isn't it great? And she didn't even know about the wedding! How spooky is that?"

"Oh I see, so you're not here for the wedding?" he asked finally, his throat dry.

"No, it's just a coincidence. I just decided I wanted to come home, so I did," Dakota explained as she sauntered down the stairs.

"Welcome home," he managed as the three of them stood awkwardly in the hall. Every urge Dakota had to kiss him and be held by him again had to be suppressed. But the hardest thing was just to keep her eyes off him. Luckily Lula was so excited that she didn't even notice. Instead she was flapping around and dishing up dinner, a 'welcome home' meal that consisted of cheese-topped shepherd's pie, Dakota's favourite.

Her stomach was in so many knots that she had to use every bit of willpower to eat her meal, all the time answering a million questions from Lula, and trying not to look at Jackson for fear their eyes might become glued together again.

Once dinner was over and they had all settled in the lounge with glasses of wine, Lula's face took on a serious look.

"I did write you a letter that was in with your invite, but seeing as you didn't get it, I'll ask you face to face,"

"What?" A stab of fear pricked her stomach, and for a second she thought that Lula somehow knew about her and Jackson.

"Will you be my Maid of Honour?"

Dakota almost choked on her mouthful of wine, and then felt she needed to swallow the rest of glass.

"Um, yeah, of course I will. Will I have to wear a silly peach-coloured dress and satin shoes?" Dakota forced a giggle, filling up her glass again.

"No! We can go shopping this week. I have the week off work, so we can go looking for a dress for you, OK?"

"Yeah, OK. When is the wedding?"

"Two months." Lula beamed. "Hey! It's your birthday in a few weeks. How fab, we can go out somewhere!"

Dakota felt terrible. Here was her only sister so incredibly happy to see her and so desperate to bring her back into her life, and yet all she wanted was to tell Lula to get out and leave her alone with Jackson.

It had all seemed so much easier before she had left for Dublin. The way she had always dealt with keeping her feelings secret from Lula seemed to have left her; all she wanted to do was tell her she was in love with Jackson. Greed had taken over her. She wanted Jackson all to herself now, more than she ever had.

The evening wore on, Lula asking all sorts of questions and showing Dakota what her wedding dress was like and what music they would have. All the while, Jackson sat drinking and staring at Dakota, only looking away to light his cigarettes.

"Isn't it time you took your sedatives, Lula?" he muttered

around ten o'clock.

"Nah, not tonight, I want to stay up late and talk with my sister. What do you think, D? Shall we stay up all night watching movies and drinking?" Lula asked excitedly. And only the part of Dakota that felt guilt stopped her from saying no. She realised that this meant she would have to go another night without touching Jackson, but she felt she could handle it. What difference would one more night make?

"Oh, I never told you about Mr Goldman next door, did I?" began Lula, pouring out more wine.

The mention of his name made Dakota go cold, and for an icy moment she thought he had been arrested.

"He disappeared!" A cold sweat pricked on her forehead as some kind of relief washed over her.

"When?"

"God, it was about six months ago now. He had a younger brother apparently and they hadn't seen each other in years, but the brother decided to come back and see him. He knocked here and asked if Goldman still lived there, and I said he did but I hadn't seen him in a few weeks. The brother went round the back and his back door was open, but Goldman was gone. The place was messed up as if someone had broken in or had a fight and then he found the pictures," Lula explained and paused to sip her wine. Dakota could feel her hand shaking.

"What pictures?"

"It was horrible. I am so glad I didn't find them. They were all of little girls and things, you know? He had been molesting them, and taking pictures. They also found pictures of dead ones. The police have been looking for him ever since. Seems it was him who killed that little girl there was a big thing about, Michelle something. Do you remember?"

"Yeah, I do. And they don't know where he is?" Her mind flickered between what she was asking and the thoughts she was having about the photographs of herself and Jackson.

"Nope, the news has been full of it for ages, but they think he might have left the country. I hope they catch him. I keep thinking he could still be out there hurting little girls, sick bastard. They said he was responsible for all the other little girls' bodies they found out in the woods."

"I'm sure they'll catch him one day," replied Dakota, wondering if she really believed that.

"Oh, we're out of wine. I'll get another bottle from the kitchen. Hang on a sec," Lula said as she got up and left the room.

Dakota turned to Jackson, her eyes wide, asking the question he knew she would: had he killed Goldman?

"Don't be stupid, D, but I wish I had," he whispered, leaning forward. For a second it looked like he was going to kiss her but the sound of Lula returning made him stand up suddenly, his eyes never leaving Dakota's. "Soon."

"But what about the photos?"

"Taken care of, don't worry."

So the night passed by until around 5 am, when Dakota realised she was tired, and, leaving Lula on the sofa with Jackson, she wandered off to bed, her desire for Jackson burning in her stomach, unsatisfied.

The next morning, Dakota found a note on her pillow as she woke.

All it said was:
'Meet me in the woods at midnight by the witch tree.
I'll make sure Lula sleeps heavy.
It's good to see you again, I missed you,
Jackson.'

Just as she was slipping the note between the pages of her diary, Lula came in unannounced.

"Morning love, you all right? It's nearly afternoon actually. Fancy going shopping?" she began, wandering into the half-lit room and opening the curtains.

"Uh yeah, OK. You want to look for a bridesmaid dress?"

"Yeah, why not? Hey, is that your old diary? God you've had that for years. I see you taped some new books to it; had a lot to write about, have you?" she asked, nudging and winking like a school girl.

"Heh heh, oh yeah, you know how I have to write

everything down," she replied slipping the diary under her pillow. "Right OK, give me five minutes, I'll be ready for some shopping!"

Dakota spent the day making sure she kept Lula happy. Everything Lula wanted to do, Dakota did, and every awful dress she had to try on, she tried on with a smile. Everything she was doing was not what she wanted to be doing, but it was all bearable because she knew she would be seeing Jackson again that night, and they would be alone at last.

It seemed to be the longest day of her life. As it wore on, it got harder for her to smile and keep up the act of the little sister home from her adventures, home for good, back to the bosom of her family.

Her family.

What had become of her family? A row of tiny stones to mark where her brothers and sisters lay, one big one to mark where her beloved parents lay, all of them turning to dust over the long years. And all that was left on the earth was Lula, her older, manic depressive, drug-dependent sister. Dakota had spent most of her life picking Lula up out of her depression, making sure she attended her therapy sessions and took her medication. What kind of a life was that? The only things her family had taught her were that people die, and what sort of antidepressants are sedatives. The memories were suddenly painful; the sweet memories of her mother and father were replaced by dark moments of grieving and having to spend all her time making sure Lula didn't accidentally overdose. All there was in her memories now was death, madness and loneliness.

TWENTY-EIGHT: History Repeating

Darkness came late in the July evening, the sky pausing in shades of peach and amber before slipping into darker hues and secrecy.

Dakota had taken herself off to bed early that night, leaving it up to Jackson to make sure Lula took her tablets in time to be deep in slumbers by midnight. All night long Dakota had waited for Jackson to look into her eyes, but not once did he turn those Caribbean blue circles on her; not for one moment did he chance a glance at her with a wink as he used to before. He seemed so different since she had returned. Even though she still sensed the desire in him, radiating out to her, he did not show it in his eyes, that look of wanting she had so often seen, a signal that promised he would come crawling up to her bed in the small hours.

She heard Jackson and Lula go to bed together around ten, and all was silent until half past eleven when she heard him leave the room, pause on the landing, and then head downstairs. At that signal, Dakota slipped her hooded jacket on and crept out of the window onto the garage roof, then jumped down onto the driveway to head off to the woods.

It was a clear night; the sky was endless stars and the soft whisper of the wind through trees was a warm sound of comfort to her. It was only minutes before she reached the edge of the woods.

And she paused.

She had not set foot in the woods since the morning she had found Michelle Taybury. Before that day she had never been afraid of the woods, but now, as she looked into the deepening dark she thought of all the ghosts that wandered there, all the lost children trying to find their way out of the woods and back to their mothers. The shuffling of the trees sounded like their souls, moving through the undergrowth, their still hearts unafraid of the dark now it was all over, now the bad man couldn't touch them anymore. Then she wondered; was he there? Had Goldman returned to these woods to haunt them, to chase down the ghosts of all those children he stole? Would he stand by and watch her walking through, down those paths she always used to take to get to the grove to meet Jackson?

As fear reached its peak in her, she set foot in the forest.

Walking through the routes she could take blindfolded, suddenly the fear left her and was replaced by a feeling of safety, as though she was coming home to warm comforts and familiarity. The trees groaned above her, and shuffled their mighty branches as though they were wings; distant cars hummed briefly in the midnight world and then were gone. No birds chirped; they were all asleep in the high branches, their eyes closed to her and her journey. Only squirrels and foxes whispered in the blind gloom a conspiracy of secrets in the undergrowth, old bird bones and stolen eggs, and weasels grinning in the dark.

But even in the endless night, she could find her, the Witch Tree, and even though the fear had left her, she could not pass her and enter the grove. In her mind, Dakota could still see that little girl with glassy eyes and feared slightly that her ghost would remain there, only standing upright, still and staring with shining eyes and dirty clothes, leaves in her unkempt hair, at her, the girl who let her die.

Jackson arrived only moments later but neither made a move to touch. Only the trees spoke, then finally she found her voice.

"I missed you, that's why I came back."

"Last I heard you were in love. Didn't miss me then, did you?" he began, lighting a cigarette.

"Yeah I know, it didn't work out, I made a mistake. I realised it was you I loved, that I'd been terribly wrong to leave. But I'm back now and I want us to be together... properly," she explained.

"I see... did you read any of my letters?"

"Yes, I read them all, the night before I came home. I kept them all as you sent them, but I didn't want to read them because... well, because I was trying to leave you behind."

"I see."

Something ran across the clearing behind Jackson and Dakota jumped forward, clinging to him. For a second he was rigid under her grip, then slowly, she could feel softness entering the tight muscles of his arms and he put his arms around her, held her so tight that she thought she might never draw breath again. Tears pricked her eyes as the warmth she had dreamt of returned to her. That feeling of being loved and wanted was there again. Jackson made her feel like no other person in the world had: complete.

The kisses that followed were as passionate as they ever had been, as though they were about to devour each other, as though they were the only sustenance left in the dry dead world.

Then suddenly Jackson pushed her away.

"What?" she asked, breathless.

"No, not anymore, this isn't happening anymore," he muttered, turning away, shaking his head to the dark woods.

"What do you mean?"

"I mean it's not going to happen anymore, Dakota. You left me, and you made it clear you didn't want me anymore." He paused as emotion began to surface in him. "I loved you so much and you loved me, but you ruined it!"

"I was wrong, OK? I made a mistake; I thought it would be best for us all if I left because there was no way we could continue without someone getting hurt! I did it for Lula!"

"Yeah I know, but you hurt me in the process! What about me and my feelings? You were mine, and I was yours and you didn't want me anymore, so you threw me aside to get on with a new life. So you could meet new men and do everything I taught you!" He was getting angry and Dakota was getting desperate.

"But I was too young to understand! I can see it all now. I made a mistake and you were right all along; we are meant to be together!"

"No! No, you don't get to change it all anytime you like! You left me and that's your choice. I can't take you back now, because I have learnt to live without you." He shook his fist at her as though he wanted to hit her, and yet the fear of him never returned. She wanted him more than ever now, and he was putting up a fight. This wasn't right!

"Hang on a second. Are you saying you don't love me anymore?"

"No! I love you and I can't help it but I don't want to anymore! You broke my heart, Dakota Grace. After everything I showed you, all the love I gave you, you passed me over for some other bloke you didn't even last five minutes with. That's not love." She thought he was about to cry but he turned away again.

"You can't do this. I do love you and I can't live without you. Please, can't we just calm down and talk it over?"

"No, it's too late. I am marrying Lula and that's it! You had your chance and you showed me you didn't care so I moved on. I have spent the last six months trying to get over you and now you come back and do this? I could kill you!" He growled at her.

"Oh yeah, do you think Lula would be marrying you if she knew what kind of a man you really are? The kind of man who would defile a twelve-year-old girl?" She smirked, suddenly turning on him, his unwavering rejection of her beginning to send shockwaves through her.

"It wasn't like that and you know it! You think she would feel so loved up about you if she knew you wanted me to come to your room every night? That you got pregnant when she never could and then killed it?"

A swift slap across his face stopped his outburst. Rage burned in his eyes momentarily, then cooled.

"Don't try and turn this around, Jackson. You are just as guilty as I am," she snapped angrily.

"I'm going home, and I think you should go back to Ireland soon as the wedding's over, OK?"

"No, it's not OK! I love you!"

In the dark, quivering night, the two figures stood, bruised by the dark, the trees whispering malevolent lies in their ears. As bats flitted through the high trees, life went on elsewhere in the world, and the crimes that had taken place here were forgotten. This place was killing ground, and ghosts peeked out from behind the trees to witness the great battle of love continue in its last weak stages.

Jackson allowed a tear to break from his eye as he looked at her: the one he loved, the one he adored and the one he had promised himself to until the end of time. But, Dakota could see, her Loverman was fading now. All the resolve he had when he wanted her had turned around on her. She had broken his heart and he was punishing her for it, denying her the one thing he knew she could not live without. Him.

"It's over, D," he whispered and turned away, the wind ruffling his hair as his blue eyes looked away from her and down to the floor. Slowly, he began to walk away, ignoring her calling his name.

Seeing him leaving, she knew there was nothing she could do, and as a mixture of grief and rage overtook her she reached down for a rock at her feet.

"But Jackson," she muttered, trance-like, in the gloomy woods, "you should know by now, it's never over."

The rock struck him hard just as he turned his head back towards her on hearing her words, in moments that passed in slow motion. He fell to the ground before he could even turn completely. Silence passed through the woods, trees and animals suddenly still in the summer night, and Dakota felt her legs give way.

She scrambled across the dry earth towards where he lay and took one look into his eyes and knew it was over.

She had seen those eyes before.

He was dead.

TWENTY-NINE: The Sound of Guilt

Dakota felt as if someone was strangling her, her useless throat constricted with shock as she closed the book and turned away from the table where it lay. The images were playing over in her head like a video tape being rewound and played again over and over. Each time the last image was his dead blue eyes looking back at her.

She could feel all that pain again, the same pain she had felt in life at realising the love of her life, her soul-mate, was gone forever. All the horror and disgust she had felt during the re-learning of her life had vanished, replaced by those real feelings, the pain of love, the shock at what she had done. She had taken a life, the life of the man she loved.

All the time she had felt responsible for Michelle Taybury; all that guilt and shame paled in comparison to what she felt now.

She was a murderer.

At last she knew into which category she fell here in Purgatory. She was amongst killers. She was no better than Goldman.

The sound of her sobs echoed through the library, the rain humming in the background as if it had quietened the storm in favour of this new sound.

The sound of guilt surfacing.

What on earth had she done? What had made her a killer? Why did she snap so violently, and kill Jackson for turning his back on her? It was ridiculous, in her earlier years she would have given anything for him to turn away and leave her alone. She must have lost her mind, she decided. The years of abuse had made her mentally unstable and Jackson had finally pushed her over the edge.

Dakota came back to herself, leaving the dark forest behind a door she closed in her head.

The library loomed around her, dark and uncomforting. She needed to get out, and tell Betty.

Tell Betty that she was a murderer, too, just like her. And she thought of the feeling she had when Betty had told her; that slight revulsion at the thought she was sitting so close to someone who had taken a life on purpose. Now she had to turn that judgemental gaze on herself.

She thought of Goldman, laughing maniacally at her all the time, laughing at her disgust of him being a murderer. All that time he knew she was just like him. No wonder he was laughing at her, looking down on him for being a killer when she was no better.

Dakota returned her book to the shelf, deciding she had read enough for now. The mystery of her own death would have to wait; she had to deal with this fresh news first.

The long shadows whispered and the vague outlines of others crouching by lamps or shuffling amongst the high shelves haunted the edges of her vision as she made her way out of the library, feeling again that she needed to be drunk.

As she left the library, she first headed straight to the Bar, but before she got too far down the hall, she remembered David and how she promised she would go back and see him. She felt that she needed to pray now. Knowing why she was there, she felt she needed to start praying, for help or forgiveness, or both.

Past the cockroaches and dust, she made her way to the door that led through to the Chapel, and when she got there found herself looking around to see if anyone was watching her enter the room.

Inside the Chapel, the rain muttered against the windows, shadows of dead trees shivering across the dimly lit room.

"David?" she whispered, unable to see him. Silence returned to her as she searched the room for her young friend, but he was gone.

Strange, she thought. He doesn't leave here much. She

stared at the chair he was sitting in when she last saw him. She wondered if his prayers had finally paid off and he'd been forgiven.

The loneliness of the high room with its deities looking down at her made her realise she did not want to be here right now. I'm a murderer, she thought. I'm not worthy of your gaze.

As quickly as she entered, she left the chapel and hurried away down the hall to the Bar. There seemed to be fewer people around – just the occasional shadow in the poorly lit corridor, but not as many as usual.

The Bar seemed as busy as ever and Danny was asleep against the bar again. A customer had climbed over the bar and was helping himself to bottles of whisky as she approached, searching her pocket for her cigarettes. He paused as she sat at the bar and noticed her eyeing his armful of bottles. After what seemed like a moment's careful thought, he plucked a bottle from his arm and put it down in front of her with a sheepish grin.

"Thanks, pass us some fags while you're back there?" she muttered, her last cigarette dangling from her lips as she crushed the empty packet in her other hand. After grabbing a few packs for himself, he threw two down for her and shuffled away and out into the corridor.

The Bar was quiet, although there were quite a few occupants. They all seemed to be calm for a change, no arguments or shouting, and there weren't many women around either, but Dakota didn't care about the company – she just wanted to drink and sleep, but first she wanted to talk to Danny. She had to tell him what she had found out.

"Danny? Danny?" she whispered, shaking his arm slightly. He woke with a start and stared at her bleary-eyed for a moment before calm seemed to come over him and he reached for his cigarettes.

"So, any wiser?" he asked.

"I'm a killer Danny... I killed someone, that's why I'm here... I know now," she mumbled, half-ashamed, half-pleased to know the truth.

"Well I could have told you that, but I figured you wouldn't believe me." He shrugged, cigarette smoke curling away from his lined face.

"What? How did you know?"

"Well, I just had it figured out, that's all. You certainly weren't a rapist, and I just guessed you had murdered someone."

Dakota froze, slightly angry that he hadn't told her before, slightly fearful as she realised she was truly among her own kind.

"Christ, I wish you'd told me! But you're right – I would have thought you were lying. I'd never believe I was here cos I killed someone, but I did and here I am."

"Who'd you kill?"

"My... lover, he tried to leave me and I killed him."

"I see," he mused, flicking the ash from his cigarette.

"It's true, isn't it, that we meet the same people in each life?" Danny nodded, a sad look in his eyes.

"So why do you think that I was murdered in all my lives by the same soul, but in my last one, I killed my murderer?"

"You finally got there first?" He half laughed.

"Maybe that's what it is. I guess I just wasn't going to let it happen again, eh?" She laughed but tears were pricking her eyes again as she recalled those last moments before Jackson died, that look in his eyes, the way he had held her, telling her that he wanted her but his words saying the opposite. He was leaving her. How dare he? And for that second, she felt the same rage that was in her when she killed him, that deep burning rage in her stomach, rising like bile and blurring her senses, removing all reason. She had felt in those seconds what Jackson had felt in every life before he had killed her, every time he had taken her life away.

It was almost revenge.

Revenge for every life he had taken away from her, and only her soul knew how deep that need for revenge went. It wasn't revenge for leaving her; it was revenge for being the one who decided when it would end... every time. Dakota opened her bottle of whisky and began drinking it down like it was water. The desire to be completely drunk overtook her. She wanted that numbness to take away all the feelings her discovery had put in her. She was a killer and nothing would change that, but she just wanted to forget for a while, forget the horror of it all.

"I think you should go lie down in your room for a while, sleep for a bit before you carry on. What you found out is a shock, and there are more to come, I think," Danny said, getting up and moving behind the bar.

"Yeah, I will. I have to get over this first, before I find out anymore," she agreed and got up, clutching her bottle and smiling warmly at Danny. "Thanks, I'm sorry I woke you up. I just wanted you to know."

"You know what you are now. Does it feel any better than when you didn't know?" he asked, not returning her warmth.

"No, it doesn't feel any better, but at least I know. I can be miserable but at least I know why." She laughed, but her laughter seemed wrong, and she looked around at the ugly, angry faces in the gloom.

"Go to bed," he muttered and began looking perplexed at the lack of bottles behind the bar.

"So you're a murderer too, eh? Who did you kill?"

"My Lover. She tried to leave me so I killed her," he said coldly in the distant whisper of rain. Dakota nodded, realising it was not the time for questions, and headed out of the Bar to her room.

She was too drunk to negotiate the elevator, and accidentally said twenty-one instead of her own room number of twenty. Even more confusing was the fact that when the elevator opened its doors, she was facing room twenty-one. She peered along to see her own room door and wondered why the room had moved, or if it was the elevator that had moved.

The elevator ride was no good for her equilibrium. As she stepped out onto her landing, she stumbled. A feeling like standing on a moving boat overtook her and she moved, slowly, drunkenly, as though the hotel was floating on an angry sea.

"Ugh, fuggin' whisky," she muttered to the empty corridor. As she began to rummage around her coat pocket for her keys she became aware of music playing somewhere. A low and lazy tune was creeping out from one of the rooms, and as she laid her hands on her room key, recognition of the tune clicked in her brain.

It was Nick Cave, the last song on the album Jackson had given her, and as she moved slowly and unsteadily towards her door, she knew the music was coming from her room.

For a second a burning feeling set up in her stomach; fear took form in her but also rage.

Who was in her room and how dare they?

She burst angrily through the door, to find it empty apart from the life in the stereo and the fluttering curtains. Tired of the stalking games, she kicked the stereo until it went silent and slammed her door causing moans to come from other rooms.

The loud noise was a bit too much for her own brain and she collapsed groaning onto the bed where she passed out.

Sometime later she woke up, her skull thumping just as it had when she first woke in Purgatory. As she slowly opened her eyes she realised the light was out, and she was sure she had left it on when she lay down on the bed.

Turning her head towards the rest of the room she noticed something over by the curtains.

A shape was flickering in and out of visibility like a poor TV reception or a faulty fluorescent light bulb.

Dakota's eyes widened in fear as it began to permeate her brain, the image reappearing like a strobe light until finally it stabilised in the darkness to a solid form. A tall figure of a man was standing a few feet away by the fluttering curtains, his face momentarily lit by the glow of a match as he lit a cigarette.

"Hello D," said Jackson.

THIRTY: The Reunion

Dakota wasn't sure how to react, but the first thing she did was reach over and turn the light back on so she could see him properly.

And there he was, the love of her life, looking as beautiful as he had in life, smoking a cigarette and looking at her with those eyes that always made her give in.

Tears sprang up in her eyes as she looked at him and her whole life with him seemed so clear in her head again. And as clear as any other image was the last time she saw him, lying dead on the forest floor.

"Was it you? I mean has it been you following me around here? I thought it was Woods, I mean Goldman," she stuttered, unsure at how he was going to behave now he was face to face with his killer.

"Yeah, it was me. Thought you would have guessed by the poem," he replied calmly, his eyes flicking from the bedside table and back to her.

Suddenly she remembered the poem that she had found in her bed. How stupid was she? It could have been written by him, but she guessed it was Baudelaire.

"The French poem, is it? The one I never understood?" she asked, still shaking.

"It's called The Ghost. How funny that I used to recite it to you for all those years and here we are now, and I'm still haunting you." He wasn't laughing.

*"As others reign through tenderness,
Over your life and youthfulness,
I want, myself, to reign through fear."*

His words repeating the very poem she had found in her bed set a new chill in her bones. She felt odd that she had been so intimate with him in life, even unafraid at times of his wrath, as though she knew him so well he could do nothing to make her feel in danger. But now it was different, just like it was when he first laid hands on her, a deep burning fear that she did not know what he was capable of, or what death had done to his feelings for her.

"I'm sorry... that I killed you," she managed, worried that her apology might make him angrier, but hoping it might make him calmer.

"Well, from all I've read since I got here, seems I was due a violent death. You finally managed to get in there before me, eh?"

Dakota laughed uneasily, waiting for him to turn on her. She began wondering if she could make it to the door before him, or would a sudden break for freedom only make the situation worse.

"I'm sorry, I don't know why I did it. I can't recall any of it clearly."

"Seems you couldn't remember anything clearly, been spending all that time down at the Library. Can you really remember nothing?" he queried.

"Well I remember everything up to killing you now, but no, when I got here, I had no memory. But after reading for a while and judging by our past lives, I assumed you had killed me, but now I—"

"Ahh, so it's still an unsolved mystery, eh? Hehe, that must be unbearable." He laughed coldly.

"You know... you know who killed me?"

"Of course. I followed you very closely after you murdered me, you see, D. I never could bear to be parted from you, and those feelings got even stronger after I was dead. But you don't remember any of it, do you? How amusing." He smirked as he stamped his cigarette out on her floor.

"Well, are you going to tell me?" she snapped, finding herself growing tired of his game.

"No, you are going to remember by yourself, D, and I can't wait to see your face!" he began, walking across to her bed. "How many times have I stood over your bed? How many times have you been afraid of me? And how many times have you loved that feeling? This is just one more time, D, and you have so many more to remember. We're going back to the Library together and I am going to watch you remember."

"You're sadistic. Why did I love you?" She spat back, angry that even now when they were both dead, he was still in control of her.

"It's all you knew how to do," he replied and grabbed her for a long angry kiss, before dragging her off the bed and pushing her out into the dim corridor.

The noise she made from slamming into the wall opposite caused Betty to open her own door. She stared out wide eyed at Dakota, looking a bit confused.

"You all right, love?" she asked.

"Yeah, just great. Betty, this is Jackson," she replied, rubbing her arm where it had smacked the wall.

"Eh?" she asked, peering out down the corridor. Dakota looked at Jackson who just smiled and pressed the button to call the elevator.

"Can't you see him?" Dakota asked incredulously.

"You had way too much vodka I think, girl. Perhaps you ought to get some kip, eh?" Betty spoke to her like she was an idiot in need of calming down.

"Are you saying you can't see him? He's right there!" she half shouted, pointing right at Jackson. Betty shook her head and tutted.

"You really are obsessed with him, aren't you? Get some sleep, love, we'll talk later," she muttered and closed her door.

Just then the elevator door opened and Jackson pushed Dakota in.

"Stop fucking pushing me! Why can't she see you?"

"I don't matter to her, obviously," he shrugged. "By rights, you shouldn't be able to see me either, but it seems you can communicate with souls in other dimensions."

"What? You are in another dimension? Is that why you kept appearing and vanishing?"

"Yeah, I didn't realise you could see me at all, until you shouted at me in the corridor by the library. I was most surprised," he offered as the elevator slammed onto the ground floor.

"Why can you see me, then?"

"I asked Ariel about that. She said that they can't control every emotion and the strongest feelings cause strange changes in the laws of Purgatory: killers see their victims if they end up here too, victims see their killers. And I saw you, the minute you arrived." He paused as the door of the elevator opened and he moved her out into the hall. "I was standing right here, waiting for you, I saw you pass over, D, and I was waiting for you when you finally got off the floor of the lobby. I've barely been apart from you since, but once I realised you could see me I had to be more careful. It's emotion that makes me visible to you, just as it made you visible to Lula. So your friend Betty was actually right when she said you were obsessed with me. If you weren't we wouldn't be able to see each other."

Dakota recalled her sister's screams when she saw her, how awful it must have been for her to see her dead sister.

"So you have been with me since I got here?"

"Not always right beside you but close enough to know where you were all the time." His eyes grew intense as he stared at her; he had looked at her that way so many times, she thought he was going to kiss her again and her stomach tightened. "Told you I'd never let you go," he whispered before grabbing her and pushing her down the corridor towards the library.

"Heh, so we're special, huh? Able to see each other across dimensions and all that?" She attempted a laugh as she regained her footing.

"Yep, you are walking around your dimension talking to yourself and I am doing the same in mine," he replied as they wandered past the guttering lights.

"So where are you?"

"Just another dimension. It isn't planned, but sometimes, as I said, the rules get broken and some of us break through to the other dimensions of this place," he muttered, lighting another cigarette.

"Lucky old me stuck with Goldman though, eh?" Dakota tried humour again, whilst rooting around for her own cigarettes.

"Don't worry, I can see him too, and vice versa, I suppose we must have had a 'special' relationship, too. Can you shut up now? You're boring me, D." He sighed.

They finally reached the Library in silence and she went in, heading straight for her own book on the shelf again.

Dakota settled down at a table and lit herself a cigarette as she turned the pages to where she had finished. Again the images of Jackson lying dead in the woods flooded her mind. She looked up at him sheepishly.

"Do you know what's so funny about you killing me, D?" he said, sensing what she was thinking. "I wasn't leaving you."

"What?" She looked utterly shocked and confused. "What do you mean?"

"I'm surprised you didn't know me better. I was testing you again, punishing you for ever leaving. I thought you would just cry a lot and be depressed, and then I was going to leave Lula." He was almost laughing. "Then you went and killed me! I can't believe you fell for it!" His laughter disturbed the quiet air of the Library, and left Dakota feeling unnerved. She couldn't ever remember hearing him laugh like that. The blow was equal to discovering she had killed him in the first place. It was all for nothing. She would have had him to herself anyway; she had ruined everything by not seeing through his game. She was even more disgusted with herself.

Furious, she ignored Jackson's laughter and turned back to the book, to the last chapters of her life.

THIRTY-ONE: The Killer

The moments that followed Dakota's realisation that she had actually killed Jackson were oddly calm and organised. She picked up the rock she had killed him with and walked a few feet away to the brook that babbled past the clearing, when she got to the icy cold water she washed the rock and placed it on the bed of the brook.

Returning to where he lay, she stopped to look around. She knew he might not be found for days here, so she took him by the wrist and dragged him out of the clearing and through the undergrowth towards the path. She strained hard to move him. With each second that she tugged at his lifeless body, pulling him through the ferns, she felt more and more as though the muscles in her arms were about to burst. He was heavy and though she was strong, she was not strong enough to pull him all the way out onto the path. Pausing by a tree to catch her breath, she decided she could take him no further and would just have to hope someone would chance upon him.

Her mind trawled through remembered images of crime programmes on the television as she leant down and pulled his wallet from his back pocket, all the while carefully avoiding looking at his face.

Then she simply turned away and after a few moments of looking down at Jackson's lifeless face, she walked out of the woods and back to the house, where she climbed up silently into her bedroom.

Back inside she opened her bedroom door a crack and listened to Lula's heavy breathing as she slept soundly in the other room. She had a feeling that Jackson had perhaps given her sister a slightly stronger dose that night – just one more tablet crushed up and dropped in her wine, as she had seen him do many times before.

Pulling Jackson's wallet from her pocket, she didn't even pause to look at it before hiding it under the floorboards with her diaries.

Assured that Lula was undisturbed, Dakota got changed and got back into bed; and then for the first time in years Dakota fell straight to sleep, thinking somewhere deep down in her soul that tonight she needn't stay awake, because Jackson would not be coming to her room.

Her dreams that night were dark and full of deep forests whose late night noises were strange and unnatural. She heard Goldman there, laughing his wicked laugh out in the gloom, and as she walked alone, she sensed another presence there, another being tracking her through the endless night and moaning trees. She felt slight fear in her belly, low down, just like she had those nights when she heard Jackson mount the stairs. But the fear was mixed with desire and half of her yearned for the moment that other being would step out into the path ahead of her.

Somewhere not too far from her she heard someone singing.

When Dakota opened her eyes that first morning she screamed.

As her weary eyes flickered she was aware of a presence in the room, something watchful, something too close to her bed for comfort. And in the split second her eyes opened, she saw Jackson leaning over her bed.

Her door flew open and Lula ran in. "What? What's wrong?" she half screamed herself.

"Uh... oh god Lula, sorry!" she stuttered as the previous night flooded back into her head. "I thought there was someone in the room; I just got a fright," she managed, her heart bursting in her chest.

"Oh dear, were you having a bad dream?" Lula walked across to her sister and stroked her hair. "God, you're soaked with sweat! Must have been a bad one!"

"Yeah, I guess so." Dakota wiped the sweat away from her forehead, as Lula left the room muttering about tea and how she'd better wake Jackson up.

Dakota lay back down and listened to Lula go downstairs and start searching for Jackson. Before long she heard the phrase, "It's not like him to go out so early," over and over again.

She finally got up and got dressed, repeating in her head that she had to keep her act going and that everything would be all right – no one would suspect her of killing Jackson. She just had to keep her head together and all would be fine.

It wasn't long before Lula was panicking, ringing round everyone she knew to ask if they had seen him anywhere. All replied no and the more Lula heard the word no, the more she panicked.

It was early afternoon when she called the police, but it was not long after when the police called to say a body had been found in Church Woods.

It was all very reminiscent of the night their parents had died. Lula lost control of herself fairly quickly, but this time she begged Dakota to go and identify the body for her. As much as she wanted to refuse, she knew she couldn't put her sister through the horror of seeing another dead loved one. It would have to be her, and she would have to be upset.

Lula's state was deteriorating even before she left for the police station, so Dakota called the doctor out and got one of Lula's work colleagues stay with her; she was pretty sure her sister would need sedating.

At the hospital, Dakota felt numb still, as she waited to be brought through to identify her sister's fiancé. All feeling for him and what she had done seemed oddly absent and she was unsure if this was self-preservation or whether she really didn't care at all about the fact that she had murdered her lover.

Everything seemed long drawn out, the walk to the

mortuary was eternal, the corridors endless, but when she got there and the cloth was pulled back, it suddenly changed.

She stared at Jackson's body and remembered that she had to be upset, but as she began to think about how to relate this to the people standing beside her she realised she was already sobbing, almost inconsolably, her entire body shaking with grief and loss. He was gone. The one thing that kept her going was gone forever. He would never look into her eyes again and make her feel like the only person in the world. He would never read poetry to her nor sing low and quiet in her ear about how she was her Loverman, till the bitter end.

She looked at him for only a second or two before turning away to sob, sudden guilt rising in her, quelled by turning from the body.

She pulled herself together fairly quickly and composed herself to answer any questions.

When they took her to sit down and gave her a glass of water, she heard words like: "I'm so sorry for your loss," and "He must have been like a father to you." There was a policeman there who told her it looked like murder and that they would need to know more about what Jackson had done the previous night, and as easy as that, the lies came.

"He was downstairs when I went to bed. I never heard him go out. Lula mustn't have known either because when she went downstairs this morning she said she was going to have to wake him up," she managed, wiping tears away with a withering tissue.

"Was he supposed to be asleep downstairs, then?"

"Yes, he always slept downstairs. Well, not always anymore, he mostly sleeps in with Lula now, but sometimes he doesn't make it to bed before he falls asleep."

After a few more questions they let her go home and break the news to Lula. They would be visiting the house in the next day or two to ask some more questions.

The journey home in the taxi was not long enough for Dakota to sort everything out in her head and before she knew it she was back home to face a sedated Lula and tell her that her fiancé was dead.

Lucky for Dakota, Lula's friend offered to stay the night, which meant she could go and hide in her room and try to block out the sounds of wailing sobs that continued through till the early hours of the morning when Lula passed out from exhaustion and Dakota passed out from drinking a bottle of Jackson's whisky.

The days that followed were difficult but, lucky for Dakota, their cousins rallied round to help out with watching over Lula.

The police called round the day after to ask more questions about Jackson's movements and they eventually revealed that they were treating his death as murder.

"But who would want to murder my Jackson? He didn't hurt anyone, didn't have any enemies. I just don't understand!" sobbed Lula as the detectives looked listlessly at her. Dakota felt like she was about to confess, scream suddenly that it was her, that he had been her lover and she had murdered him out of rage for spurning her advances.

But instead she lit a cigarette and looked into the ashtray.

"Is his wallet here? Only there wasn't one found on the body," asked the detective who had introduced himself as Detective Finley.

Lula sat up and peered out into the hallway to see if his wallet was on the hall table where he always left it. She choked back a sob as she shook her head.

"I haven't seen it anywhere else," Dakota added to her sister's silent response.

"So why do you think he would have gone out?" Finley asked. "I have no idea, but he did used to go out late sometimes, to the twenty-four-hour garage up the road if he ran out of fags," offered Dakota steadily.

"Hmmm, but he would have no reason to visit the woods?" asked Finley, motioning to his companion to make some notes.

"No, not that we know of," she replied holding onto her sister's shaky hand.

"Could he have been meeting someone?"

Lula snapped out of her whimpering sob for a moment and looked up at Detective Finley.

"Who? Who would he have been meeting?" she asked, agitated.

"Well, I hoped you might be able to help me with that, but was it possible he was having an affair or in any trouble?"

"Uh, well, uh... no, of course not!" Lula stuttered, dragging her hair from her face. Dakota found herself looking at Lula suspiciously as though she knew more than her.

"Lula, was he having an affair?" she asked as her mind ran away with her.

"No!"

"OK, well if you think of any reasons why he might have been out there, can you let us know? It looks like a mugging gone wrong to us, but we will have to look into it further," the Detective said as he and his colleague stood to leave. "I think we have bothered you enough today."

Dakota saw them out, her heart thumping in her chest. She was suddenly terrified that she would be found out and put in prison, with Lula finally sent to a mental hospital.

She knew that there was no way anyone would ever find out about her and Jackson now as only she remained to tell the tale.

Except Goldman.

If he was still alive, he was the only other one who knew about her and Jackson. While Jackson may have removed the evidence from Goldman's house, Goldman could still turn up.

Though she had always suspected that Jackson had finally murdered Goldman and buried him in the woods, she was unsure. He could always resurface – not that it would be in his interests, seeing as he was a wanted man. But she knew Goldman; she knew he got almost as excited about others' misery as he did about little girls.

Her racing mind was interrupted by a scream and a crash in the kitchen.

Dakota ran to the kitchen to see Lula on the floor, leaned

up against the cupboard and shaking, white as a sheet with the remains of a teacup around her legs.

"Lula? Lula, what's wrong?" she asked softly seeing her sister's fragile condition as she approached and knelt down beside her. Lula seemed to be staring at the air in the doorframe. "Lula? Tell me what's happened?"

"It was him… he was right there, just looking at me as I turned around to put the tea on… he was there," she muttered over and over until Dakota broke the spell and got her to look at her.

"Who was there?"

"Jackson," she muttered and immediately broke into tears.

Dakota felt the hairs on her arms standing up as she recalled seeing him in her room that morning. Sudden fear gripped her stomach and the compulsion to return her gaze to the doorway was unbearable.

He was not there, and she was half-grateful but half-sad.

If he had been there, why didn't he appear to her instead of Lula? So it seems he really did love Lula and want her at the end, she thought, a seed of that jealousy germinating in her again.

She had killed him but she wanted nothing more than to see him again, see those eyes once more.

It was early afternoon, and the kettle clicked off the boil as she sat holding a sobbing Lula in her arms. And all she could do was count the feelings that were fighting for control of her: sadness, fear, jealousy, loneliness and rage.

THIRTY-TWO:
The Return of Jackson Shade

The following day there was a nasty shock waiting for Dakota on the front of the newspaper.

The face of Goldman stared at her from the hall floor, as the paper carried a story about a possible sighting of the man locally.

The missing suspect in a string of child murders was sighted by a man and woman in the area of St Brigid's Cemetery.

The man, James Goldman, has been missing for six months from his home in Little Mort and is the only suspect for the murders of seven children in the same area and neighbouring villages of Marbury and Chapel Allen. His home was found to contain large amounts of child pornography and many photographs taken by himself of several victims of unsolved murders. The discovery of these pictures has placed him as the lead suspect in the 'Babes in the Woods Murders.' They involved the Michelle Taybury murder along with the murders of six other girls whose bodies were all discovered in Pan's Wood, Little Mort after an anonymous tip-off led the police to the body of Taybury. Though a local man confessed and was convicted, he has been cleared of murder charges but now faces being detained under the Mental Health Act and charges of perverting the course of justice.

No evidence was found connecting anyone to the murders until Goldman's disappearance led to the search of his home.

A man matching his description was seen yesterday in the St Brigid's cemetery which adjoins Pan's Wood. Police are asking local residents to be alert and to report any further sightings, although they also advise the public not to approach this man as he could be dangerous.

Dakota wanted to collapse but some minimal strength in her legs kept her standing up. She could picture him, skulking through the woods waiting for her, or waiting for some other little girl to wander by so that he could snatch her away, too.

As nausea wavered in her throat she made her way slowly into the lounge. For an instant, Jackson was sitting in his favourite chair, smoking a cigarette. Dakota screamed and jumped back smacking her head off the doorframe.

Next thing she was aware of was Lula's voice saying her name. When she opened her eyes, she found she was lying on the floor halfway between the lounge and the hall with the newspaper still gripped in her hand.

"What happened? I heard a scream and when I came down you were lying here!"

"Uh sorry, I hit my head, I jumped cos I saw..." She stopped and looked at the armchair, now very empty and frightening.

"Have you seen him, too?" asked Lula, a smile on her face suddenly, as though someone had just told her she wasn't insane and that everything was right with the world.

"I thought I did, but I am still half-asleep, you know..."

"I knew I had seen him! He has come back to us!" Lula was ecstatic as she helped Dakota to her feet. "I knew he would not leave me! Maybe he can tell us who killed him!"

"Lula, I think we might just be a bit upset, you know, and seeing things," suggested Dakota as she felt carefully around the lump rising on the back of her head, her eyes nervously scanning the room for a shadowy figure.

"No, I know what I saw and that's it. I knew he wouldn't leave me to cope alone. He has come to help us deal with everything, D!" Lula was happier than she had been for days, as though a new light was lit inside her.

And from that day, Lula didn't need sedating. She returned to life as it had been before Jackson had died, suddenly empowered and full of hope. Dakota had never seen

Lula so strong and she felt glad for her. She was quite relieved that she no longer had to watch over her sister and that her duties were done.

She spoke to the police regularly but always laughed with Dakota afterwards how she was going to solve the case before the police because Jackson was going to tell her himself who had murdered him.

And though Dakota laughed with her sister, deep down she was afraid that Lula was right.

Lula claimed more and more that she had spoken with Jackson and they had comforted each other, but she said he always claimed not to be ready to discuss his murder.

Part of Dakota just thought her sister had finally lost her marbles, but another part thought it was real.

Although she had not spoken to Jackson, she had seen him regularly, though only for split seconds. In her dreams he haunted the edges of her vision, always slipping away as she turned to face him; he was like a tease, a tantalising glimpse of his proximity to her, but she could not touch him.

In her waking life he was the same, a flash of an image, a shape at the corner of her eye, a shadow across her door or in the corner of her unlit room.

One night she dreamt of being in her bedroom and she could hear 'Loverman' playing somewhere. The room was dark but hot, the curtains fluttered slightly in a breeze from the open window, and in the distance she could hear cars passing, far off in their late night journeys. Beside her bed the time glowed red for 1.30am.

Low down and faint she could hear the words to the song playing:

"Loverman, since the world began, forever Amen till the end of time..."

The door to her room was haloed in a dim yellow light coming from the hallway.

Then a shadow broke up the halo as a figure moved outside the door. It was Jackson and he was humming along to the music that was playing somewhere in her room. When the door opened, all she could see was the silhouette of the man with long hair that just touched his shoulders. He had on a pair of trousers and nothing else, but she could not see his face. All he was was a black shape moving slowly and silently save for his low humming.

Although she seemed quite still and at ease there was a great knot growing in her stomach, twisting and turning her stomach over. As he closed the door and made his way towards her bed in the dark, she realised it was fear she felt.

"There's a devil waiting outside your door... weak with evil and broken by the world... shouting your name and he's asking for more..."

He had put the song back to the beginning and it was playing over again as she felt the weight of him lie down on the bed beside her and all the while he sang along quietly. Fear was becoming confusion. She knew this man – why was she so afraid of him? He said nothing to her; he just sang along, low and soft to the words of the song. He was faceless movement beside her in the dark, and he drew closer to her ear as he whispered the words:

"Take off that dress... I'm coming down... I'm your Loverman..."

The room seemed to be growing hotter and she could feel her body beginning to perspire as she smelt moisture growing on his brow. Then he put his hand under her nightdress and buried it between her legs.

She awoke sweating in the dark room and snapped the light on, shaking violently. The dream had been so real, so vivid that she was convinced it had actually happened. But her CD-player sat silent and Jackson was not in the room. Still she could almost smell him in the air, feel the pressure on her from where he had recently touched her.

The more she thought about it, the more she was sure it had happened. At that moment, her stereo exploded into life with the screaming voice of Nick Cave:

"I'm your Loverman! Til the bitter end!"

Dakota thought she was going to die of heart failure, but with a rush of fear she leapt from the bed and pulled the plug from the wall throwing the room into silence, before passing out on the floor.

The same dream began to recur for Dakota, and every time she was convinced it was real. It didn't help that Lula was acting like Jackson wasn't dead and talked constantly about how she had seen him that day. On top of that, Dakota thought she caught glimpses of him around the house and even out in the street.

She had always believed in ghosts but wondered why her parents had never come back. Now she was convinced she was being haunted by the man she murdered.

She frequently woke to the image of him standing over her bed, but his silhouette was always gone before she could blink her eyes clear of sleep, and while she was furious at his intrusions, she was angrier that he didn't hang around long enough to talk to her.

The murder investigation turned up few leads and Lula and Dakota were questioned several times by the police leading them both to realise they were suspects. Fortunately for Dakota they were more interested in Lula because of her history of mental illness.

But even though it would have taken no more than a few well-placed words for the police to arrest Lula, she couldn't have borne the guilt of sending her own sister to prison for a crime she had not committed. She had accepted that if they ever turned up the evidence to prove she had murdered Jackson, she would admit to it all and accept her fate, but she was comfortable in the knowledge that no one would ever know about her and Jackson, thus her motive was concealed. As long as Goldman didn't turn himself in and spill the beans, she was safe.

The detectives had thrown in the whole 'did you hate Jackson because he tried to take the place of your dead father' routine, but Dakota's responses were convincing due to the fact that she had never resented Jackson for moving in. Her genuine sadness at his death was beneficial because the detectives could see her cry every time they talked about his death. She told them simply, "He was like my big brother and he always took care of me. I can't believe he's gone..." and then she would sob over the death of her parents and they would feel sorry for her.

Eventually they released Jackson's body for burial after they had taken all the evidence they needed from him, and the Crow sisters began to plan the funeral.

Dakota's twenty-first birthday passed unnoticed, and she celebrated alone that night with a bottle of red wine in her room.

Lula seemed very calm about everything, still. Her nighttime visits and chats with Jackson's ghost seemed to be doing her the world of good.

"You seem so together about this funeral, Lula. You weren't like this for Mum and Dad's," said Dakota one evening as they drank wine and decided what music should be played.

"Well, maybe if Mum and Dad had visited me I might have handled things better, but now Jackson has talked to me about everything, I know it's just his body we are burying, not him!" She smiled as though she were trying to comfort Dakota.

"I guess that's true. It's just... he is gone."

"No, he isn't, not for me! I see him more now than I did when he was alive!" She laughed and sipped her wine. "I'm sorry you don't get to speak to him, but I know you see him. It's just that he and I had... well, a different and stronger bond than you had with him. That's maybe why he can speak with me."

Dakota nodded and wondered if Jackson was punishing her by not speaking to her. That's so typical of him, she thought.

"Are you going to invite his father?"

"No, his older brother will be coming but that's all," replied Lula without looking up.

"You can't not invite a man to his own son's funeral," Dakota said warily.

"D, he died a year or so ago. That's why he won't be there."

"He died? How come it was never mentioned? Did Jackson go to the funeral?"

"Look, Jackson and his father were not very close so he never talked about it. I think he may have visited his grave since, but it wasn't a sad parting so that was that. Now the music…" And with that Lula changed the subject.

Lula decided that Jackson would have liked to have the Nick Cave song 'Into My Arms' played at his funeral and there would be a poem read by herself and, if Dakota wanted to, she could read one, too.

Her mind strayed to the Baudelaire book he had been reading the day Lula met him, and she wondered if there was anything suitable in there. But how could she stand up there, in front of everyone, and pretend not to be saying goodbye to the love of her young life? Even though she kept it all together quite well most of the time, sometimes, late at night, she sobbed into her pillow – great, shuddering, back-arching sobs fed by her deep loss and unbearable guilt. She would ache for him, long for that touch again, the feel of those hands, to be at the mercy of his gaze and feel his burning kisses on her.

How could she hide her deep, bone-crushing sorrow from all those people as her eyes fell on the coffin where his dead body lay?

Two days before the funeral, Lula took Dakota to the funeral home so that she could see Jackson one last time. They arrived in the quiet lobby where paintings of trees and fields adorned the walls along with old-fashioned photos of the local area. Dakota waited patiently and silently as Lula spoke to the funeral director about payment and the funeral arrangements in between tears. All the while she became more aware that Jackson's lifeless body was lying in a coffin in a room not far away. His presence was there; she felt it as the hairs on her arms stood up. Even though he was dead, she could still feel his presence nearby, invisible and daunting.

Moments later, Lula followed the funeral director around the corner to the room where Jackson was laid out. Dakota was close behind, her head bowed, dreading seeing him again. She had seen him twice since he died and now she had to see him again.

"Lula, do you mind if I go in after you? I think you should be alone with him, you know?" Dakota asked just as her sister was about to enter the room. Lula turned and nodded, her eyes already glassy with tears.

The long minutes passed as she listened to her sister sniffling and whispering to her dead fiancé's body and eventually she came out, eyes red but with a smile on her lips as she looked at her sister.

"It's OK, he looks fine. I'm glad I saw him. You go on in there and say goodbye," Lula managed with a broken voice, touching her sister's arm.

Dakota walked past her sister towards the door that lay open. She could already see the foot of the coffin as she moved slowly into the dim room with flock wallpaper. She wondered for a moment if they had actually made the room look gothic on purpose, but the thought soon left her head as she moved towards the coffin and looked in.

A sudden stillness overtook her, as she stared frozen at the body in the coffin. When she had seen him the moments after he died and later at the morgue, she had not looked at him properly.

But now she was staring at him and she could not tear her eyes away from him. He looked like he was asleep and at any moment would open his eyes, but there was something wrong. Even though her eyes showed her what looked like the Jackson she knew, there was an absence of something that gave her the deepest awareness that he was truly gone.

Dakota felt as though he was there in that tiny gothic room, but he was not lying in the coffin; he was somewhere else, leaning against the red walls and watching her intently. She was certain that if she turned away she would see him standing there, but she did not turn away from his body. It was all so raw and real: the stillness of the room, the knowledge that Jackson would never move again, the sense that his soul had gone and all that was left was a shell, the hard outer casing that was the appearance of Jackson Shade.

But what had made Jackson a person, a living being, was gone. Now he was an empty church, still and cold.

Without moving or shaking, she was crying. Tears were streaming down her face and dripping down her neck, but she could not feel anything except a gaping hole inside her, as though in killing Jackson, in robbing him of that thing that made him real, she had also lost a part of herself. She felt that part of her soul had been taken by Jackson as he slipped away that night, and now she was only half-alive. Half of her was lost to the woods and she would never get it back until she, too, stopped breathing.

THIRTY-THREE: The Funeral

That morning it was autumn suddenly.

Dakota stood and looked out of the window and saw the first leaves had fallen and the wind was pulling more down to sleep for the winter. Jackson would have liked it: the earth going to sleep for winter just as he was interred. He would have thought it poetic.

She turned back to her bed and blinked rapidly to allow her eyes to adjust from the bright sun outside to the darkness of her room. As her eyes grew accustomed once more to the dark she noticed a sheet of paper poking out from under her duvet. Wondering what she had left lying around, she walked over and picked the sheet up from where she had recently been lying. The paper was creased in a way that led her to believe she may have slept all night on it.

However, her calm demeanour slipped into sheer panic as she recognised Jackson's distinct block capital writing.

All that was written was a four-verse poem, entitled 'The Ghost' by Baudelaire. Written beneath it was a French title, 'Le Revenant' and at once she realised what it was. Jackson had many times recited that poem to her in French and had never told her the English version. It seemed that now he was dead, he was quite happy to share the information with her.

"Like an angel of wild eye,
I shall return to where you lie
And towards you, noiseless, glide
With the shades of eventide.

I shall give you, dusky one,
Kisses icy as the moon,

*Embraces that a snake would give
As it crawled around a grave.*

*When the sombre morning comes
You will find your lover gone,
My place cold till night draws near.*

*As others reign through tenderness,
Over your life and youthfulness,
I want, myself, to reign through fear."*

Nausea washed over her and she sat down weakly on the bed; it was too much for her. Today of all days.

The sounds of Lula getting dressed woke her from her trance and she ran out into the hallway.

"You all right, D?" asked Lula, looking more fabulous than she had ever done in her life, with a sharp suit and perfect make-up.

"Uh, yeah, I just need to get washed up and dressed and I will be ready, all right? Are you OK?" she asked, mildly perturbed by her sister's almost sinister calm.

"I'm just fine!" Lula smiled and went downstairs.

Within a couple of hours all the family had arrived at the house and Dakota found herself standing in the hallway waiting for the funeral cars to arrive to take them to the church. The silence was unbearably uncomfortable, nobody knowing what to say to each other as Lula busied herself with nothing in particular.

Dakota was standing once more facing the photograph of the Dakota Badlands her father had taken. And again that feeling of utter loneliness washed over her, and memories of her mother comforting her were enough to make the tears start.

"What's wrong, D?" asked Lula, appearing at her elbow. Dakota noticed a faint smell of whisky, weakly masked by perfume and mouthwash.

"Nothing, just thinking of Mum and Dad," she replied,

wiping the tears from her face. "It's a bit early for whisky, isn't it?"

"Don't tell me what to do, D. Let's just try and get through the day, shall we?" her sister answered sharply.

When the cars arrived, Dakota found herself with Lula and another person she had not yet met, but was alarmed when her eyes met his to recognise something of Jackson in them.

"Oh D, this is Marlon, Jackson's cousin. He has to ride with us because he is the only immediate family from his side," explained Lula, unable to take her eyes off the man sat beside her.

Dakota felt badly for her sister, seeing that look of adoration that she reserved only for her Prince Jackson. She wondered if Lula would ever get over his death properly. Or would she spend the rest of her life having late night conversations with his ghost?

The thought then occurred to her that if Lula was staying awake at night, she couldn't have been taking her medication. She realised that it wasn't a good time to discuss this with her sister, so she contented herself with looking out of the window for the short drive to St Brigid's church.

The church was sadly empty apart from about fifteen people, a poignant indication of Jackson's solitary life and how he had only really had Lula and herself for many years. Dakota wondered where his father was buried and what had happened to his mother. She found it hard to believe that after all the years she had shared with Jackson, she still knew so little about him. She had tried often to find out more about his background but had been met with silences.

Dakota had declined Lula's offer to read something at the service, but when it came to be Lula's turn to read the poem she had chosen, she was so distraught she begged Dakota to read it for her.

She walked up to the front, nervous and desperately aware that all eyes were on her, and after a few breaths she began to read a poem that she had heard before, only last time it had come from Jackson's lips.

"Lula wanted me to read this poem by James Joyce, on her behalf… It was one of Jackson's favourites." She paused before she began to read words about rain and dead lovers.

"Rain on Rahoon falls softly, softly falling,
Where my dark lover lies.
Sad is his voice that calls me, sadly calling,
At grey moonrise.

Love, hear thou
How soft, how sad his voice is ever calling,
Ever unanswered, and the dark rain falling,
Then as now.

Dark too our hearts, O love, shall lie and cold
As his sad heart has lain
Under the moongrey nettles, the black mould
And muttering rain."

It felt odd for her to be reading a love poem to Jackson in front of everyone, but they all knew it was supposed to be from Lula's lips, so nobody could have guessed that she was indeed speaking her own feelings for him, too. But for one moment she feared that Lula might have read something in her eyes, in the quiet tears that slipped down her cheek as she read those words. Could she have seen it? The heart of her broken in two, pulled out on show to everyone? Or was she really that practised at hiding her feelings that she managed to even hide that deepest of emotions? Loss.

Dakota could not help but shed some tears when his coffin was carried away and out into the waiting cemetery to be interred. In her mind, she could see him walking away from her in the moments before the rock struck his head and he hit the floor. She felt like he was still walking away from her and always would be.

"Oh D, this is the very graveyard where we met, where I first fell in love with him, and here we are again, only he is going to be a part of this place now. He should be here, lying on one of the graves, reading his books as though no one else mattered." Lula sobbed as they walked slowly to where the freshly dug grave yawned up from the earth, waiting for its latest guest.

The sun that had been shining that morning was gone, and the first spots of rain were falling on the headstones, on all the graves that lay around, her family, her dear mother and father and all her dead brothers and sisters. Now she would have another grave to visit, another place to sit in the rain.

As the priest began his graveside eulogy, Dakota's eyes wandered around the quiet cemetery, over the many headstones and statues, to the distance where she could just make out the Boncoeur crypt where Lula and Jackson had consummated their relationship, and where she and Jackson had briefly paused to kiss.

Further to her right lay Pan's Wood, a source of complete gloom in the grey daylight. What secrets those trees knew, she thought. How many tales could they tell if they could, stories of passion, of lies, secret meetings and of murder. How many people had died in those woods she did not know. There had been seven of Goldman's stolen children, and there had been the murder she had committed – the murder of the man whose grave she was now standing over.

She looked down at his coffin and the sudden panic of being found out surged in her again, that deep down fear of the truth coming out somehow. But it passed as it always did after a moment or two and she regained control of her mind and realised that Goldman could not be so stupid as to turn himself over to the police and tell them about her and Jackson. Anyway, she repeated again in her head, he has no evidence anymore.

She was brought back to herself by Lula's fresh sobs as she dropped a handful of earth onto his wooden death suit, along with spots of autumn rain.

Before any amount of time had passed, they were back at home, settling into the thin wake where the few relatives were helping themselves to triangle-shaped sandwiches and sausage rolls. Lula was gliding around the gathering with her make-up re-applied and was now doing the social butterfly act. Dakota had had quite enough and disappeared into her bedroom with a bottle of vodka and a carton of orange juice. She lit up her cigarette and sighed with relief that her tearful pleas with Lula for some time alone had been met with sympathy.

The light early autumn rain had continued through the afternoon and yet had not let the heat escape. The gardens that lay below her window were still in the gloom, save for the occasional shudder of a bloom over-heavy with rain. In her heart, she dreamed of Jackson returning to her across the carpet of late flowers that adorned the forest floor, lavenders brushing his feet as he made his way towards her, a love as deep as all roses flowering in his heart.

Dakota turned away from the window, blowing a steady stream of cigarette smoke around the room, but paused when something on the bed caught her eye. Sitting up against her pillow was a white envelope bearing her name. Her knees turned to jelly and her hands shook a smattering of ash onto her carpet as her mind reeled and raced to make sense of why she was looking at Jackson's handwriting for the second time that day.

Before going any further, she took a huge swig of vodka and orange as she began walking to the bed, picking up and opening the envelope.

'My dearest D,
Meet me by the witch tree at midnight, we have to talk....
Your Lover man, till the bitter end,
Jackson.'

Her heart was beating so fast it burned, there was no mistaking his writing; she had seen it a hundred times before. She had been right; he had returned from the grave to haunt her. Why was he calling her back out to the woods? To get his revenge and kill her? Just like him to get the last word. She half laughed.

Part of her knew it could be suicide to return to the

woods, but she was also aware that if it was Jackson she wanted to see him.

She also contemplated the fact that it could be Goldman, returned at last with the perfect way to get her out to the woods, a letter forged to make it seem her dead lover had returned from the grave. No matter who it was from she was going out there, in the desperate hope it was actually Jackson.

Lula noticed her sister's pale complexion later that day when she finally made her way back downstairs to say goodbye to the mourners.

"Hey, are you feeling OK, D?" asked Lula.

"Not really. I feel sad and a bit drunk. I think I drank too much," explained Dakota weakly.

"Don't be sad; he isn't gone, you know!" Lula said with a wide smile of perfect teeth.

"You really think he has come back? You don't think it's just your way of dealing with the grief?"

"No, I know he is here, D. Don't question me," replied Lula as something like rage flickered in her eyes. "I needed him so he came back, and he is going to stay. Don't worry, you will see him soon. He told me he would let you see him soon."

"Oh, I see." Dakota sighed, catching sight of her ashen complexion in the mirror.

"Well, I am going to take an early night, hun. Will you be OK?"

"Oh yeah, I'm just going to drink till I pass out." Dakota smiled and kissed her sister who gripped her tightly.

"It will be all right, D. Don't worry, his killer will be caught, I will find out who did it and they will get what they deserve," Lula said strongly, and after staring briefly at her sister she went up to bed.

THIRTY-FOUR: Pan's Wood

Just before midnight Dakota put her jeans and favourite grey sweater on and hid a knife in the pocket of her coat before climbing out of her bedroom window and heading for the woods.

The roads were quiet and still and the birds had all gone to sleep, but there was life out there in the inky night. As she crossed the road to head into the woods, a fox darted out onto the road, pausing to stare at her. The moment was brief but Dakota felt as if time had slowed to a halt. There they stood, the girl and the fox, in the middle of the road a few feet apart, watching each other. There was something there between them, as though they were acknowledging the fact that they were both creatures of the night, a wildness about them that they had no control of, a need to be there while it was dark and everyone else was sleeping.

And then the fox padded away into the night to look for food, and the girl walked on into the woods to look for answers.

She could have found her way to the Witch tree and the grove blindfolded by now, but she never thought she would be out there again; the night Jackson died, so did any reason she should ever come back to their grove. But now she was not sure if it was he who had called her back or the sick individual she had hoped was dead. Goldman should have died, she thought, and with her hand on the knife in her pocket, she wondered if she was up to committing another murder.

A low wind moaned through the trees, the cackle of leaves an undercurrent she wanted to ignore. She could feel someone else nearby, watching her from the darkness, carefully moving in time with her like a shadow she did not know she needed.

Every time she paused to listen, the footsteps would stop also. A slight shuffle was all she could make out in the various sounds that filled the woods that night: the small rustling of animals in the undergrowth, the steady wind above her head and the movement of an unknown creature, stalking her towards her destination.

As the Witch Tree appeared in front of her, a wind kicked up and disturbed the already fallen leaves into a small whirlwind. But as they flew up into the air, her eyes registered the presence of many pieces of paper flying alongside the brown reminders that summer was gone.

It seemed as though someone had ripped hundreds of pages out of a book and thrown them on the forest floor. As she stepped forward, the wind brought one of those pages up against her leg, and stooping down she brought the page to her face, angling it so that the dappled moonlight could illuminate the page.

'....*I know it's all wrong but I can't help it, he makes me feel so loved and wanted and like I finally matter. Lula seems too crazy to care whether I am all right or not, Jackson knows how to look after me...*'

Dakota's head spun as she realised she was reading a page from her own diary.

The forest floor felt like it was rising up to meet her as her head grew dizzy and a wave of nausea crept up from her belly.

Her diaries were the only way she had ever been able to talk about her life and she had kept them secret and safe beneath one of the floorboards in her room for as long as she had been writing them, which was since she was nine years old. She had written down every single experience she'd had since that age in detail and had been glad she could express herself freely in those pages.

A lifetime of secrets all in those books, secrets that she had always hoped would stay between her and those lined pages. But someone had found them and someone was letting her know that all the evidence the police needed to prove she had murdered Jackson was right there.

Her entire body was shaking as she ran grabbing every page she could get her hands on before they blew away into the grim distance of the woods. Her arms full of paper and her heart hammering its way out of her chest, she only stopped when something caught her eye.

Ahead of her, just beyond the Witch Tree, she could see the burning tip of a cigarette glowing around the entrance to the grove. Only the trees and leaves moved as Dakota felt her heart stop in her chest with fear, her eyes glued to the orange dot that glowed then dimmed as the owner sucked the air out of it.

Another movement caught her eye then. To the left of the grove she could see the outline of a figure shaded from the moonlight by the trees. Dakota wanted to speak, to ask who was out there, but her throat felt as though it had collapsed.

Jackson stepped out of the trees and into the moonlight. Dakota fell to her knees. The sight of him had taken all the energy out of her body. He had come back from the dead; Lula wasn't crazy – he was really there. He stared at her intently, with neither hate nor love in his eyes. His skin was the colour of the sky just before it snows and his eyes looked bluer than ever. Every inch of her body was crying out for him, every cell in her body was bursting with love for him, and in turn her heart felt like it was going to explode with the pain of having lost him. She had killed him, and she missed him more than she had ever missed her parents. In those few moments while she looked at his ghostly form standing in the clearing, she realised she could never live without him, and she prayed that he had come back to kill her.

"Jackson," she whispered through a cracked and suddenly useless throat.

"I think I'd offer an apology if I were you," said another voice from the grove. At first she couldn't place it, but she did know it. It just seemed like her mind had capsized and all she had ever known was slightly foggy in her mind.

As the wind picked up again and blew a page from her

diary into her face, Dakota felt her heart seize up as Lula stepped out of the grove, one of Dakota's diaries in her hand.

THIRTY-FIVE: The Bitter End

Dakota was frozen to the spot as her eyes flicked from Jackson, now leaning arms crossed against the Witch Tree, to her sister, smoking and smiling in a way Dakota had never seen before. Perhaps it was the fact that her mind was racing so fast that her body had lost all movement, but she couldn't make out singular thoughts anymore, nor could she move from her kneeling position in the centre of the clearing.

"Surprised? I bet you are, you sneaky little thing!" Lula laughed, stubbing her cigarette out on the side of a tree. "Thought it was just going to be you and your Loverman, huh? Sorry to disappoint but I thought I should make an appearance. You know how it is."

Lula stood and opened the diary she was holding, beginning to read from it as the wind blew leaves across the clearing and she sauntered over to her kneeling sister.

"I can't believe he's gone, Diary, I can't believe what I did. I didn't intend to do it but the anger just took over when he said he wouldn't leave Lula. I killed him. I killed my Jackson..." Lula slammed the book shut in Dakota's face. "Interesting reading, hun! I have to admit I didn't believe Jackson when he told me it was you who had killed him, but now I have read it all, it's quite believable."

"How did you find my diaries?" managed Dakota, shivering.

"Jackson told me where to find them, didn't tell me what else I would discover about you when I read them though. You can imagine my surprise when I discovered you had been fucking my boyfriend since you were twelve!"

"He made me do it! I was just a child!"

"Save it, I have read it all, D, and there didn't seem to be too much resistance from you. You're right you were a child, and he should've known better. But you never made much of an effort to stop it, did you? You could've told someone!"

"You would never have believed me, and I was worried you would get sick..."

"Go mad, you mean? Just flip out?" Lula screamed at her, and suddenly punched Dakota in the face, knocking her back onto the floor, the diary pages scattering like freed birds.

"You're right I would have, but believe me I would have taken your side cos you were only a child! Now I take no one's side. You are both filthy fucking bastards!" Lula stepped back and by way of trying to calm down, lit herself a cigarette. Dakota winced slightly as she sat up, holding her bruised jaw and looking at her sister who was now staring at Jackson who was staring at Dakota.

"Lula... how long ago did you stop taking your medication?" Dakota asked as the thought that had occurred to her at the funeral crept into her mind again.

"A while ago. Jackson told me to, said they weren't worth taking and that he wouldn't be able to see me at night anymore if I was sleeping."

"You shouldn't have stopped taking them, Lula. You need them! You aren't feeling yourself, are you? You have never hit me before. You need to calm down and realise that not taking your medication is making you sick." Dakota tried to get through to her sister, but Lula was just shaking her head, still staring at Jackson.

"You are such a bastard!" muttered Lula to Jackson. "Of all the people you could have had an affair with you picked my baby sister? You are a fucking paedophile, just like that Goldman bloke next door. Did you used to get together and talk about fucking little girls?"

Jackson shook his head slowly without looking away from Dakota.

"Yes, and on the subject of Goldman, D, seems you have been keeping another pretty big secret for the last few years, haven't you?" Lula returned her attention to Dakota whose thoughts had now turned to Michelle Taybury suddenly.

"Yes, you know what I mean, that poor little girl, her poor family, and you knew all along, lied to the police over and over again. Mind you, you must be pretty good at lying by now. Been doing it for a while, haven't you?"

"I'm... I'm sorry, Lula. Really I can't explain it to you any other way than that I was thinking about how you would react..." and even as she said it she realised how stupid it sounded.

"Really? So when you were caught by Goldman you were thinking of me?"

"Yes."

"Were you thinking of me when you were fucking my boyfriend right there in that grove? Were you thinking of me when you had your... abortion?" Lula could barely say the word and suddenly she was crying. A hysterical torrent of emotion escaped from her; she wailed as though someone had ripped her heart from her chest. And for the first time, Dakota felt complete guilt.

In such a small space in the heart of the woods, so much had happened. This clearing was off the beaten path by a long way, and while people had occasionally stumbled upon the Witch Tree, nobody would find it at night. Dakota was aware of this as she sat before the tree. Just beyond it lay the quiet, secret grove, and she knew somewhere deep down that as she had lived her secret life out there in those woods, so her secret life would die out there too. Nobody would chance upon them now, just as no one had chanced upon her and Jackson the night she had killed him.

She was suddenly very aware that she was about to die.

The pages of her diaries rustled around the clearing, and reminded her that now, she had no secrets. Lula knew everything, about the abortion, about Michelle Taybury's murder and about how she and Jackson had been having sex while she laid in her drugged sleep night after night only a few metres away.

Poor fragile Lula. All the hard work she had done over the years to get over the grief of her siblings' tiny deaths, and the death of their parents would now be undone. Any security

Lula had ever felt would now be gone, smashed to pieces by a handful of notebooks and secrets.

"I should have known, I should have seen it. Maybe I would have if I wasn't full of drugs and romantic notions," Lula muttered bitterly into the piles of torn paper that lay around her. "I am so stupid. All those times I thought I was getting you two to get along by leaving you alone, I was just giving you more time to betray me. Oh my god! My God, it's all my fault!"

"No Lula, it wasn't your fault..." Dakota began but realised her sister wasn't listening. She was in a world of her own, a nightmare of memories.

"If I hadn't asked Jackson to live with us he never could have had the chance to get near you like that! I invited him to take you! And I forced you to be alone so he could do it over and over again. I might as well have given my consent! I let him rape you. I made him bring you back when you ran away! My God, what have I done?"

The night fell silent save for Lula's sobs. Even the wildlife had abandoned the place where the two girls and the spectre performed the last act of the play.

Then suddenly Lula stopped crying. Dakota looked at her sister heaped on the forest floor, her hair covering her face, and slowly Lula's eyes raised, glinting, up from the ground and focused on Dakota. Neither of them moved as they stared across the littered floor at each other.

"You wanted him back and he didn't want you anymore so you killed him. You came back from Ireland to get him and he didn't want you," Lula half whispered.

"Yes. He said he wanted you and that it was over between us." Dakota felt relief in her stomach, as though this might be the thing to calm Lula down, the fact that in the end Jackson had wanted her.

"But if he had said yes, you would have stolen him from me finally. You would have left me and taken him with you, wouldn't you?" Dakota had no answer that would make anything better so she just sat silent. "But he should have known better than to turn you down, shouldn't he? He should have known it would never be over…"

Something rational clicked in Dakota's mind. She had not written about what actually happened that night in her diary; she only wrote that she had killed him and did not have it in her to record the details of the murder.

How did Lula know what had been said? Unless Jackson had told her.

But why would Jackson give her all the details? God knows Jackson had never told Lula the details of anything in his life. Why would he choose that evening to let it all out, tell each damning, maddening detail?

Jackson wanted Lula to kill Dakota.

And in that moment that Dakota realised, that was when it happened.

Lula stood up, leaves in her hair, madness in her eyes and began to speak again.

"It doesn't matter what way I look at it, D. It's all very simple. You had an affair with my boyfriend for nine years, you murdered an unborn baby, you let a small girl go to her death at the hands of a paedophile and you murdered my boyfriend, your Loverman. Three people are dead because of you, Dakota Crow. If it were possible that you could die three times, maybe that would be payment enough. But you can't."

In split seconds, Lula had launched herself at her sister and was upon her, raining blows on her head with a strength Dakota did not know her sister had. In a brief pause as Lula lifted her arms above her head, Dakota noticed the rock in her sister's white hands. In the second that followed, as the rock made its way towards Dakota's head, her eyes dropped and she saw Jackson standing a few feet away, watching, waiting.

Her body had no register for the sort of pain she was in. Blow after blow with the rock she slipped away, and pain had no part in it, only numbness and fear.

In the seconds before everything stopped, her life passed before her in a random barrage of images that arrived like photographs slipping past her eyes.

Her mother kneading the scone mix, her father polishing

his motorcycle, Lula styling her hair and laughing in front of a mirror, the photo on her hallway of the Dakota Badlands, the blue dress her mother was wearing the night she died, her father looking smart in his suit as he closed the car door forever, the first second she laid eyes on Jackson, the hug he gave her as she wept at the hospital, " a murder of crows" he had said, and the words of a Baudelaire poem he only ever said in French, steady autumn rain falling on the garden and the first fall of apples, rain on the churchyard , the face of Michelle Taybury, the photos Goldman had sent her of her and Jackson making love, tears on Lula's face, Jackson's eyes, Jackson's cold blue eyes.

And she was gone.

THIRTY-SIX: The After-Life

Dakota was not crying, but there were tears on her face. She felt as though her soul was leaking, but no sobs came.

Jackson was staring straight at her and smoking a cigarette.

She couldn't find any words to say, and the last thoughts before her death continued to fall across her vision as she lit a cigarette for herself.

"Poor Lula, what did we do to her?" she said, her voice cracking slightly with dryness.

"It wasn't our fault, D. When are you going to realise that?" Jackson tutted and shook his head.

"You took advantage of me; you were a paedophile!" She wanted to shout at him for his indifference.

"Did you ever see me look at another child? Did you ever suspect I might leave you once you got too old? Do you think I wanted you because you were a child?" he asked her steadily, as though he had expected he might have to ask her this for some time. "And you remember that first time, it wasn't me who instigated it, D; it was you. I tried to stop you."

"But I was a child! And you turned me into a bitch of an adult as well!"

"That was incidental. Have you learnt nothing since you've been dead? WE were supposed to be together, just as we always have been in every life. There have been obstacles, but we always came together anyway."

"Yes, and then you murdered me!" she said incredulously.

"Yes, I did, because you always tried to leave me, when I knew we should never have been apart. If I had known about our past lives, I would never have said I would leave you, and you would never have murdered me. It was our last chance, D, and we fucked it up."

"I knew about our past lives – my dreams, remember? I knew you had killed me before, and I thought you would do it again one day. But I got you first..."

"And here we are, and it's too late," he sighed, stubbing his cigarette out in the ashtray. "No matter what way you look at it, I always knew we belonged together, in every life we went through, and you always thought you knew better! You were the one who ran away, and I was always the one to stop you. But last time I didn't; I waited for you to come back and when you did, I wanted you to beg. I didn't think you would kill me!" He laughed the way he always did, without smiling. "One thing you don't know and couldn't because you never got to read any of my books; was that I committed suicide in every life after I had killed you. I killed you and in doing so removed my reason for living. Every time. Every time except the last."

"What God would put two souls together over and over if they could only harm each other? And what God would put us together when I was a child and you were an adult? Every time, we were put in a situation where we were not allowed to be together, and every time the rules got broken and ruined our lives!"

"Perhaps we were a game? Maybe he wanted to see if we could resist temptation?"

"Oh fuck off, Jackson. Why would he bother?"

"To see if he had any control over human nature?"

Something Ariel had said to her jumped back up in her mind: how God could not control humans because he had given them free will.

Whatever the game, Dakota knew that somehow her soul was tied forever to Jackson's and in that lay the ruination of many lives and lifetimes.

"You know, there was never anything beautiful about my life, until I met you. You were the first and only truly beautiful thing I ever had. I knew, the second I saw you, that I loved you, that moment I saw you sat on your sofa at home, a little ten-year-old girl, whose eyes I knew from lifetimes ago. For some reason, something I could not explain, you were more than a child to me, and I never questioned myself for that reason. From the outside I knew how it looked, but I knew how it felt and I had no choice. I loved you in a way I thought was only possible in books, but you made it all real.

I knew it would be harder for you because you were so young, but I also knew that in time you would realise that you felt the same. I know I did it all wrong, but there was no easy way of doing it. How could I have a relationship with a young girl without being called a paedophile? That is why I stayed with Lula, so I could hide behind the façade of a normal relationship until you were old enough to become accepted as my lover."

"Shit Jackson, you really have read 'Lolita' once too often. Why didn't you just kill Lula off and run away with me?" she mocked, shaking her head.

"You don't have to be afraid anymore, D. We're dead and we're paying for what we have done. Don't pretend you don't care about us," he snapped and lit another cigarette.

Dakota noticed that the world of Purgatory was still continuing around her. Lightning still bleached the room occasionally, the rain still battered the windows and the distant sound of another soul in torment still shivered in the air.

"I watched you die, Dakota, just as you watched me die. I stood there and watched. You had the eyes of a spooked horse, frantic, losing control. I saw that panic turn to calm as somewhere inside you began to die. I knew that you were seeing your life flash before your eyes… amazing. I always thought that was just a myth, but it does really happen. I could see it there, the acceptance that it was all over, and you were seeing all the things you loved best about life, the things that you hated most, too, probably. It was amazing, watching you go, seeing you slip away like that. You were never more beautiful." He spoke more animatedly than Dakota could ever recall. In life he had only ever seemed so alive when reading from a book, a poem or some prose, but always someone else's words. But these were his words and he wasn't afraid to say them. There was something like blue fire in his eyes and she couldn't tear her gaze from him. As thunder crashed outside, Dakota snapped out of her trance.

"Did you want Lula to kill me? Is that why you came back and told her about my diaries?"

"Yes, that's exactly right. I came back at first just to see you. That first morning you awoke without me, I know you saw me. And once I had seen you again I knew I had to make sure we were together again. Plus I was sort of pissed off with you for killing me so I thought it was only fair you met a similar end." He smiled wickedly at her before continuing. "So I came back as often as I could to watch you, and eventually found out where you had hidden your diaries all these years. I had never considered that you would hide them under the floorboards when you had a fitted carpet in your room, but there you were, pulling back the carpet and lifting floorboards to reveal a pile of notebooks dating back to before I even laid eyes on you. I knew that was all I would need to tip Lula over the edge."

"You made her a killer! Now she won't go to Heaven either; she will end up here with us! Why did you have to do that? Ruin her afterlife as well as her life? What if she gets charged with my murder?"

"She won't; they'll think Goldman did it," he said, a smile creeping across his thin face.

"What? Why?"

"Well, Lula will get on her acting shoes and make out that you were being stalked by the missing murderer, the diary confirms you knew each other and that he had attacked you before. When they find your body, Lula will 'discover' your hidden diaries, the ones she didn't rip to pieces, and not only will she prove the connection between you and Goldman, she will prove that you murdered me! Lula and I had it planned all along. You told your diary that the only person who knew about me and you was him and that since his recent sightings, you were afraid he had come back for you, having guessed you had murdered me. So he lured you out to the woods, and murdered you because he believed you had turned him over to the police. That's the story she will tell them when they find your body. Until then they think you have run away. Lula told them you had done it loads of times before," he explained.

"But Goldman is dead! He arrived just after me," Dakota exclaimed.

"No, he arrived a long time before you, but he just couldn't bring himself to leave those woods, till you showed up. I know he was already dead because I killed him." The ease with which he confessed to murder caught Dakota by surprise. There had always been the possibility that he had killed Goldman but it was never real to her, just a thought. Maybe there was always a part of her that didn't want to believe Jackson was capable of murder after all.

"Jackson! I thought he ran away!"

"No, he tried to blackmail me while you were in Ireland, so I met him out in the woods to pay him off and decided to kill him instead. I buried him behind the base of the Witch Tree and went back to his place to take away the photos of us and pack a bag for Goldman to disappear with. I messed up the house, to make it look like he had left in a hurry, it wasn't long after that, by coincidence, that his brother showed up looking for him. He reported him missing and when the police turned up they had all the evidence they needed that he had murdered all those little girls."

"Didn't the police wonder why he hadn't gotten rid of the evidence?"

"No, they suspected that he fled suddenly and didn't have time. They were too consumed with the evidence to worry too much about whys and wherefores. They just started hunting him down, looking for a man on the run, not a body in the woods. They had only just done scouring those woods after turning up all the bodies of the girls. It was the perfect time for a burial out there."

Dakota was slightly in shock, but somehow was unsurprised that Jackson had finally killed Goldman.

"What about the sightings around the woods and

cemetery?"

"Amazing how many people can see an angry ghost. He couldn't stop himself from going back to those woods, just as he couldn't when he was alive. I think if you asked him now why he was so angry about being dead he would say that he wanted to kill more children before he died. He seems quite at home out in our woods here though, no wonder they call him 'Woods'"

"I thought he was stalking me when I got here; he seemed to be everywhere I went, but then so were you."

"Hmm, well, he does still love a good stalk," muttered Jackson standing up.

"Where are you going?"

"For a drink. You coming? There's something else I need to tell you, something that isn't in your book."

Dakota nodded and got up. In her mind, all she could see was her own dead body, lying out there in Pan's Wood, undiscovered and alone. She remembered how she had felt about leaving Michelle Taybury's body out in those same woods, and thought sadly how nobody had felt enough about her to not leave her to rot out there alone. All the days and nights that had passed on earth since she had arrived here in Purgatory, all those days and nights her poor broken body had lain out in the dark heart of the woods, her dead eyes staring but not seeing every small animal that passed by and stopped to look at her body, confused by its stillness.

She closed the book of her life and returned it to the shelf where it belonged. One tiny life amongst a million others, new souls and old souls, all lined up for eternity in that old library. Leaving the library, she felt an odd sense of comfort, of at last knowing what had happened, of what she had done wrong and why she deserved to be in Purgatory amongst the dregs of humanity. She was a murderer who was in love with a murderer. It seemed at last she knew there was no hope for her soul.

THIRTY-SEVEN: One Last Thing

Dakota followed Jackson out of the library and down the corridor that led back to the lobby. She felt slightly dizzy, as though the remembrance of her last days was too much for her and was setting her off balance Ahead of her, Jackson walked slowly, his long coat opening out behind him like lowered wings, as he reached into his pocket and lit a cigarette, his match illuminating the gloom of the corridor momentarily before it faded back into its normal state. The shadows grew back again, reclaiming the hall, strangling the glow from the small lamps as they shifted back and forth from bright to dim. Nameless shapes huddled into the darkest edges of the hall, insects twitching at the corners of Dakota's dizzied vision. In her head she could hear the piano strains of a Nick Cave song, the corridor twisted side to side ahead of her as Jackson hummed the tune.

Finally they passed from the long gloom into the odd comfort of the Bar, but as they reached the doors Dakota paused.

"Wait," she said, and Jackson stopped and turned back to look at her. "I have to go see Ariel; I need to talk to her. Can I just see you in there?"

"Yeah, I'll get one in for you, but don't be long, I haven't finished with you yet," he replied, a touch of humour in his voice but no smile on his lips.

"Uh yeah, I don't think I'd be able to get too far away from you. Do you?" she muttered sarcastically as she turned away from him. Jackson's hand reached out and grabbed her wrist causing her to jump slightly.

"I mean it, don't be long... please. Now that we are talking again, I don't want to stop. There's so much I want to tell you..." There was a softness in his tone, one she had heard before only in their most quiet and intimate moments.

As she turned and walked away, she wondered how it was that after all that had happened, she was still in love with him. She had killed him and in effect he had killed her, and yet she still had the same feelings she'd had on her return from Ireland: complete acceptance that he was all she ever wanted, and that nothing else mattered but how close he was to her.

As she approached reception, Dakota found Ariel was waiting there for her, a calm look upon her face that developed into a soft, encouraging smile as she stepped aside to invite Dakota back to the room where they had talked before.

"So you finished your book?" asked Ariel as they took their chairs.

"Yes, it's all over; I know it all. I must say, it was a surprise ending. I never suspected Lula, never thought she could do that..." Dakota broke off as a wave of sadness washed over her.

"And Jackson?"

"Yes, well that was another surprise. I never saw that coming. I had higher expectations of myself," mused Dakota, fiddling with a cigarette.

"Higher expectations?"

"I never thought I could be a murderer; I don't feel like one."

"And how do you suppose a murderer should feel?" Ariel asked, a faint smile ghosting her lips.

"I don't know. I suppose I thought there would be the whole... evil thing, but I don't feel evil. I feel like I always did, just guiltier, but then again, I always did have something to feel guilty about." She paused to light her cigarette. "I'm not who I thought I was when I woke up here. I didn't feel like a killer; I felt like a victim. Now I am starting to wonder how everyone else here feels. Something David said... where is that 'just' God?"

"You don't think God is justified in sending you here?"

"In a way, but I was a victim all my life. I didn't know any better. I was too young to cope with what I went through. David was a victim who defended himself... so was Betty! Why do we have to suffer alongside people like Goldman – people who kill because they like it?"

"Perhaps because no matter what way you look at it, you all took a life, and that is not God's plan."

"Yes, but death is predetermined! How can we be punished for what God lays out for us?"

"God doesn't lay it out, God doesn't lay anything out. Humans make choices. Humans die. There are miracles: babies get pulled from wreckages of earthquakes, people survive tsunamis, which is God's hand. But God doesn't take lives... She saves them. And as I said before, the eternal balance must exist, for every life She saves. One must be lost, and how that happens is left to humanity. People die of cancers and AIDS, both diseases created through evolution, through mankind's mistakes, and whether you believe it or not, God is not responsible for evolution. All She did was create the earth and the first amoebas. The rest was nature."

"Forgive me but I have hard time believing that God couldn't have stepped in whenever He... sorry She wanted to!"

"You're right, She could have... but She didn't. That was Her choice, Her Plan..."

Silence filled the small room, with its plush chairs and useless fireplace. It felt like a Victorian parlour – too much velvet and rotting lace. Dakota watched, partly amused as her cigarette ash slipped from her cigarette and disappeared into thin air before it hit the carpet.

"I don't get it..."

"You will, when you get to meet Her. That's how it works," Ariel explained, her cool eyes glowing in the dimly lit room.

"If I ever get there. I think I have a long way to go yet, a lot of work to do, and I don't even know where to start... or how to start," Dakota said, a touch of despair leaking into her voice.

"You will find a way. God has not shut you out forever, and the opportunity to make amends is there. You just have to do the work. But you have to ask yourself, how much do you want it?"

At those words, Dakota thought of Jackson, and of leaving him behind in this place. Could she bear to be separated from him again?

As though Ariel had read her mind she added, "He has been your downfall in every single one of your lives, he murdered you four times and managed to completely destroy any hope you ever had of a normal life in your last incarnation. How is it you still love him?"

Dakota looked up at Ariel and could see it was a genuine question. Ariel really did not understand.

"Do you know what it's like? I mean, were you ever human?"

"No, all angels were the first creation, created by God as companions and helpers. We have never lived a normal life. We've spent time amongst the living – for some of us it's all we do. But no, none of us were ever human," she explained.

"Not that it would make any difference if you had, but if you had, you would know, there's no way to explain why you love someone. I know now that it's because of your last lives together, but in that first life, the first time you get to live... what is it that draws you to that particular soul? I always thought that I loved Jackson because of how important he made me feel, but looking back, he made me feel pretty shit, too. After a while I think I came to realise that we had been together in other lives, but I don't know why I fell in love with him the first time around." Dakota paused, the distant sounds of the storm making her think of the rain falling on every part of the hotel, every window haunted by the cold eternal night. "I don't know what happened in my first life. Betty never read it cos we just sort of thought... well, we knew what happened. Maybe it was different?"

"Maybe. You should read it, Dakota. It might help you understand your love for Jackson. And when you do, perhaps you can explain it to me?" Ariel almost laughed as she said this, realising that while she was an angel, there was something Dakota might be able to understand that she couldn't.

"I'd like to tell you that you're missing out on something by not knowing about love, but to be honest," Dakota swallowed a huge lump in her throat as a tear rolled down her cheek, "love has never made me happy. It just hurts."

Unable to find anymore words, Dakota left Ariel and headed for the Bar. She felt that odd pull towards Jackson that she had felt in life, as though they were invisibly attached by an umbilical cord. The Lobby was more empty than usual, but still the odd soul shifted in the shadows, the glow from the fire offering false comfort.

She thought about her first life, and whether she might learn the truth about why she and Jackson ever fell in love in the first place. Another life to take on board, more pain to deal with. Could it be worth it?

When she walked into the Bar, Jackson was sitting by the bar smoking, watching Danny who was slumped asleep in his usual place...

Dakota sat between him and Jackson as he motioned at her to poke Danny into wakefulness.

"Hey you, what's a girl got to do to get a drink here?" She laughed, prodding Danny till he sprang up like a robot and stood behind the bar, blinking his eyes into clear vision. Something like horror flitted across his face as he looked at her and Jackson.

"Hey, he can see you, too!" Dakota noticed, mildly amused.

"He's the Barman; he can see everybody," replied Jackson.

"Did I tell you, Jackson, this man is the first friend I made here? I only have two friends here but Danny was the first. I take it you've met him before, I mean everyone who comes here must come straight to the Bar," she said, lighting her own cigarette.

"Oh yes, I've met him before, haven't I, Danny," Jackson

said, emphasising the name at the end. Dakota could see there was something between the two men, but she wasn't sure what so she asked if there was a problem.

"No, not a problem for me, but it might be for you D," Jackson muttered without taking his eyes off Danny.

Lightning lit the room for a moment and Danny didn't move.

"Tell her what your real name is," instructed Jackson, reaching over and taking a bottle of whisky to swig from. Danny looked bitterly at Jackson, shaking his head slowly.

"OK, what is going on? I am actually interested now," Dakota stated, looking from Danny to Jackson until one of them looked at her.

"It's interesting stuff, D, really," smiled Jackson, and straight away she knew it wasn't going to be interesting in a good way.

"Why are you doing this? Hasn't she been through enough? Aren't I paying for it now? Can't we just leave it alone?" begged Danny. Jackson shook his head silently.

"Tell her your name," Jackson repeated.

"I know his name, Jackson," Dakota interjected.

"No, you don't. You know him by his middle name."

"My name is William Daniel Shade." The old man addressed Dakota, his tired blue eyes fixed on her with a look that expected imminent upset.

"Shade?" Dakota's brain began to sift through information because something was calling to her from a long-ago memory. Finally she found it.

That night she had seen a man standing under the streetlight opposite her house drinking cans of beer, she had only seen the halo of his grey hair in the light that was resting on him from above, throwing his face into darkness.

"You're Jackson's father?" she asked. "Did you know who I was? Why didn't you say anything?" Her memory reminded her of Danny's often odd behaviour when she mentioned finding out about her life, and even the odd look on his face when she first told him her name. "I'm sorry I murdered your son," she said suddenly which surprised them all. Both men looked at her oddly, and then she saw that soft look in Danny's eyes which she knew meant he forgave her.

"Oh, it gets better," Jackson mocked. "Did he ever tell you why he is here?"

"No, actually you have avoided that question ever since I got here. I never knew why, I just guessed you weren't dealing with it very well and didn't want to talk about it. Why are you here, Danny?" asked Dakota.

Danny sighed deeply and lit up a cigarette before beginning.

"I did tell you, remember? I said I had killed my lover, same as you." Dakota nodded as she recalled his brief response to her last attempt to find out why he was in Purgatory. "Well, all that is true. I was having an affair with a married woman, and had been for many years. Then one night I followed her as she went out with her husband, to steal a few moments with her. She managed to get away from him for a while and came out to see me in my car where I was waiting. She said that she didn't want to see me anymore, that enough was enough and she wasn't going to leave her family for me. She looked so beautiful that night, in a summer evening dress, a warm wind shifting her hair. She had always been so beautiful. Since we were children, I had loved her and she loved me, too. But when she got older she got bored of me and only came back to me when she wanted what only I could give her. She always said I could never make her happy – that's why she didn't marry me – but she still wanted me, so she always came back to me. But this time she said it was really over, that she was worried about her family ever finding out and she cared too much about them." He paused to smoke and rub his eyes. "You know how it feels, that moment when you realise it's over and they really don't want you anymore," he said, looking straight at Dakota who looked briefly at Jackson and nodded.

"Well, that was it. She said what she wanted to and wasn't interested in my pleas. I could see in her eyes she didn't want to end it with me, but she was going to do it anyway. And she got out of the car and walked back inside to the party, in her beautiful dress, and she didn't even look back at me. My heart felt like it had caved in. I thought I was going to die right there, and when I didn't, I decided I would kill myself.

"So I sat in my car and drank the bottle of whisky I had with me and waited for the party to finish. When it did, I saw her again, leaving the hall with her husband and getting into their car. I suppose at this point I should be saying, 'I don't know what possessed me,' but I would be lying. I know exactly why I did what I did. I followed them in my car, drunk as you like. I could barely focus but I concentrated on that car with all my strength. We were out in the country, a moonlit night, nearing midnight, and out there on the deserted road, I ran that car off the road. I chased them and forced them off into a ditch." Silence sat between them for a few moments. Everything was still except for the storm outside, rattling the windows angrily. "I left them there and drove off. I found out later that they both died, and luckily for me her husband, who was driving, had been drinking, so they assumed it was an open and shut drunk-driving accident. But her death ripped me apart and after that I was never the same. I just drank all day long, lost my job, survived on pocket money given to me by Jackson, but eventually I gave up completely and one drunken night I decided to visit where she had died and as fate would have it, a lorry ran me over as I stumbled out of the ditch and killed me. And here I am."

"What are you leaving out?" Dakota asked, her fists bunching inexplicably as though some kind of bottled rage was pushing the stopper out and she did not know why.

"The woman I killed was your mother, and your father died with her, getting the blame for both their deaths because he had drunk too much Guinness at the wedding party."

Something like acceptance passed through Dakota momentarily, before she said, "So you thought you were following the woman you loved, but you accidentally killed my parents. Is that right?"

"No, Dakota. I was following the woman I loved. I knew your mother since we lived in Ireland, and I followed her over here after she and your father finished their tour of the

States. She married your father because he loved her and he would look after her. He had inherited a lot of money from his family and I had nothing. And when I followed her here I still had nothing, but she still loved me and still saw me whenever she could. So I married too, had a son and waited around in the wings for her, for Hannah."

The mention of her mother's name was too much for Dakota, and her head began to ache again as memories of her mother swam back to her across the years: how much she had loved her and how beautiful she was. And all those years she had been lying to them all; she wasn't happy with her husband, she was in love with someone else, someone they would never know about.

It seemed to Dakota that now, even after all she had found out about her life, this was the final crushing blow. She had accepted how her life had turned out with Jackson, but the only true and pure thing in her whole life was her mother. Her beautiful mother, baking scones on a Saturday afternoon, dressing for church on a Sunday morning, brushing her brunette hair into perfection before leaving their house to take the short walk up to St Brigid's for morning Mass.

None of it was real, none of it was pure. Her mother had loved her though, loved her enough to stay with a man she did not love just to ensure their happiness. There could be no doubt that Hannah Crow was a good mother, but she was not a good wife.

Dakota had no words. Rage seemed pointless now, here in the dirty Bar at Purgatory Hotel. Her anger and tears would be wasted, for all they could do was to disappear against the grim walls, be drowned out by the endless storm at the windows. She saw finally that no matter what else she could possibly hear, it would do her no good to lose her calm.

"So you knew about it all, I take it?" she half whispered to Jackson, snatching the whisky from his hand.

"Yes, I did, only from my own snooping. I found out where you all lived, and on the way there found the cemetery. I went inside and chanced upon the graves of your brothers and sisters, and after that I went there a lot. Then I met Lula, and the rest you know," Jackson replied.

"You even knew about my brothers and sisters?"

"Yes, Dad was so obsessed that he kept the burial notices of them all. I suspect part of him always knew they were his." This set off a whole new direction in Dakota's head.

"Oh Christ, please don't tell me you're my father."

"I'm not your father, Dakota, I'm not, I'm not Lula's either. But the others were mine and they all died. I guess God knew better than to let them live." Danny sighed and finally came around from behind the bar and sat back down beside Dakota. "That's another thing, you see, Dakota. Your mother was my first cousin; our relationship would have been frowned upon anyway, whether she married someone else or not."

"You were cousins? Christ, my dad thought you were family?"

"Your father never knew about me, but it seemed that my genes mixed with your mother's caused cot death in the babies. Back then nobody asked a lot of questions. Cot death was cot death, babies died sometimes."

"But so many, one after the other?"

"Well your mother and father were both questioned to ensure that neither of them harmed the babies, but in all cases death was natural. Your father assumed that they were only lucky to have Lula, and that somehow he and your mother were incompatible for making children. As it happened, one night they got lucky and she fell pregnant by your father and you lived. You were their miracle baby, and after you were born she saw me less and less. She said all her other babies had died because God was punishing her for her adultery, but because she had returned to the arms of her husband she was allowed to keep you. The truth is, we were too close genetically to have ever had children."

"And yet you still had Jackson? Didn't your wife ever suspect anything?"

"I don't know, she never said, but she seemed happier once she had a baby. After he was born, I never touched my wife again." Danny looked ashamed, and Jackson looked disinterested, as if he had heard the story a million times.

"Did you know all of this while you were alive?" she asked Jackson.

"Most of it. I didn't know that the reason I had no siblings was because my father did not want my mother; I didn't learn that till I got here and he told me for certain that all those babies were his. But the rest, I already knew."

Dakota sipped at the foul-tasting liquid as she considered the fact that all stories start somewhere, every story has a beginning. She knew now that her story began long ago, when Hannah O'Leary met her cousin, William Shade. Through their own twisted and dangerous love they destroyed the lives of everyone they touched, and through this both had paid the ultimate price with their own lives.

Her mother's love for the 'wrong man' meant that one day she would have a child, and she would call her Dakota, and Dakota would meet a man called Jackson, and together they would start the story all over again, falling in love and destroying so many other lives all on their own.

Dakota looked at Jackson and knew that even now, in the afterlife that they had earned, a dark and dismal existence on the edge of forever, she still felt that fire in her stomach for him, that even now she might destroy lives because of her love for him.

She wondered what sort of afterlife her mother had gone on to. Did she get to go straight to heaven, to a more beautiful hotel, somewhere where the sun shone and gentle breezes ruffled her brunette hair, and live out her eternity holding the hand of her husband, the man she had loved enough to have a family with? Enough to leave the man she had first loved? Dakota felt sure that wherever she was it was more beautiful than this place.

But then again, maybe Jackson had been right that day in the cemetery, all those years ago. Maybe her mother was alive again somewhere, a new person in a new life, and it was a part of that low murmur that was the backdrop of the Library of Remembrance. Her mother's life was somewhere else now with other people. But she would not be with Danny this time; maybe she had a chance at a normal life.

And how long might it take for Dakota to pay for her crimes? How many years might she have to spend in David's temple praying for forgiveness?

But part of her knew that she might never see Heaven, never feel the sun on her face again that this was it for her: occasional visits to earth to remember what living was like, the endless dark night of Purgatory yawning out in the storm as she wandered the hotel corridors forever, trying not to earn the wrath of the Punishers. She knew this because she felt deep down that there truly was no hope for her soul. She loved a murderer, and would suffer the aching stretch of eternity in this Godless place, just to be by his side. Dakota knew that she could take any kind of punishment as long as she was with him. He was the last trick up God's sleeve for her, the one thing that would keep her in Purgatory, the one thing that she could never seek forgiveness for.

And here she would be, as long as they allowed it, an eternity with Jackson, the devil at her door, her Loverman, until the bitter end.

And yet might she be able to resist? Able to fight it out and earn a place in Heaven, able at last to be rid of Jackson Shade and be forgiven for her crimes? Only time would tell, and that was something she had plenty of.

Fantastic Books
Great Authors

CROOKED CAT

Meet our authors and discover
our exciting range:

- Gripping Thrillers
- Cosy Mysteries
- Romantic Chick-Lit
- Fascinating Historicals
- Exciting Fantasy
- Young Adult and Children's Adventures

Visit us at:
www.crookedcatbooks.com

Join us on facebook:
www.facebook.com/crookedcatbooks

Printed in Great Britain
by Amazon